Hopeium

NEXT IN THE
MESSY BUSINESS OF LOVE SERIES:

Detachment (Kylie & Marcus)
Suite Haven (Elyse & Brayden)
Sunrise Nights (Riley & Mike)
Reverie (Senna & Trey)
Rosewater (Angela & Slater)
Our Unicorn (Henley, Mason, & Addison)

ADRIAN EVERLY
D.J. THOMPSON

MASTERLESS
PRESS

www.masterlesspress.com

Masterless Press
www.masterlesspress.com

This book is a work of fiction. Any references to historical events, real people, or real places are used fictitiously. Other names, characters, places, and events are products of the author's imagination, and any resemblance to actual events or places or persons, living or dead, is entirely coincidental.

Hopeium
Copyright © 2020 by D.J. Thompson
Cover design by Vanessa Mendozzi

First Masterless Press print edition: October 2020

Printed in the United States of America

ISBN: 978-1-7323064-9-3 (print)
ISBN: 978-1-7350801-3-0 (ebook)

Welcome to the Messy Business of Love!

If you're looking for a sweet and spicy read imbued with the perfect amount of steam, you're in the right place! Especially if a no-nonsense, raunchy, sass queen of a heroine and a sweet, witty, gentleman of a hero are the types you like to root for.

The Messy Business of love is a standalone, HEA romance series filled with twenty-somethings who are trying to succeed in both relationships and entrepreneurial ventures. Each novel is a complete story with some light to medium crossovers so they can be read individually in any order or you can check out the series in the intended sequence to keep up with your favorite couples and see how happily ever after is treating them as time goes on!

Hopeium is a bit of a special story as these characters are from D.J. Thompson's *Angels of War* series—a military technothriller set in a dystopian version of today's world. If you're a fan of that kind of thing, and if you're curious to see what Dion and Isabella's relationship was like in an alternate world ravaged by a global war, please give the series a read! Only then will you truly understand that some people are always meant to find each other and fall in love, no matter what universe or timeline they're in!

While *Hopeium* is co-written with D.J. Thompson and based on characters from his series, voice-wise and stylistically, this an Adrian Everly novel that will echo throughout the Messy Business of Love series. As such, it's best to read this before *Detachment,* though it was written to be enjoyed in any order.

Before you dive in, please take a second to sign up for the newsletter at https://www.masterlesspress.com/romance to get free bonus chapters and fun, exclusive crossovers!

Enjoy, loves!

1
Isabella

Saturday

BEING DRUNK OFF YOUR ass and having a great night out with friends is one thing, but there's a certain euphoria that comes with being way past tipsy and dancing on a famous DJ's livestream at an exclusive rooftop party overlooking Los Angeles.

The biggest influencers on social media, musicians and actors big and small, aspiring and legit models—no matter where I turn, there's at least three famous socialites mixed in the clusters of nobodies who are trying to get noticed.

Nobodies like me, hoping to become somebodies…

The only reason I've even gotten an in to these events over the last few months is because of TyDie, Los Angeles's up-and-coming DJ. Back before he *blew* up a few months ago, I was front row at his show, giving him fuck-me eyes while showcasing my sexiest dance moves until he took notice and summoned me up on stage. And then, in a backstage bathroom after his set, I *blew* my way into becoming his "groupie." The weekend after, we hooked up in his penthouse. Now I'm pretty much out with him, his boys, and his thot-flock every weekend. Can't say that being in LA pretty much from Friday to Monday is doing any justice for my GPA, especially when I keep missing Monday's 8 A.M. behavioral psych class…

"Ayo!" Ayden, one of TyDie's friends, hollers as he carries a tray of glasses back to the table. "Shots!"

"Yasss!" TyDie's groupies cheer in unison while trotting over to him.

Ayden is waving for me to come over, but I'm too busy posing for a picture with Allyson and the girls I made nice with tonight.

"I just followed you!" I shout, watching her type up this basic-ass caption. "Don't forget to tag me!"

"Sis, I got you!" Allyson says, rhythmically moving her hips to the Rihanna "Work" song that just started. "At Isabella... Monroe? Right?"

I lean in. "Izzy Bella's my name on Insta, but the username is Izzy-underscore-Does It! One word," I almost shout in her ear. I point at my profile when **@Izzy_DoesIt** pops up in the suggestions. "That's me!"

She taps the name then hits **Share**. "Done." She thumbs her screen a few more times. "And I followed you back, girl!"

"Sweet! You're the best!" I say.

"Can't wait to see your videos!"

"Well, I've already seen yours but I'll totally be creeping on your new stuff!"

"Yass!"

"We definitely need to collab!"

"No doubt, girl! I'm always looking for some fresh talent to dance with! DM me!"

"Izzy, come on!" Ayden calls.

I nod and start toward the table. "Alright, Allyson! Talk soon!"

Flirt with all the right artists and photographers, be friendly with all the right people, and get tagged in as many Instagram pictures and videos as possible. That's the name of the game. That's the only reason every other wannabe model and SoundCloud rapper comes to these things. All of the musicians and producers here tonight are surrounded by flocks of girls taller and debatably prettier than my five-foot-six ass, so I couldn't get into their orbit tonight if I tried. But at least I managed to get in nice with a chill bunch of girls, two of whom happen to be repped by a talent agency called RTA that places dancers in high-end gigs. The cherry on top of the pie is that Allyson's aunt is an award-winning choreographer affiliated with that very same agency.

Hopefully this pans out better than my last attempt to get signed with an agency...

Glasses clink together and then I throw back tequila shot number five—drink number eight for the evening. This is bad-decision territory now. And, despite telling myself that I'd exercise some restraint tonight, I'm already looking for someone to leave here with.

TyDie is out as an option. Like every other night, there's too much newness buzzing around for him to focus on something he's already had. The lead singer of a band I've been eyeing has his arm around an Insta-model. The DJ I met earlier is nowhere to be found. TyDie's friends don't interest me in the least, especially not Ayden's thirsty ass. The bartender who chatted me up earlier is pretty cute, so maybe that's who I'll go for if a better opportunity doesn't present itself.

I sit at the edge of the L-shaped couch, cross my legs, and skim the dozen or so notifications I've missed in the last hour. The snapchat from Chase catches my eye immediately. And instead of ignoring it like I know I should, I open it right away.

It's a reply to my snap story that reads: **Where you at tonight?**
Me: **I'm at Spire! A-list musician's party.**

His little Bitmoji pops right up in the corner. Chase: **Can you get me in? Or do you wanna go somewhere and grab a drink? Maybe some food?**

To be honest, he could get himself in. He's a comedy content creator who knows a few of tonight's attendees, like his close friend and my acquaintance Maisie Marie, who looks like she's filming a skit right this very moment. But having him here isn't a good idea. "No" should be my response, but that last shot of tequila is hitting me hard and all I'm thinking about is the good dicking he always delivers.

I'm in bad-decision territory.

Sunday

It's like seven in the morning by the time I wake up. Chase is still fast asleep, snoring like a goddamn bear. I need to get out before he awakens and starts whining for me to spend the day with him. He's been getting annoying lately, bugging me about being together when he knows I want to be single after my last relationship—my first serious relationship—blew my life up. That drunk, horny alter ego of mine that everyone calls Bella just had to go and invite him to the party last night...

I quietly get dressed then loiter in his living room while I wait for the Uber, which shouldn't take long since he's already in the neighborhood. When he's a block away, I slip out of Chase's apartment with my shoes in hand, sliding them on out in the hall. The elevator is busted so I clop my way downstairs. A gray Honda Civic pulls up outside not long after I reach the lobby exit.

"You Isabella?" the driver asks as I step onto the sidewalk.

I check the app to make sure he's the right guy. *Yup*, and he looks even better in person. "That's me, Austin!" I say, grabbing the rear door handle.

"I dig your accent! Where are you from?"

"Texas," I say in a more exaggerated drawl with a slam of the door. "Grew up in Austin."

"Awesomeness! I'd live there if my name wasn't the same as the town." He laughs, shifting the car into drive. "What brings you out here? You a model?"

"Something like that," I say with a smile.

"Sweet." His eyes look me over via the rearview mirror. "You had a good time last night?" He palms his face. "I'm sorry, that didn't come out right."

"Relax, hon," I say, patting his shoulder. "I did have a good time. Thanks for asking." I squirm in my seat. "My crotch is kind of sore, though. Last night was a bit of a marathon, if ya know what I mean!"

In the rearview, I watch his face go beet red. "Uh, sure." He clears his throat then silence follows. "Do you mind if I play an audiobook?"

"Go on ahead."

From what I gleaned from the Uber driver's navigation, it's going to take about ten minutes longer than normal to get to Pasadena. Because LA traffic. At least that gives me extra time to catch up on all my social media and missed texts from last night.

So glad I didn't look as fucked up as I felt, I think, swiping through the pictures I was tagged in and those that I posted last night, half of which I don't remember taking. The Instagram stories of me taking shots, twerking, and throwing it back don't do me justice.

Each of the photos I was tagged in got almost a thousand or so likes. Of course the ones I'm in with TyDie have, like, twice that. Last night got me 106 follows, mostly from guys. Obviously. Damn near 1200 likes per picture/video posted by me with dozens of new ones on my older posts from thirsty new followers. Impressive stats considering that I grew this account to seven thousand followers from scratch after I basically had to scrub all of my social media from the internet a little over a month ago…

Checking my texts reminds me of why I went ghost online in the first place.

Kevin, some guy I used to party with, messaged me: **Isabella, what dat mouth do?** Sent at 12:05 A.M.

That's the caption under the attached pic of me looking up at the camera with a mouthful of that skinny carrot my ex Zach called a cock…

Me: **I don't know who you think this is, but you just sent a text to a cop, pal.** *That should scare him good. Aaand… number blocked.*

A text from Jason Dunn from Kappa Sigma reads: **Hey! So, is it true you do private strip shows? I'm looking to throw something epic for my frat bro's 21st. Our frat had a fundraiser so money's no issue!** Sent at 1:21 A.M.

Number blocked.

Those are just two of, like, ten texts and snapchats I got last night from guys who were supposedly *friends* as well as from numbers I don't even know. It's fallout from Zach's revenge porn campaign against me following our breakup. As if outing me as a stripper to my family and friends in private messages and essay-length Facebook posts that he tagged me in wasn't enough, that prick leaked all of my nudes and the contents of his explicit album containing our sexy-time photos and videos to a bunch of my guy friends, along with my number.

Since I don't really use Facebook and haven't really added anyone on there since, like, freshman year of college, it was mostly guys from high school harassing me at first. Then there were a couple guys DMing me on Instagram before I deactivated both accounts. Things died down after I changed my number and went dark online, but now this is the second weekend in a row that I've gotten messages like this from guys at Cal State, which means Zach or some other asshole is circulating an email or some shit around the San Bernardino campus…

Fuck me… FUCK!

Being harassed like this is stressful to the point of crippling anxiety. This is why I've been keeping my head down the last six weeks or so and stopped associating with anyone at the San

Bernardino campus. Not that ghosting dudes I used to be cool with isn't just helping create more bitter fuckboys out of the pretend-nice-guys who are looking to get back at me for not being the easy slut Zach made me out to be...

"Right here is fine," I say as the driver approaches Los Roble apartments.

"I can take you to the entrance," he offers.

"No, it's fine. I need to stop at my car." I open the door. "Thank you, Austin!"

"My pleasure. Um, I don't usually—" It sounds like he's starting to say something else when I slam the door, but I'm not really in the mood to be social before I've had my caffeine. Especially not when I'm mildly hungover.

I get my bag of clothes and toiletries out of the trunk of my Volkswagen Golf and then head up to Riley's. This *luxury* apartment is my second home. I'm pretty much here every weekend. If I don't end up going home with Travis or some rando, that is...

I slip the key in and unlock the door as quietly as I can, just in case she's still asleep.

"*Well*, good morning!" Riley cheers from the kitchen.

"Morning, Ri!" I say flatly.

She looks over at the clock. "Damn, it's not even nine yet! Is this what you meant when you said you'd be back early-ish?" She smirks.

"By early, I meant, like, one or two last night..." I set my purse on the counter.

Riley halts scrambling the eggs then searches my face. "Uh oh... Bad night?"

"No, it was a great night. Just hasn't been the best morning..."

"You wake up next to an uggo?" The grimace that follows quickly morphs into a grin.

"I woke up next to Chase."

She rolls her eyes. "Ugh, again? I thought you were cutting him off."

"Oh, I was doing good for a while there, but you know Bella... When she wants some man meat, she gets her man meat."

"Sounds like Bella needs to try being vegan for a while."

It's hard not to crack up at that.

She scoops the eggs in the pan onto her plate right as the toast pops. "You two get into a fight this morning?"

I shake my head as I pull up one of the less graphic texts. Then I hold it up to her face. "More guys from college this time..."

"Shit... Not again." She resumes buttering the toast.

"Seems like it only happens on weekend nights or some shit. Like, just because I'm probably drunk that means I'm down to say yes to every booty call. Come on."

"I'm sorry, Izzy."

I toss the phone back in my purse. "Meh... It'll pass eventually, I suppose."

"You going to do something about it?"

"Well, I contacted the student conflict affairs last week and got an email from the associate dean on Friday about meeting with him after my first class on Monday. I'm hoping the university can file criminal charges on my behalf or, at the very least, expel anyone involved."

"I'm sure it'll all work out." She extends the plate of food to me. "Here. Eat."

"What about you?"

"It'll take me five minutes to make more. Now take it."

The gesture makes me smile. "Thanks, bae. I don't know what I'd do without you."

"Well, for one, you'd probably be way more motivated to keep hooking up with Chase so you'd have a place in the city to stay at."

"Yeah, no," I say.

"I mean, Chase is kind of a douche, but aren't all guys these days? He's not *that* bad."

"I guess. But a relationship isn't something I can handle right now. And another scornful guy trying to sabotage me is the last thing I need. Especially when he's connected on social media." I shovel a forkful of eggs into my mouth.

"Understandable after everything that's happened."

"Mm-hmm." I chew in silence for a while, watching her dump the eggs she just beat onto the pan. "How's your roommate hunt going, by the way?"

"No luck yet. Why? Scared you'll be back to couch surfing?"

Smirking, I shake my head. "More like I might need somewhere to relocate to if things get worse and I decide to drop out... Because dropping out is starting to seem like a better option as the weeks go by."

"If it comes to that, and someone has already signed the lease, I'll evict a bitch for you."

A snort precedes my laugh. "Appreciate it."

"You know I'd do anything for my bestie!"

"Um, duh!"

Riley giggles. "Soooo... you sticking around for a while or are you leaving after breakfast?"

"Wasn't planning on heading back home until early Monday. Why, what's up?"

"Perfect! Well, I was hoping we could go out tonight to celebrate instead of waiting until next weekend."

"Okay, I'm down. But what exactly are we celebrating?"

"After you left yesterday, my friend from the studio texted me saying that I, uh... got the dance instructor job!"

"Holy shit!" I spring up from my seat and almost knock her over as I'm hugging her. "Riley, that's freaking amazing! Congrats!"

"Thanks! I mean, it's not like I'll be teaching choreography to any big-name artist or anything, but at least I can quit working at that damn store!"

"Hey, don't downplay this achievement, girl. You've always wanted to teach. And you'll finally get paid to do what you love!"

"No, you're right!"

"Um, of course I'm right, betch!"

Seeing as how I got obliterated last night and I'm planning on leaving early tomorrow morning, my intention was to go easy tonight. The thing is, when I'm upset, I drink more. So, on top of those texts ruining my day, it hasn't helped that Mom has been ignoring her disappointment of a daughter all day, yet again. Also, after drink number four, I typically keep drinking. And drink four happened during the pregame, on an empty stomach. So those shots chased with White Claws hit hard and fast…

Now we're sitting here at Bestia in downtown LA for dinner with platinum-blond party girl—our mutual friend Candice— drinking our first round of this expensive tequila-based cocktail while Riley maps out all the bars she wants to hit tonight for her celebratory girls' night out. Something's telling me that making it to my 8 A.M. class tomorrow is going to be out of the question, yet again…

2
Dion

Sunday

THE FIRST STOP ON the ten-mile, forty-minute drive from LAX to the Airbnb is to pick up beer and liquor. Not food or groceries. Alcohol. Because Penn Stater priorities.

"There's a Mexican place about two minutes from the house," I say, pinching the screen to zoom in on Google Maps during the walk back to the Nissan Pathfinder. "Plancha Tacos. Four-and-a-half stars."

Mike gets that stupid smirk on his face that often precedes something nonsensical. "But here's the thing, Dion… If we drink on an empty stomach, we'll get drunk faster and then we won't have to spend as much when we get to the bars. Then we can use that money to spend on the ladies. Plus, there's calories in beer!" Classic Mike logic.

I scowl. "True, but the calories issue aside, how many times have we done that and still ended up spending a shit-ton of money only to end up feeling nauseous as hell by the end of the night?"

"Only all the time," Jeremy pipes up from behind me.

"Oh, you mean like last night?" Tommy says with a grin, patting his stomach. "Bleh…" he pretends to gag.

Mike holds up a hand. "Guys… Guys… Trust me, I'm a scientist."

"You're a kinesiology major," I grumble, opening the driver's door.

He lifts the trunk for the guys hauling cases of beer. "It ends in ology so I'm pretty sure that's a science, Mr. High-and-Mighty Biologist!"

I smirk. "Whatever helps you sleep at night." Once behind the wheel, I turn to the guys in the third row. "You foolios down for some burritos, or do you want to wait until we Uber down to a restaurant where we might have to wait to be seated and then wait to be served?"

"Um," Han hums, "considering it's, like, uh… 7:45 P.M. Eastern time and we haven't eaten since noon, food now!"

"Yeah, I ain't trying to wait," says Stefan.

"Ditto," Tommy says, climbing in the passenger seat.

I add Plancha Tacos to our route. "Food it is."

Mike slams his door. "Fine, but now we're going to double up during power hour because you guys are bitches." He laughs.

The Airbnb in Beverly Grove is dope as hell. The house has four bedrooms, three bathrooms, a high-end entertainment system in the living room, Bluetooth speakers everywhere, smart devices throughout the house, and a Jacuzzi out back. Seven days of luxury, all for $330 per person. Not bad. If we hadn't booked this back in August of last year, there's no way we would've found anything this nice that was ten miles from Santa Monica Beach and ten miles from Downtown LA.

The song "La La Land" by Bryce Vine starts bumping once Mike connects his phone to the speakers. "Um, fellas, there's no way we leave here without throwing at least one party in this place."

Stefan raises his rum and Coke. "No doubt, boy," he says with that rich Brooklyn accent of his—an accent I lost after having lived in Orlando for four years and in Pennsylvania the last four years.

Jeremy slams his empty beer can on the table. "All we need to do is rally a bunch of valley girls and we're set."

Mike turns his phone to face our side of the table, a big grin stretched across his face. Bumble is open and there's a hottie on his screen. "Dude, don't worry, I'm working on it."

There are a few chuckles.

Stefan starts laughing. "Same here!" he says, swiping through Tinder.

Han silently joins in.

Jeremy fishes his phone out of his pocket. "Oh, word! I should probably get in on that, too!"

Mike snorts. "Why? So you can get shot down again like you did last night?"

"Ooooooooh," we all harmonize.

Jeremy throws his head back. "Wow... Damn... Okay, you know how it is with Karla." He looks to me. Because I tried talking to Karla many times for him, even though I had a thing for her. But I was friend-zoned, so...

I hold up a finger. "Karla." I put up two more fingers. "The chicks who shut you down on the dance floor. Yeah, I saw that." My pinky goes up. "Karla again at the end of the night."

Jeremy throws a balled-up tissue at me. "That's different... That was Pennsylvania. We're in California now. It's more progressive. The girls out here have the kind of mindset that will vibe with woke brothas like me and you." He nudges me, grinning. "Watch. You'll see. You'll all see!" he says dramatically, throwing his beer back after.

All we can do is laugh.

Tommy and I are the only ones not prowling dating apps for hookups. He's busy watching a video on his phone. And me? I'm over here scarfing down this delicious burrito while texting Jessica Stewart.

The aforementioned Karla introduced me to her old roommate Jess a month ago and we clicked right off the bat, which is awesome because she's sweet, pretty as all hell, and, personality-wise, definitely my type. And I'm pretty damn picky.

She and I only hung out twice since meeting, thanks to midterms, projects, and her job getting in the way. But last night at the club, we finally linked up again. In fact, she's the reason I talked everyone into hitting up the club last night instead of staying in and saving money like we planned. Anyways, she and I pretty much danced together all night and, when we weren't, she was all over me. So, at the end of the night, I finally manned up and asked her out. Our first date is the Friday after we get back to Pennsylvania. And she's been blowing up my phone all day, so now she's all I'm thinking about.

By the time the Uber drops our rowdy pack off at the first bar in downtown LA, we're all straddling the line of tipsy and buzzed. That's the Goldilocks zone of inebriation for me. That's when I'm the best at beer pong, pool, and video games, and when I'm my most confident.

Not that I'm shy by any means. I'm just not super sociable unless I'm surrounded by more people that I know than strangers in any given group. And I'm not one to put myself out there and just walk up to a group of girls sober. When there are too many eyes on me, I shut down. Sober me is also too hyper-analytical, which means I often end up reading too much into facial expressions, body language, and word choices with girls I don't know, and the second I detect a hint of disinterest, suddenly I'm unable to keep the conversation going or crack jokes. And I don't care how attractive a girl is, if I'm not being mentally stimulated, it's hard for me try and run game. Because it's hard to pretend to care.

But when I'm buzzing, that's when the jokes flow, that's when it's all just so easy. Drunk me could care less if there's a connection or not. I'm just present in the moment and my inner extrovert emerges, and his only mission is the same as any single guy's.

Mike nudges me as we carry the pitchers and tray of shots back to the table. "Four girls at the high top. Table with the hippy girl in the forest green army jacket and the blond hottie with the bangs."

"Oh my damn…" I say in awe. "Gotta love California."

"Yes indeed. Oh, and dibs on the blonde." He sets down the tray at our table, removes one, and picks the tray back up. "I'll be right back, gents. Mikey Mike has to go to work."

"Where the hell is he going with our shots?" Stefan blurts out, craning his neck to track him.

"He's doing what Mike does," I say, tilting the pitcher of blood orange IPA to fill my glass.

Stefan pours himself some lager. "As long as he knows he owes us a round…"

Unlike me, Mike is more of an alpha when it comes to picking up ladies. He's the kind of guy that will go up to an entire bachelorette party or a flock of gals having ladies' night out to chat them up. Even if he was wearing a dress he could probably still walk away with a number or take one of them home. Back in State College, that brown-haired, green-eyed country boy cleans up pretty much every weekend. That's why no one is surprised to see him leading the pack of hipster girls back to our table five minutes later.

"Fellas, I'd like you to meet Alexia, Saffron, Winona, and… Emma," he says pointing to blondie with the bangs, then to the hippie, the tall one, and the Asian, respectively. "We were over there talking and they said they'd be willing to give us the lowdown on all the things to do while we're visiting for the week."

Alexia giggles. "I mean, it's the least we could do after that down payment you so generously presented us with!"

The girls are all really friendly and down to earth, a refreshing change from a lot of the ones I've met while living in PA. And they're a lot more interesting too. Alexia is in a band. Saffron is a cannabis and lifestyle blogger, which is somehow her bread and butter. Winona and Emma run a food truck together.

The girls end up sticking around long after giving us the list of things to do in LA. Maybe that's because we bought them another round of drinks. Or maybe they dig us. Alexia is definitely all about Mike. She's hardly taken her eyes off of him once since coming over. Han's a big foodie, so he and Emma connect on that. Them both being second-generation Chinese-Americans might also contribute to their connection. Stefan and Jeremy are left vying for the attention of Winona since Saffron and I have been off in our own little world since she sat down beside me. From the sounds of it, Jeremy the marketing major is using his knowledge on the topic of Winona's sales tactics to dominate the conversation.

Saffron smells of patchouli and weed, and is not only pretty and super chill, but she's also a bio major and a comic movie nerd, so I'm all about her. Since our second round of drinks together, she's gotten a bit flirty. And every time I crack a joke, she's either leaning into me while she laughs or hitting me playfully after I tease her. Suddenly, Jessica is the farthest thing from my mind.

The girls take us to a whisky bar a few blocks away. Then when hunger strikes again one shot later, they lead us to what Emma Chan calls the "*best kept secret in LA.*"

There are maybe a few moments in life when you witness something that captivates you to the point that all other input fades into nothingness and the only thing in focus is this hypnotizing spectacle of a sight. That moment-causing spectacle comes into view right as I'm walking arm in arm with Saffron to the door that Tommy is holding open for us.

Not sure if it's my blood alcohol level or not, but one of the three girls walking toward us… gorgeous might be an understatement. She's wearing an unbuttoned burgundy and black flannel with a white crop top underneath, black pants, and black sneakers. Compared to her friends, she's more tanned, like she's of Greek or maybe Italian descent. Her honey-brown curls bounce against her shoulders as she walks.

As this paragon of a woman who might just be the walking incarnation of allure gets closer, her sad yet alluring eyes meet mine and a confused smile stretches across her face, probably because I look stupid gawking the way I am as I'm being dragged toward the bar's entrance by another girl. That's the last thing I see before I tear my eyes away and step inside.

Saffron snickers. "Are you that drunk that you almost walked past the door your friend is holding open for you?"

A nervous laugh escapes me. "No, I just got distracted… Shiny object syndrome kicking in."

It's almost 9:30 P.M. on a Sunday, so this place isn't too packed. That's probably the only reason we find ourselves two unoccupied tables. And as I'm sliding a chair up to the tables the guys just pushed together, I see that girl again. And she catches me staring as she takes her seat in the booth, her image disappearing behind the wall of guys who just congregated at the bar between us.

From the vibe I'm getting, Saffron seems like a sure thing. But a sure thing doesn't interest me right now. That girl across the bar that my eyes keep wandering over to… all I want to do is talk to her. She probably has a boyfriend. She'll probably shoot me down. But I don't care. For once. Everything in me is telling me that I have to meet her. And that's a first, even for drunk me.

This girl has me so shook I feel sober again… I can't just walk over there. I need a plan.

Saffron is talking to me, but I'm only responding with "Mm-hm" and "Oh yeah?" and "That's crazy!" That's all I can muster, because I'm all up in my head trying to formulate the best strategy to interject myself into this curly-haired, model-looking girl's night out.

Time is evaporating the way it does when you don't want it to. And no smooth openers are coming to mind. Our loaded nachos, sliders, and bacon-cheese fries come out ten minutes before the kitchen closes, which means there's only two hours until last call. If I don't act soon, that's it.

Stop being a bitch! Just walk over and say hi!

As I guzzle beer with the hopes it'll restore the liquid courage I had earlier in the night, a server comes out with a tray of food and, as he's banking around the bar to her side of the watering hole, the loud, douchey-looking frat guy near the door backsteps and throws his arm back, smacking the serving tray out of the waiter's hands and sending loaded nachos and bacon cheese fries everywhere.

All the onlooking bar patrons harmonize with one long "Awwwwwww!"

Across the bar, the curly-haired girl throws her head back and shakes her hands up at the ceiling like she's cursing at the bar gods for forsaking her. Then she and the girl beside her are all pouty.

"Shit, sucks for them," Emma says. "The kitchen is closed now."

They're hungry and the kitchen is closed. That means they'll leave as soon as their drinks are done…

That's when the smell of loaded nachos wafting up my nostrils sparks an idea.

As Jeremy is reaching over for the nachos, I smack his hand away and then grab up that still pretty hot plate along with the fries.

"Dion, what the eff?!" Jeremy frets.

"Hay!" Emma shouts.

"Wait, is he going to give those girls our apps?" Winona says.

"Aww, that's kinda sweet!" Saffron says right before I'm out of earshot.

As the waiter leaves the girls' booth, curly hair is all pouty until she realizes I'm walking up to her table with food. The brunette follows her gaze and then the head of a girl with platinum blond hair peeks over the booth at me, prairie dog–style. In my peripheries, it's clear that pretty much everyone I'm walking by is staring at me now.

"Hey," I say, trying to keep my voice casual while preventing my subtle smirk from turning into the cheesy grin that wants to manifest from just how damn pretty she is.

"Uh, hi," she says with a partial smile and the most confused look of all time. It's only being this close to her that makes it clear she's probably as drunk as I am.

"I… saw what happened. And uh… you all seemed so damn upset, I would've felt bad enjoying this deliciousness while you all were over here all hangry." I set both plates down.

The curly-haired girl's face lights up. "Are you *serious* right now?" Her voice sounds a bit country, southwestern maybe.

"Oh, very serious," I say as coolly as possible.

"Awww! Thanks!" her very inebriated brunette friend cheers. "That's so effing sweet of you!" She proceeds to shove damn near ten fries into her mouth.

The platinum blonde is too busy munching on nachos, so she just gives me a thumbs up and a head nod.

"You're welcome," I say, trying my best not to laugh at how sloppy drunk they are. "And sorry that we kind of picked over them already…"

"Oh, no worries," the brunette mumbles through her potato- and cheese-filled mouth.

The curly-haired goddess searches my eyes. "Kitchen's closed, you know."

"Oh, I know."

"Hm… Well, FYI, your friends are practically glaring at you."

I glance back at them. "Eh, they'll be fine. Besides, something tells me you could use a good end to your night tonight."

She squints, smiling faintly. "And what makes you say that?"

"I don't know. You seemed bummed or something when I saw you outside earlier."

"You're not wrong," she mutters, cheeks reddening as her mouth stretches into a grin. For a moment her glassy, hazel eyes hold my gaze. "Well, this is, like, the sweetest freaking thing anyone's ever done for me."

"Done for *us*," the brunette chimes in.

Curly-hair shoots a look at her friend, her half-shut eyes flick back to me. "Thanks for making my night, hon." She shoves several fries into her mouth, shutting her eyes while she chews. "Mmmmm… Ugh, yassss…"

Walk away and play it cool or ask for her number?

"Alright… well, you all enjoy!" I say, turning around.

"Whoa, wait!" curly locks blurts out before I can turn around to ask what I wanted like it was an afterthought. "You want to join us? Or can I get you a drink or something as a thank you?"

Screw a drink, ask for her number!

"I'd settle for a chance at getting to know you, if that's an option."

She smiles shyly, biting her bottom lip as she side-eyes the brunette.

The brunette nods subtly.

"That's definitely an option!" curly-hair says with a grin. "Anything for the someone who saves my night by feeding me." A cute giggle follows.

"Feeding *us*," the brunette chimes in.

I chuckle a bit. "Awesome. Well, I still have a full glass back there that I should get to before it gets warm. You going to be here for a while?"

The brunette nods rapidly.

Curly-locks nods too. "Probably staying until close!"

"Perfect. How about you finish eating while I'll go work on beer number…" I pretend to count on my fingers. "I forget which drink I'm on." Her laugh makes me laugh. "Shoot me a text when you're done, then we can meet up at the bar?"

She cocks a brow, flashing me a coy smile as she unlocks her phone. "Oh, clever move. Yes, you can have my number, sweet stranger who made my night." She hands it to me.

Smirking, I extend a hand. "Dion. Johnson."

She shakes it. "Isabella. Monroe," she says, mocking the James Bond–like cadence that I spoke in for some reason.

Our handshake lasts a while. When she finally lets go, I enter my name and number then hand her back the phone. "Don't forget about me once your belly's full." I arch a brow.

Her thumbs tap away at the screen, then my phone vibrates in my pocket. "Oh, I won't. Don't you leave until I repay my debt, okay?"

"I wouldn't dare, Isabella."

3
Isabella

Sunday

"THAT GUY LITERALLY JUST up and brought us pretty much all of their food without even hesitating," Riley says as we all watch him walk away. "Talk about a romantic gesture."

"Right?" I say, turning my attention back to the fries my stomach so desperately needs. I can't stop freaking smiling, even while I'm chewing. "That was, like, the sweetest thing ever."

"Like, genuinely sweet, even if he clearly wants to bang you," Candice says. "He seemed pretty cool, too. He had this whole Childish Gambino vibe to him."

Riley sips her drink, her eyes flicking back and forth between mine. "You think he's cute? I think he's cute?"

"I mean, I don't usually go for black dudes, but he's definitely a good-looking guy."

"Wow," Candice drags. "That's not racist at all."

I scoff. "Oh, hush, Candice. I'm not saying I wouldn't try sweet chocolate. It's just that I usually go for douchey white guys, is all."

Riley lifts her drink to her mouth. "And look where douchey white guys have gotten you." While she drinks, she stares over her glass at me with judgy eyes.

"Valid point," I groan.

"Mm-hm... So maybe you should give a nice black guy a try."

"Maybe I should," I say, finishing my water and then palming my White Claw.

"Maybe? Did you see the way he was looking at you? That was fucking adoration. And the poor guy is hungry because he wanted to make your night. If you asked him, I'm sure his ass is drunk enough to chow down on your carpet without a second thought."

That makes me cackle. "I don't doubt that. We'll see."

"Well, if you don't go home with him, Isabella, I will," Riley says, rapidly waggling her thin eyebrows.

I roll my eyes. "Give me a chance to get to know the guy first… Geez."

"Yes, because *you* need to get to know a guy before you take him to pound town."

"Wow." I throw a fry at her. "Judgy much?"

She shrugs, leaning forward with her arms on the table. "No. Come on, Izzy, how well do I know you?"

"Better than anyone."

"Yeah, exactly. And that's why I know that Nelly Furtado 'Promiscuous' song is, like, your theme song, betch."

Grinning, I shake my head. "Maybe, for *once*, I'm trying to keep myself from getting mixed up in any more trouble by thoroughly screening guys before I grant admission to Cooterville."

Riley's snickering explodes into full-blown laughter. It's loud enough to draw eye from our hero and his friends on the other side of the bar. "That's probably a good idea. But 'asshole' isn't the vibe I got from him."

"Same," Candice says, open-mouth chomping on a nacho.

I sigh. "Well, if recent history has taught me anything, it's that *nice* guys aren't really all that nice for long…"

Riley arches a brow. "Only if you don't chew them up and spit them out."

That subtle truth bomb gives me pause.

Once my belly is content, I wipe my hands and finish my White Claw. Now that I'm no longer starving, Bella is in the mood to flirt with the guy I've thought about with every bite.

My eyes wander across the bar. Dion's over there at that high-top table laughing with the wannabe flowerchild that he walked in all arm-in-arm with.

If he's with her, why the fuck did he do what he did and ask to get to know me?

I guess there's only one way to find that out. Though curiosity isn't why I'm about to follow through with my promise to have a talk with him…

I tap the text icon. There's a response from Chase, but I ignore that shit and open the message with Dion.

Me: Haayy! It's Izzy! Thanks again! That's what I texted him when he handed me my phone back.

My unopened response from him was: **Yo! You are very welcome!**

Now I text him: **Done nursing that beer yet?** Then I turn my attention to him.

He urgently looks down at his phone and then turns to me, raising his empty glass with a big, bright smile. Now he points at the bar and raises his brows as he gives me a thumbs up.

Smiling, I make a slow, suggestive *come here* motion with my pointer finger and then grab my purse. "I'll be back, y'all."

Riley grins. "Should I expect you back at the apartment tonight?"

I shut my eyes and stick my tongue out at her.

"Have fun, Bella!" Riley cheers as I walk off.

I put my hand behind my back and stick up my middle finger.

"Hello again," he says, clearly struggling to fight off a smile as we come face-to-face at the bar.

For some reason, I grin. "Hey, you." I hold eye contact with him as I pull the bar stool back. "So, what are you drinking?"

"You don't have to buy me anything. I'll get this round."

"Something you should know about me is that I never pass on free drinks. Never. And I don't *ever* spend money on dudes I'm not friends with. But I'd feel better about eating your guys' food if you let me treat you."

"Now I feel special."

"Oh, you should." I smile.

He nods slowly. "Alright then, treat away."

"Excellent. So, what'll it be?"

"Dealer's choice. Unless the dealer, who I imagine is a whisky girl, wants a shot. Because I'm one shot away from being obliterated, and I'd rather not blank out on any part of our time together."

I giggle. "Considering I'm in the same boat as you, skipping on the whisky I love so very much sounds like a smart call." To the bartender who hasn't taken his eyes off me since I came over, I say, "Uh… two Stella Artois?" I look to Dion.

He nods in approval. "Excellent choice."

"What can I say? I'm feeling classy tonight."

He just smiles, his caring brown eyes staring into mine and not drifting down at my tits. Shit, he didn't even sneak a peek when he came by earlier.

"So, wait… how'd you guess I liked whisky, hon?"

"The accent. The way you say *hon.* Southern or southwestern, I'm guessing."

"Southwestern!" I say, pointing at him with a finger gun. "Guess which state."

"Uh, Texas?" He shrugs. "Because finger gun?"

"Damn, you're good!"

The bartender sets our pints down, and I slide a twenty over to him.

I raise my glass to Dion. "Here's to you for saving my night."

"Cheers to you for doing me the honor of letting me steal you away from your friends."

We clink glasses and then gulp down a mouthful of beer.

"So, you from around here, Dion?"

"Nope. Here on vacation."

"Oh, thought so. I wasn't getting a California, cookie-cutter hipster vibe from you."

He pretends to grimace. "Is that a good thing or a bad thing?"

"Good thing. Trust me. There's too much of the same infesting this city. Or this planet, for that matter."

He smirks. "I hear that. Well, your turn to guess where I'm from."

I look him over. "Uh… I'm guessing East Coast by the accent and style?"

"Yup."

"You come off pretty polite, but you're not southern, that's for sure… And you kind of have the swag of a city boy. Since you seem more *Blackish* than rapper, I'm guessing a nice neighborhood in Philadelphia or New York? Maybe Connecticut?"

He's cracking up. "I'll take the *Blackish* bit as a compliment." More laughter follows. "And you were right about New York." He touches his glass to mine.

"Awesome!" I say. We both drink. I don't stop until he does. *Why am I mirroring him?* "What part are you from?"

"Brooklyn."

"Okay, sweet! I walked across the Brooklyn Bridge with my parents way back when. I hear it's hipster central there now though."

"I hear the same. I actually don't live there anymore. Haven't since eighth grade. Jeremy, the light-skinned guy at my table, I've known since fifth grade. The darker-skinned guy, Stefan, is my best friend from kindergarten. Now Stefan and I are both at Penn State together, with the rest of the guys at the table. Except Jeremy. He's at a nearby university you probably never heard of."

"Wow, that's pretty wild! So, did you move to Pennsylvania after eighth grade then?"

He shakes his head. "I actually went to high school down in Orlando."

"Seriously? It's pretty cool that you went from big city to swamp to farm." I giggle.

"I like to think so. Moving and being far away from family sucks, but I wouldn't trade the experience for anything."

"Life's all about experience!"

"Damn right… So, what about you? Texas then you moved here when?"

"Came here from Austin almost three years ago for college. And the California dream, like everyone else who moves here."

He smirks. "And what's the dream you came to chase?"

"Let's see if you can guess by the end of the night."

"What do I get if I guess?"

"I don't know… A burger?" *A fur burger if you're lucky.* The dirty thought makes me smile and bite my lip.

"Challenge accepted," he says, raising his glass.

"Excellent. So," I say while he drinks, "you guys are here for spring break, I take it?" Now I drink.

"Yup, yup. We landed today around four Pacific time and we've been bar hopping since six."

I snicker. "Damn! You guys know how to vacation!"

"That's how Penn Staters roll!" He laughs.

"Wait, you said the *guys* all go to college with you, right?"

He nods.

"What about the girls at your table?"

"Oh, they're locals we met earlier."

I smirk. "Oh yeah? You boys work fast then."

"Eh, some of us more than others."

"Hmm… Now I'm curious." I lean toward him, planting my elbow on the counter, and rest my chin in my palm. "That girl who's been glaring at me—the one that you came in with? She seemed pretty friendly with you…"

"Oh, Saffron is *very* friendly. Pretty sure that was a sure thing." He smirks.

I laugh. "Really? I mean, she's a good-looking girl… Why the hell would you give up a sure thing with that hot hippie to take a risk getting to know me? For all you know, I could've had a boyfriend or straight-up curved you."

"Sometimes the best things require the greatest risks." He gets lost in my eyes for a moment. "Also, do you have a boyfriend?"

My smile turns into a scowl. "You recognize me or something?" *Have you seen me on any porn sites?* is what I want to ask.

He cocks a brow. "No, should I? You an actress or something? Wait, no… I bet you're a model."

Or something, I think, chewing on the inside of my lip while searching his eyes. Doesn't seem like he's lying. And thirsty pervert who's seen my nudes online isn't the vibe I'm getting. Now it feels like my paranoia is showing. "No. I mean, I do model from time to time as a brand ambassador for clothes and shit on Instagram, but I'm not, like, Insta-famous or repped by an agency."

"Well, that's pretty cool still!"

"Yeah, I guess… And thanks for basically calling me hot enough to pass for a model." I smile.

He grins. "It was the most logical guess since you seem too genuine to be an actress."

That makes me blush. "So, you gonna tell me why you gave away your table's food and why you've been looking over at me all night?" I nod slowly. "That's right, I caught you."

"Oh, I know you did, because I caught you catching me a few times. And you were smiling whenever you looked over. Now, whether or not you were cheesing because you and your friends were talking shit about me is to be determined."

Smirking, I lean closer. "Answer the question, Dion… And be honest. I'm good at detecting bullshit, even when white-girl wasted."

"Obviously it's because you're friggin beautiful. Okay? But I've seen tons of pretty faces since I've been in LA. Like Saffron. I think she's pretty as hell. But with you… I didn't see just another pretty face when I spotted you outside earlier."

I'm cheesing now. "Oh please," I scoff, rolling my eyes as I bring my beer to my mouth.

"Hey, don't *oh please* me," he laughs. "You asked for honest? I'm being honest, Isabella." He pauses for a moment as if he's gathering the right words. "Fun Dion fact: I'm over-analytical and it makes me freakishly good at reading people…. And as cheesy as this will sound, there was just something in your eyes when I first saw you, something kind, sweet, interesting, fun. But also something kind of sad."

I can't help but smile. "Ouch, my lactose intolerance is flaring up from how fucking cheesy that was." I laugh, as does he. "Cheesy, but also, weirdly sweet." I take a quick sip of beer right as he does. "So, you got a soft spot for sad girls or something?"

Dion shakes his head. "Not just for any sad girl… Fun fact number two: I'm pretty damn picky. I don't just pursue anyone. Take Saffron, for instance. If my boy Mike didn't bring her and her friends over, I wouldn't have gone over to say hi or whatever."

"Interesting… So, what do I have that Saffron doesn't?"

"Aside from what I already said?"

I nod eagerly.

"Well, you also seemed super approachable, unlike a lot of these girls out here, so you don't come off like you're too good for people or whatever. I just liked the vibes you were giving off. I don't know…" He snickers, looking down at the counter and shaking his head. He's flustered, and it's kind of cute. This is much different than the rehearsed game or straight-up assholery that I'm used to. "It's hard to explain… Let's just say the second I saw you, all I wanted was to talk to you, even if that meant I had to give up an easy lay for a few seconds with a girl who'd probably shoot me down or who likely had a boyfriend."

My cheeks get warm, and I can't tell if it's the alcohol or the flattery. "Okay," I say, brushing my curls back as I turn my body to face him, "I *guess* I believe you."

He's all smiles. "Well, good. I'm glad." He brings his glass to his mouth.

I stare at him as he chugs the nervousness away. "Oh, and for the record? I'm single."

He gulps hard and pants like he forgot to breathe. "That's even better news!"

I wink, turning my attention to my drink. "Hey, you didn't by chance pay off that drunk guy to assassinate our food just so you could play at being my knight in shining armor, did you?" I look back at him, squinting.

"No. If I planned it, I would've ordered double the food so my friends wouldn't be pissed at me." He snickers.

An embarrassing snort precedes my laugh. "Yeah, that'd make more sense."

"Mm-hmm. But now that you mention it, that does sounds like a great play for the future." He chuckles. "You know, if I can't convince you to hang out with me for the remaining six days that I'll be in town…"

I grimace. "Sorry, but we may just have tonight together, hon. I go to Cal State in San Bernardino, which is, like, a two-hour drive if I left right after class. Because traffic… And I have dance class on Tuesday and Thursdays. Plus midterms."

"Well, that sucks… Guess I'm going to have to enjoy your company while I can then."

I wink again, as Bella often does. "Guess so."

He gulps down some Stella. "So, what are you studying at Cal State?"

"Psychology."

"Nice! I frickin' love psych. I'm actually minoring in it!"

"Guess that explains why you're supposedly *soooo* good at reading people."

"Hey, if you ever meet sober me, it'll be a different ball game."

"Sure it is," I say with heavy sarcasm.

"Come on. I think drunk me has been doing a Stella job proving it," he says, raising his Stella Artois.

"Ha!" A cackle follows. "Nice pun. You're clever! Cheesy, but clever."

He chuckles. "Thank you."

I'm still shaking my head. "What about you, Mr. Penn State? What are you majoring in?"

"Want to try and guess?"

"Going off of how observant you are and how quick-witted you come off while being visibly drunk, I'll have to say something that requires more than half a brain?" I look him up and down. "Too much personality, style, and humor for computer nerd or anything *Big Bang Theory*. Something in the life sciences maybe?"

He sticks his lower lip out and nods slowly. "Yup, biology. Impressive… You're scary good. You CIA?"

"If I tell you…"

"You'll have to kiss me—I mean, kill me?"

My eyes reflexively snap to his lips then flick back to his eyes. "Wow… Smooth." Now I'm imagining his full lips against mine.

"Meh, I have my moments."

I hold his gaze as I brush my hair back again, clinking my glass into his when he raises it to me. *Refreshing*, I think during our unspoken race to finish chugging the remainder of our pints. *He's refreshing compared to the guys I usually meet.*

Dion beats me to the bottom of the glass, then smirks when he set it on the counter.

I smile, rolling my eyes. As I do, I see a guy strolling into the bar who makes me do a double take. *Chase…* I turn my face and lean forward as fast as I can to hide behind Dion. *Shit, I forgot I told him I was here.* I grab my phone and start texting Riley.

Scowling, Dion turns his body to me and leans in. "Everything okay?"

"The guy that just walked in?" I say, pausing to feverishly text: **Chase here! Distract him!** to Riley. "I'm avoiding him because I'm trying to cut him off and he's not exactly taking no for an answer."

Instead of turning around like an idiot and drawing attention, Dion uses his damn phone as a mirror. Smart as hell. "Stalker situation?" he asks, straightening his posture.

"No, more like it's my fault because I keep texting him to meet up with me when I'm drunk downtown," I say, watching Riley call Chase while waving frantically. "Except I didn't today. Well, I mean, I told him where I was when he asked… But that wasn't an invitation this time. Yet here he is."

"Oh, gotcha."

"Yeah…" I watch Chase talk to Riley and Candice. Now I look back to Dion, searching his face as I chew the inside of my lip the way I do when I'm nervous. "Hey, you're hungry, aren't you?"

"Sooo hungry. I gave my food away to this model and now I have to live off Stella Artois."

I snicker. "Ha. Funny." I grab my purse. "How about we get out of here and I take you to the best diner I know? Maybe we'll smoke a little weed on the way? You know, give you a proper LA experience."

His face lights up. "That sounds like an amazing time."

I nod toward the door. "Great! Let's go!" I say with wide eyes. We hop off our seats at the same time. "Cover me," I say dramatically. Of course, he's already in the process of shielding me from sight before I get the words out. Now I interlace my fingers with his. He squeezes my hand gently without missing a beat. "If he does spot me, maybe seeing us hold hands will get the message across that I don't want anything to do with him."

Dion glances at me, a smug smile plastered on his face. "Yeah, that's why you're holding my hand, Isabella."

4
Dion

Sunday

"BY THE WAY, DION," Isabella says once we're clear of the bar windows, still holding my hand, "that whole cell phone as a mirror thing you did back there? That was some real Jason Bourne shit." She scans my face. "Maybe *I* should be asking *you* if you're CIA."

Dramatically, I look from left to right. "I could tell you, but then—"

"What, you'll have to *kiss* me... oh... uh, I mean, *kill* me?" she says in a mocking baby voice, arching a brow after.

I snort. "No, I was going to say then you'd have to skip classes one day and come out here to give me the full California experience. Food trucks, the beach, sites I can't leave until I visit..."

"Hmm, maybe I might be willing to do that for you... If I knew you a bit better."

"Ask me anything."

"*Are* you CIA, Mr. Observant Counter-Surveillance Guy?"

"No. I'm just good at not drawing attention to myself. And I'm very situationally aware because of how my dad raised me. And because martial arts."

"So... your dad's a spy?" She smirks.

I snicker. "No, but he grew up on the mean streets of New York back in the sixties, so he had to learn to watch his back. Lessons he imparted to me in my youth."

"That's good parenting right there! My dad served in the Gulf War so he taught me to defend myself too." She holds up a fist. "And, like any true Texan, he taught me how to shoot when I was, like, nine." She makes a finger gun, closes an eye, and pretends to fire.

I laugh. "Your dad sounds pretty great."

"He was…" Her words trail off. "He died my freshman year of high school. Cancer."

I squeeze her hand, caressing her thumb with mine. "Shit… I'm so sorry."

Her hand clenches mine as she sighs. "It's alright. Not your fault. The government, however, I will blame." She looks up at me, squinting. "Call me a crazy conspiracy theorist and I'm going back in that bar to hang with Chase."

"If I did call you a conspiracy theorist, it wouldn't be in the demonizing sense, because I'm right there with ya. I'm not an antivaxxer or anything, because… scientist… though, with the government's history of illegally experimenting on people by dosing non-consenting citizens with radioactive particles and shit like LSD in MKUltra, it's hard not to believe they wouldn't do something like that today."

"Oh my gawd! Exactly!"

"And, as a scientist, it's hard not to imagine there isn't an agenda with all the shit they allow in the food and water supply, even if it is just a few *parts per million*. Especially when you look at the spikes in cancer and other diseases these days and how the pharmaceutical companies make more profits the more sick people there are."

She smiles hard. "Okay, I think I'm starting to like you now."

"Oh, *now* you're starting…"

She winks then cranes her neck to look down the alley we're passing. "Come on. Let's go down here."

"Is this where you rob me?"

"Nope." She releases my hand and starts digging in her purse. "But if someone tries to jack us, I have a feeling you'll keep us safe."

"I'm not the best fighter when drunk but, at the very least, I wouldn't let anything happen to you."

She looks up at me, smiling. Then she produces a small tin, a pipe, and a lighter from her purse. "The only thing you or I are getting robbed of tonight is our ability to focus." She cheeses. "Do you smoke weed? It's okay if you don't, so don't feel like you have to lie to impress me."

"I once had a batch of brownies that left me high for sixteen hours."

"Um, damn… Even I haven't been that high and I smoke almost daily. Sounds like an amazing day, though!"

"Yeah, it was a great experience after I realized I wasn't dying in hour five." I laugh.

She does too. "Okay then. So, we can have the gummies, but they won't kick in for about an hour. Full disclosure, they're pretty strong, so that might not be a good idea considering how drunk we both are."

"You might be right. Edibles and whisky messed me up once during State Patty's day last year."

She giggles, putting the gummies away. "Okay, pipe it is." She and I lean against the wall by the dumpster, shoulder to shoulder, and she packs the pipe. "Ooh, you know what? Let's do a pre-smoke picture!"

"Only if you send it to me."

"I can do that."

I wrap my arm around her shoulders and she wraps hers around my waist, holding me close and mushing her head against my cheek.

"Damn, perfect picture on the first try!" she says, swiping through filters. "What's your Insta? I'll tag you."

"At-Dion-underscore-the-John."

"I like it." She holds her phone to my face. "Is that you?"

"Yup!"

"Sweet!" She types up a caption. "Okay. Posted! Let's get high now. She sparks up and takes the first hit, passing it to me after. She watches me while I replicate what she just did. She blows a cloud of smoke in my face. "Okay, now I know you're not CIA or something." She laughs, nudging me.

I return the favor with my puff. "Same goes for you."

After three hits each, we walk the last four blocks, talking conspiracy theories, taking more pictures, and just straight-up goofing around. It was her dad that got her into questioning official narratives of those in power. Then after he died, she, her mom, and her little sister lost their house, forcing her to change schools. That's when she went from cheerleader to stoner after falling in with her new burnout friends.

Now she's telling me about her second semester of college, when she joined an activist group that got involved in Second Amendment rallies and protests against the Federal Reserve and college tuition costs.

"So, at one anti–police brutality protest, I fucking got arrested for filming a cop beating up a peaceful protester. And the other time was because our group was protesting in a freedom of speech free zone or some shit."

"Hot damn… you're probably on the No-Fly List."

She snickers. "Dude, I probably am! Especially with all the Second Amendment shit I posted on Facebook back then… But I haven't been as active in that group since I decided to focus all that energy on dancing again. Actually, it was Riley—the brunette I was with earlier—who got me to sign up at the studio she was at back when she was living in San Bernardino."

"Wait... that's it!"

Her eyes go wide. "What's it? I'm drunk and high and already forgot what I was just talking just about." She cackles.

I erupt into laughter. "Why you moved to LA. The dream you're chasing. You're a dancer! You want to dance. And to model, I think. But dancing is your main thing, right?"

She jumps in front of me and starts walking backwards, squinting and smirking. "You—" she boops my nose, "got it!" She twirls around until she's beside me again. "You're way too focused, mister. I don't think you're high enough."

"Oh, I am. Give it a few minutes. I'll forget that I figured it out."

"Yeah, but that doesn't mean I don't still owe you that burger for figuring it out. I'm a girl of my word, after all." She points at the neon sign ahead that reads **Hollie's Diner**. "There it is!" She loops her arm underneath mine. "I hope you're ready for a weed-enhanced flavorgasm!"

"I am so ready, it's not even funny!"

Isabella and I are seated pretty much as soon as we walk in. It takes all of our focus to scan the menu, so we don't say much, except for when we read the best-sounding food options out loud to each other. The second the waitress brings us our waters we both get to chugging. Because dehydration from drinking all night and the cotton mouth is no joke right now.

"Okay, get the California burger. Bacon, avocado, pepper jack cheese, chipotle mayo... Trust me when I say you'll cream your jeans after that first bite." She bites her lip, staring at me with squinty eyes.

I snort as I fold over laughing. "You're wild. And I dig it."

She sighs. "Silly Dion. This is me being tame." She winks slowly.

"Well, damn… Now I'm eager to see the full you."

"Oh, honey, trust me when I say you're not ready to experience *all* of me." Her voice is all sultry as she slowly writhes in her seat.

I can't tell if she's flirting. "Try me."

She leans forward and crosses her arms on the table. "Fun Isabella fact? I don't have a gag reflex," she whispers, sensually putting her straw in her mouth.

Shaking my head and blinking rapidly—that's my reaction.

"You ever hear of the Gluck-Gluck 9,000?"

I shake my head. "The what-what?"

"*Gluck-Gluck* 9,000. Spelled like Glock but with a U. It's from the *Call Her Daddy* podcast. Google it. I'll wait." She leans back in her seat.

After a quick skim of the texts from my bros cheering me on and one from Saffron saying: **Wow… way to leave me…** I google it and tap on the Urban Dictionary link. *Sloppy, wet, noisy BJ.* My jaw hangs.

"See? Speechless already." Her foot briefly rubs the inner side of my calf under the table. "You're not ready, hon."

"Isabella, if you were a condiment, you'd be raunchy sauce."

She throws her head back in a fit of laughter. "What. The. Actual. Fuck!" More cackling. "Okay, that was fucking hilarious!" She shakes her head. "You know, if I said that whole gag reflex thing to any other guy, they'd be all, like, '*Oh, hey let's get out of here and maybe you can show me what that mouth do,*'" she says in a deepened voice.

"Ha, probably. But I'm not that thirsty. And I *actually* like you."

She blushes, her eyes flicking back between mine.

All of the sudden, the waitress appears at our table and scares the shit out of me. "You two ready to order?" she asks, confused by my reaction.

I gesture to Isabella, who's laughing quietly at me.

"A California burger for him," she finally says, "and the West Coast Special omelet for me, please! Ooo, with home fries. Oh, and apple pie. But could you bring that out later? Like, after we're done?"

"Certainly."

"Oh, and more water, please!" Isabella chirps again.

The woman smiles. "I'll bring you a pitcher."

"Thanks!" Isabella and I say in unison, looking at each other afterward.

"Alright, I have to ask… Why'd you guys come to LA of all places for spring break? Why not Miami or Cancun or some shit?"

I shrug. "I'm over Florida. And I'm not in the mood to worry about combating a cartel while drunk."

She laughs. "All very good reasons."

"I don't know, I've just always wanted to visit here. See what the fuss was about. Figured I'd do it before the San Andreas and Cascadia subduction zone levels the entire coast."

She's cracking up again. "I'm loving your dark sense of humor, by the way."

"Is it only a dark sense of humor because I'm the color of milk chocolate?"

A snort precedes her laugh. "Oh my god! No, you goof!"

I wink. "No, but in all seriousness, I graduate in May and I'm thinking it's time to leave the East Coast for something different for the next chapter in my life. You know?"

She nods. "Oh, I completely get that. But don't move to LA though. The gun laws suck. Taxes are insane. The cost of living is ridiculous. There are too many wannabes and fakes out here. And there's sooo much bitterness here due to how many people come here and fail to achieve what they come here to."

"I was actually thinking San Diego. Might venture down there this week since I have a friend at a pharmaceutical lab out there.

"Ew, big pharm…"

"I know, right. At least then I'd get all the inside knowledge."

"Know thy enemy," she says with a scowl.

"Yes, indeed. And whistle blow once I uncover atrocities."

"Ooh, your style. I likey."

I snicker. "I like yours too." I suck down the rest of my water. "So, what about you? Are you content with where you're at in your journey or are you bitter like the rest of this city?"

"Well… yes and no? I'm in school, so I have that going for me if I don't make it as a professional dancer or whatever. I'd drop out in a heartbeat if I ever got an offer though. But I'm twenty, so I've got plenty of time."

"Wait… *twenty*? Were we or were we not drinking together at a bar?"

She puts a finger to her lips. "Shhh… I have a really good fake. Don't tell anyone."

"And here I thought we were both twenty-one." I shake my head. "You are just full of surprises!"

"Oh, you have no idea, hon."

"What else haven't you told me?"

"Many things."

"Tell me something interesting then," I say.

"Um, do you watch *So You Think You Can Dance*?"

"Yup! I used to back in high school all the time with my mom. Now I only watch the audition rounds, if I'm not studying."

"Well, guess who auditioned last year only to flame out after the first round," she says.

"Damn, that sucks. Well, I'm sure you did great either way."

"Thanks."

"You're welcome. It's pretty cool that you at least put yourself out there and went for it!"

She rolls her bloodshot eyes. "I guess…"

"Was your audition on TV?"

"Mm-hm."

"Is that why you asked if I recognized you?"

"Yup. it was either that or Instagram." There's something off in her voice when she says that. "What about you, Dion? Tell me something interesting about you."

"Well, my life isn't super interesting. Uh, let's see… I was in Brooklyn when 9/11 happened. I was young, so the whole ordeal of terrorism and planes deliberately flying into buildings was confusing, but I'll never forget that smell of burning buildings that washed over my area."

"Geez, I didn't even think about that when you said you were from there. Did you lose anyone?"

I shake my head. "My cousin was one of the people running through the dust clouds. But he made it across the bridge."

"That's fucking nuts."

"Yeah… On a lighter note, I once went hiking drunk in the woods after midnight with friends and we lost our one flashlight. Um… oh, I might have had alcohol poisoning once after drinking for twelve hours. Thanks to beer Olympics. And I've only been kicked out of one bar in my whole college career."

She giggles at most of that. "Why'd you get kicked out?"

"Do you have a strong stomach?"

"I've waded through pools of vomit at more parties than one person probably should in a lifetime, so yeah."

"Okay. Well, it was earlier this year. The bathroom line was stupid long and I was nauseous after chugging two pitchers of a sickeningly sweet blue mixed drink. I projectile vomited all over a friend's shoes as I heard a girl screaming, '*Oh my gawd, it's blue! Why is it blue?*' which made me laugh during the uncontrollable spewing."

She's cracking up. "Your life sounds pretty comical for a science nerd."

"You have no idea…"

Suddenly, the waitress is looming over our table with the tray of food. I only jump a little this time.

I cut my burger in half to share it with Isabella as she's cutting her omelet to share with me. We're too busy moaning as we devour the food to talk, but when we do take breaks in between chewing for what feels like forever, we continue on the track of sharing crazy college stories. Considering one involved her randomly going to Tijuana after a bout of day drinking, she has me beat.

It feels like we've been here for three hours, but it really only took us about an hour to get most of the food down. Had we not been so engrossed by our conversation and hindered by never-ending laughs, we probably would've finished eating twenty minutes ago. When the waitress returns with the boxes for our food, Isabella snags the check while I'm still struggling to get my wallet.

"Come on," I plead, "you already got me the beer. Let me treat you."

"You already treated me tonight. And I owe you a burger, remember?"

"I guess you're right."

"Of course I'm right. Don't worry, I'm not hard pressed for money."

"Fine, but when I see you next time, I get to buy you dinner."

She cocks a brow. "Next time?"

"Yeah. Perhaps I'll drive up to San Bernardino to take you out after class, if you're free at any point."

She nods. "Maybe I'll take you up on that." She slaps her bank card on the table.

"So, what do you do part time that makes you enough to not be hard-pressed like the rest of us broke college kids?"

"I'm a stripper," she says very matter-of-factly.

I search her eyes. "No, you're not…"

She just stares back in silence.

"Wait… really?"

"Kidding. Good at reading people, huh?" she says.

"Maybe you are an actress, after all…"

"I'm no actress. Or a stripper. But would you judge me if I was? A stripper, that is."

"Nope. Not at all. Some people have to do what they have to do. Or want to do, I guess. Like all those girls selling nudes on Only Fans nowadays. Your life, your choice! Props to anyone who can make money without suffering in a cubicle!"

She claps. "Preach! That's some open-minded, Californian thinking, right there."

"Close-mindedness ain't my jam."

"Good to know!" She leans forward. "Different question. Would you date a stripper? Or, like, a camgirl?"

I twist my mouth to the side. "It'd definitely be something I'd have to acclimate to, but I wouldn't say no if I met someone that I was crazy about who was. Honestly, it's not much different than going to a nude beach with your significant other, right?"

She smirks. "Yeah, pretty much the same, aside from all the pole spinning and dildos."

I snicker. "Raunchy sauce…"

She cracks up. "Shit, I don't know why that's so funny to me!"

"Might be because you're drunk and high."

"You know what, that might be it, genius." She checks her phone and then stares at me in silence, smiling. "So… my Uber is almost here. Would you like to come back with me to Riley's place for some Perrier water and weed? It's the only way to end a night out in Cali."

"Hell, if you asked me to come back and help you paint, I'd probably say yes if that meant our time together didn't have to end."

She blushes. "Perfect. Because, for some reason, even though I'm supposed to be up early tomorrow, I'm not ready to call it a night yet." She pats my hand. "Let's go." She slides out of the booth and leads the way to the exit. "Oh, and don't presume that because I'm *raunchy sauce* and a bit of a flirt that this is me trying to hook up with you because you sacrificed an easy lay and gave up food for me," she says as we step outside.

I bump against her as we walk. "The thought didn't even cross my mind, because you owe me nothing. Also, I try not to presume or expect things. That's the best way to avoid disappointment, after all." I open the Uber door for her. "Whatever happens, happens."

She looks at me. "I may actually believe you."

"You should. I haven't lied to you all night. And I'm not going to start now."

She smiles and then climbs in the back of the car.

The Uber pulls up to Riley's apartment in fifteen minutes. Isabella unlocks the door and shuts it quietly behind us. She then kicks off her shoes by the door, holding onto me so she doesn't topple over. I do the same, using the wall to balance.

She sets the Styrofoam box with the untouched pie on the counter. "Bathroom is the first door on the right," she whispers. "The door next to it is mine. Well, not mine... but you know what I mean." She hands me her purse, bouncing in place. "Grab some Perrier waters from the fridge, then go on ahead in the room and get your smoke on while I pee. Kay?"

"Alright," I whisper back.

Hunched over, she waddles hurriedly to the bathroom.

After shoving a bottle in each pocket and two in her purse, I step into the room and flick on the light, then shut the door as quietly as I can. This room is bare, aside from the floor lamp by the door and a bed with unmade lavender sheets topped with two pillows. I sit on the edge and then scoot back until my back is against the wall. Then I crack open the little green bottle and get to chugging.

There's a flush, the sink goes on, then the door ahead opens and Isabella steps out. "What. A. Relief," she pants.

"I went before we left Hollie's and I'm about ready to go again!" I smirk, extending a bottle to her as she crawls across the bed.

"Never underestimate the power of chugging half a pitcher of water ten minutes before you leave a restaurant," she says, slumping against the pillow I'm holding against the wall. "Thank you. Such a gentleman. Last of a dying breed." She chugs her sparkling water.

"Gentlemen and people with common sense—all endangered species."

She laughs, picking up the pipe and lighter resting between us. "God, you are so right about that." She sparks up and takes a pull.

I go next.

"Can I confess something, Dion?"

"But of course."

She takes another hit, holds it, then blows it out slow. "I was having a really shit day and then you came along and turned it all around and legit made my night." She turns to me. "Not just with the food thing earlier but, like, just hanging with someone who's so chill and witty and genuine—it was super refreshing compared to the fuckboys I usually meet or waste my time with." Her hand falls on mine. "And I'm really glad that we met."

"Thanks for the compliments. It goes without saying that I'm glad we met too. I should probably text Saffron to thank her. That bar we met at was her idea." I take a hit, then hand it off to her.

She giggles. "Oh, I'm sure that'd go over well." She takes one more pull and hands it back.

"I'm good for now," I say, coughing after.

"Same. I'm baked." She sets it near the edge.

I stare up at the non-spinning ceiling fan. "You know, I don't think I've ever hit it off with anyone the way we did tonight."

There's a snicker. "I was *literally* sitting here thinking that just now." She turns to me right as I'm turning to her.

"Like, it's never been this easy hanging with someone I just met. Never." I lay my head back and stare into the bathroom. "Things between us feel so… natural."

"Right? Like we've been friends for years or some shit!"

"Exactly!" I turn to her. "But not, like, friendzone friends, right?"

She grins, her chest jumping with each silent laugh. "No, not friendzone friends…" She stares in silence for a moment, eyes half closed. "Speaking of which, I can't believe you haven't made a move all night. Like, most guys would've tried the second we left the bar. And then again in the alley. And in the Uber. And as soon as I sat on the bed."

"Oh, trust me, I wanted to all those times."

"Yeah? So why haven't you yet?" Her voice is softer now.

I shrug. "I've got a bad habit of acting too slow when I meet a girl a really like. Call it my fatal flaw."

She flashes a sleepy smile, planting a finger on my hand. "Funny, my fatal flaw is that I've got a bad habit of moving too fast." Her words give me pause but then she slowly traces a line up my arm. "Something I learned from losing my dad is that life's too short not to live it like any day could be your last." She gives me this alluring-ass look. "Gotta go for what you want while you can, you know?"

"Maybe we meet somewhere in the middle then?" I finally say.

"What does somewhere in the middle look like?"

I lean in and kiss her on the cheek, holding my lips a breath away from her cheek after.

She turns and presses her mouth into mine. Her soft lips make my body buzz in a way weed and alcohol don't.

I cup the side of her face. She rakes her fingers through my short afro. Her tongue slides into my mouth. Mine slips past hers.

The longer we kiss, the more we caress and explore each other. The more time that passes, the hotter things get. Then, as we're shifting around in bed, the pressure in my bladder hints that it's better to pause now rather than later.

"Sorry," I say breathlessly after I pull away just a bit, "but I really gotta pee."

She giggles. "Go ahead. I'd rather wait a minute than have to explain to Riley why the bed smells like piss tomorrow."

I laugh into her mouth, then peck her lips once more before I maneuver off the bed. "Don't go anywhere!" I say, walking backwards, watching her sprawl out across the bed.

"Right now, I'm too high to even leave this bed, sunshine." She clutches the pillow to her chest.

"Valid point." I shut the door behind me.

"Oh, hey, when you're done, can you bring the pie in?"

"You got it!"

It feels like I've been here peeing for three minutes. When it's finally over, I wash my hands and then sneak out to the kitchen.

What the hell did I come out here for? I hate being high sometimes. I go to the fridge and look around for something to jog my memory, my eyes lingering on the Perrier water. Then I turn and see the food from the diner. "Pie," I whisper to myself. I grab the container, then slowly open drawers until I find the forks. I snag one tiptoe back to the room. Of course, when I shut the door and turn around, I find that Isabella is fast asleep.

Shit.

Can't blame her. I'm beat too. Being stoned, buzzed, and jetlagged has me ready to KO. I grab the bunched-up blanket at the end of the bed and drape it over her. Then I lay on the edge of the bed that she's not taking up.

Not too fast, not too slow. Somewhere in the middle...

5
Isabella

Monday

IT'S A FULL BLADDER, not my phone that wakes me. Perfect, considering I forgot to set an alarm last night. And judging by the amount of light shining through the blinds, I'm probably already too late to make it to my first class. Not that I care.

I roll over and sit up to find Dion curled near the bottom corner of the bed, head on the mattress instead of a pillow—since I had them both, no covers on him at all, one arm dangling off the edge.

Didn't even try to spoon with me. Such a gentleman.

Not gonna lie... That make-out session had me so ready to go and I am hella *pissed* at myself for falling asleep before we could get it in.

Oh, the things I would've done to you last night, sweetie.

I mean, it's not like I can't wake him up to give him a proper goodbye. Given how much he was drooling over me, something tells me he wouldn't last too long. I could probably get off and get out of here in time to still make the meeting with the dean.

And given the nature of this meeting, something tells me I could use a good start to the day.

Nah, I think, smiling at the guy who made my night. On the off chance that he can withstand the ride I'd give him and somehow contain himself for more than five minutes, I don't think

I should chance it. Especially if he's good and can keep his shit together, because then I'd want it to last, which would be problematic as the dean said today was the only day he could meet until two weeks from now. And this harassment shit needs to be taken care of today.

Maybe I'll have to see you later in the week, after all…

Or maybe I'll let last night be the end of it. He seems like too good of a guy, and he legit was acting like he caught feelings for me already. Seeing him again will only end with me hurting him. Or maybe he'll just end up disappointing me before then. A funny, smart, open-minded, kind, caring guy in a strong, handsome package, a guy that doesn't act like he just wants me for sex—I think I'd rather keep that illusion of the perfect gentleman in my head intact. That way, there will always be hope that if there's one person worth being with out there, there could be more. Should I ever decide that monogamy is something I'd be willing to try again, that is.

I grab my phone, then lift the covers and drape them over Dion. The time is 7:31 A.M. Class is definitely out, but the meeting can still happen, so long as there's not some crazy accident on the 210.

I bring my overnight bag into the bathroom without bumping it against the wall, then I pee without flushing, in case he's a light sleeper. After washing my hands and splashing some water on my face, I slip into the living room, where I find the early-bird, Riley, curled up on the couch reading like she typically does on weekends.

"Morning, Izzy!" Riley sings. "I was just getting ready to wake you up!"

"Morning," I whisper, holding my pointer finger to my mouth. "I'm trying to sneak out without waking up food guy."

She arches a brow. "Um, any particular reason other than the whole you don't like goodbyes thing? Like, was last night super awkward? Or is he a creep? If it's the latter, don't you dare leave him here." She squints at me.

"No! Dion's really friendly and sweet, actually. A real gentleman. I just know he's going to want to talk some more, and then I'm going to indulge him for a bit because we kinda hit it off. Then I'm going to want to do *other* things. And I can't miss this meeting."

Riley waggles her eyebrows. "Well then... He must have been something else if *you* want to get it in again the morning after a hookup, missy."

"Oh, we never even fucked last night, girl. We made out, then he went to the bathroom, and that's when I passed out."

She snickers. "And, even sober, you're thinking about picking up where you left off... Interesting."

"Don't read too much into it."

"Give me the Cliff's Notes on this guy and your night together before I decide if I'll let you leave him here with me."

I sum up everything as quickly as possible.

When I'm done, the faint smile Riley maintained during story time broadens. "Fine. I'll let him crash here for a few more minutes, but you owe me."

After Riley ducks into her bathroom, I quickly scribble up a note for Dion that I tuck in his shoe. Then I'm out the door.

For the last forty minutes of this drive, all I've been thinking about was last night. Honestly, that was the best night I had in a long while. Odd considering the circles I roll in now. It was so fun, so real, so different from any date or night out with a rando that I've ever had. That's probably due to the fact that he was so unlike anyone I've ever met, yet... somehow so familiar to me.

There was even something different about making out with him, which is weird because I've made out with dozens of guys.

Pretty much every one I've ever hooked up with grabs ass or slips a hand between my legs or down my pants within the first minute or so. Last night? Dion wasn't handsy at all. Every kiss, every slither of the tongue, it was something foreign… like slow, sensual passion versus the sloppy, primal lust I'm accustomed to.

And I liked it.

Like, I don't get it, though. I basically told him I can swallow swords, I flirted, I brought him *home* with me, I told him I typically move fast, I gave him *fuck-me* eyes… He should have been voracious after I kissed him, like all the rest. He should have been fumbling to rip my clothes off and racing to pound me into ecstasy like I wanted. But instead he was all slow and tender, thoughtful with his touch, like every peck and caress and probing of his tongue in my mouth was something to enjoy and appreciate.

And I liked it.

Oddly enough, I wasn't racing to undo his pants the way I set out to, the way I always do. I was right there in sync with him— kissing slowly, touching lightly above the waist. Like, what?

Ugh, and there was something weirdly hot about how spending time with me legitimately seemed to be enough for him, despite how badly I know he wanted me since he walked across that bar and sacrificed his meal as an opener to talk to me. I'm not sure why that's a turn on. Maybe because this is the only instance that comes to mind where someone wanted *me* more than they wanted to get in me?

One-night stands always start the same way, with me drunk and seducing whichever guy caught my eye that night, or day. I've never been turned down by a single guy. Hell, I've even convinced a few guys who were spoken for to give in, including my roommate's boyfriend. Having to find a new place after wasn't worth the six minutes of mediocrity.

My body count had been on a steady uptick since starting college. Having fun without committing was great, especially when one guy after another kept turning out to be an asshole. And then Zach Schmidt came along. Like every guy I've dated since junior year of high school, he and I began as a drunken hookup. Making out at that frat party turned to a dicking in his dorm later that night.

It took three weeks of hooking up before it even felt like he liked me. Even after the *I love yous*, there wasn't a change in the way he kissed me or how he was with me in bed. It was just slightly less sloppy, a little less rough, a little more satisfying once he figured out what I liked. Overall, unfulfilling, to say the least.

Sure, we were very close, but our relationship was mostly sexual in nature, which is fine because I'm a *very* sexual being. But I always felt like there was something missing. So, eventually, although I loved him dearly, my interest began to fade. When I began feeling like something was missing, I wondered if it was because maybe one person could never give you everything.

Now that I've gained this new experience, I'm wondering if I've finally a discovered a missing piece to the puzzle.

And the more I reflect on it all, the more curious I am to see what I missed out on last night.

I get to San Bernardino a little after nine, which gives me enough time to stop at my apartment to shower quickly and put on something that doesn't smell like dank weed. Since the line isn't long at my go-to on-campus café, I stop in for a bagel and an iced cinnamon sugar latte on the way to the meeting.

I rap my knuckles against the door three times. "Good morning, Dr. Wentworth."

The hefty, older, balding man looks up from his laptop. "Ms. Monroe, I take it?"

"Yes, sir."

"Excellent, close the door and have a seat."

I shut the door quietly, then take off my backpack and set it beside the chair as I sit.

"Well, first off, Isabella, my apologies on behalf of the university for what you are going through."

"Thank you, Dr. Wentworth."

"Please, call me Donovan." He rolls left and opens a notebook. "In your email, you said that the people harassing you are male students from this campus?"

"Yes, sir."

"Do you have any proof?"

I nod, unlocking my phone and tapping my way to the screenshots. "I compiled some screenshots of the messages I got from the guys from here. I also still have the original messages if you need to see those to confirm that these numbers were not altered." I slide him the list of numbers that have been texting me, then I hold the phone out to him, swiping through the pictures slowly so he can read the texts and see the nude images I've blurred from the neck down.

"Now, the student who began this revenge porn campaign, is he a student here?"

"No. His name is Zachary Schmidt, my ex, and he goes to Redlands. But I think he is sending links or emails to people he knows that I know here."

"I see…" When he's done jotting down notes, he leans forward and clasps his hands. "I'm going to be honest with you, Isabella. After looking into the allegations, it may be a little difficult to penalize anyone involved considering what… came to light during my investigation."

"Um… well, what came to light, exactly?"

He reaches over and drags his laptop before him. "Upon factchecking the claims on the website that you cited as the source for the photos being disseminated around campus, I discovered comments referencing your profile on CollegiateCams.com, an amateur porn webcam site."

Shit…

He clicks once, then turns the laptop around to me, and there it is—Bella Roeman's profile. In hindsight, that was a shitty pseudonym for my name that any pornoholic with an average IQ could've probably figured out. But I never thought anyone actually would.

Suddenly, there's something discomforting about having thumbnails of my work on this bastard's screen while I'm in the room—especially when he brought it up with a click, which means he already had that up on his computer for who knows how long before this meeting.

Being uncomfortable about it is kind of odd, considering I enjoy being nude online and doing kinky shit for faceless pervs for money. But I try my best to keep that shit separate from my personal life, just like I did when I was a stripper at The Library. Lots of makeup, glasses, wigs, contacts—I thought I could maintain a secret camgirl identity and keep the men paying my bills from recognizing me. But a pervert who frequents revenge porn sites and camgirl sites finally went and connected the dots.

Arms folded, I lean back in my seat. "Alright, so I do webcam work to pay for this school's outrageous tuition. Big whoop! How does that discredit my sexual harassment claims?"

"Well, one could argue that an amateur pornography model who's willing to openly please herself for hundreds of customers doesn't have the right to file suit against male students passing around nude photos from a private stock."

My eyes widen as I bring my chin to my neck. "Are you being serious right now?"

"Would you still be in here today if the pictures being circulated around and sent to you with harassing messages were from this Collegiate Cams?"

"If I'm being sexually harassed while I'm here trying to learn and have a social life? Um, yes… Harassment is *harassment*."

"How are the texts you showed me any worse than the comments on this website?"

I scowl. "Well, for one, the men who comment on there can't track me down when I'm going to class or going home."

"Perhaps." He clicks once, scrolls a bit, then clicks again. "But there is also the matter of the video on this camgirl site of you wearing a sweater brandishing this university's logo while you… *masturbate*."

I cringe at that word rolling off his tongue. My eyes start to burn. "Okay… There are, like, twenty-something CSU campuses. It'd be a little hard for any one of those men to track me down. Anyone could buy a sweater and film themselves doing anything, no?"

"That's not the point I was trying to make. You see, this university cannot be associated with pornography, especially if a student is making money off said content while wearing the name or logo of this institution."

"So, what, now *I'm* in trouble? I'll just take down the video. Whatever."

"Isabella… I'm sorry to say this, but it's the internet. You take it down, and I'm sure it'll pop up on a free site somewhere the next day, if it's not already."

"I'm sure you know all about how free porn works," I mutter under my breath.

"Excuse me?"

"Can you help me or not, Dr. Wentworth?"

He rises from his seat then paces slowly to the window. "Even if we punish the students involved and somehow scrub the leaks your ex-boyfriend disseminated, what's to say it won't keep happening from those who discovered your camgirl account?"

"That doesn't mean you can't try. I'll deactivate the account and then the university can make an example of the guys who have been harassing me. Then maybe seeing people get expelled will keep anyone from taking part in this harassment. Send out emails to everyone. I don't know."

Wentworth walks around to the front of his desk, then rests his ass on the edge. "Considering there's a video with you wearing the CSU logo–embroidered sweater, the university might prefer to take action against you rather than hurt their bottom line by expelling dozens of students."

My eyes are watering up now. "Are you saying that the person getting harassed will get expelled instead of the one violating revenge porn and sexual harassment laws?"

He curls his lips into his mouth as he walks past me, looking all deep in thought.

"Did you already disclose that video of me with the sweater? Can't I just delete it?"

"I haven't. But I am required to present all of the evidence to the university. Unless," he places a hand on my shoulder and my body becomes a statue, "you'd be willing to perhaps provide me with a very *convincing* plea as to why I should keep that video to myself until you remove it." His hand slowly moves down my arm.

I smack it away and abruptly lean forward before darting out of my seat over to the bookshelf. Many men made inappropriate passes at me when I used to strip, so this isn't new territory. But that doesn't mean it doesn't piss me the eff off. "You're fucking disgusting!"

"Excuse me?" He plays at being all confused.

"Really? I come in here to report sexual harassment to you and then *you* sexually harass me?" I shout.

"Ms. Monroe, please calm down. I simply asked you to plead your case to me."

I sling my backpack over my shoulder, then back away to the exit. "No! Don't you try to act like you didn't just touch me and *indirectly* imply that you wanted a sexual favor in exchange for keeping quiet about the video with the fucking CSU logo!"

"Please, keep your voice down. If my colleagues hear you yelling and getting all hysterical over nothing, it surely won't help your case. Especially if you're accusing the associate dean of students, who's been leading conflict resolution here for the last six years, of something I certainly did not do."

I open the door. "Lie all you want. You and I both know what happened here. And I won't let this go." I storm out of the office.

6
Dion

Sunday

IT'S ALWAYS SO DISORIENTATING waking up slightly hungover in an unfamiliar place and not being able to immediately recall where the hell you are or how you got there. Most nights out end with me back in my own bed or on a friend's couch, so squinting through one eye at a bare room throws me for a loop.

Seeing the Perrier water bottle on the floor beside the bed makes her face flash in my mind's eye. *Isabella... So glad that wasn't a dream. Which means this isn't the Airbnb...*

Upon rolling over, it's clear she's already left for San Bernardino. Which means she left me in this apartment with her friend, who may or may not know I'm crashing here.

A random black guy emerging from a white girl's spare room and scaring the shit out of her—sounds like a good way to get the cops called on me, I think, picking up my phone. Of course, it doesn't power on when I press the button. It was on 10 percent when I got here last night, and I forgot to ask for a charger.

Since we made out last night, it doesn't matter if the bottle of flat, room temp sparking water I'm now guzzling is Isabella's or mine. If she has mono or something, it's already too late. As I finish what's left, a noise outside steals my attention. Heading out to the living room and getting this potential surprise over with seems like a much better idea than using the bathroom first and scaring her with a flush. So I palm the doorknob and open it slowly.

"Hello, stranger sneaking out of my spare bedroom," the brunette says nonchalantly as she walks into her kitchen.

"Hey... Not the reaction I expected."

"Oh, this happens all the time."

Frozen in my tracks, I cock a brow. "Does it really?"

She smirks. "Nope. You're actually the first guy she's ever brought back here."

"Consider me honored."

"You should be. Oh, and FYI, she warned me that you were still here this morning."

I smile back. "Good. I was worried I'd freak you out... Riley, right?"

"That's Ms. Collins to you when you're in my home," she says in a posh yet stern accent, glaring at me.

"Um..."

Her expression softens. "Kidding, *Dion*. Just something my mom used to say to my friends. Any who, you hungry? Isabella told me to remind you that you guys had leftovers in the fridge."

"Oh yeah... I might take that pie to go."

"Uh, yeah... the pie stays." She grins.

I raise my hands in surrender. "Home fries and a piece of omelet it is."

She opens the fridge and retrieves the Styrofoam box. "I'll heat them up for ya."

"Hey, do you happen to have a charger for a Galaxy phone?"

"Ew, who the hell has an Android?"

I scowl. "Excuse me for not wanting to join the iCult."

She laughs. "I'll tell ya what," she says, setting the microwave, "I'll just get you an Uber and Isabella can pay me back later."

"That works for me! Uh… 333 North Croft in Beverly Grove. Thanks!" I take a seat at the table.

Now she picks up her phone. "Don't thank me, it's the least she can do for leaving some rando in my apartment. And I guess she kind of told me that you were sweet and to be nice to you, so you can thank her."

"I'll be sure to do that once I can charge my phone."

"Mm-hmm. Bet you're real eager to text her so you can get to arranging round two. You know, to pick up where you two left off before you have to fly back east."

"Of course she told you."

"Best friend, duh."

"Did she also happen to mention if she wanted to see me again?"

Riley shrugs. "Sorry, I don't do spoilers."

"Of course not."

Riley grins. "I will tell you that she did say you were a lot of fun and that you were a *gentleman and real sweetheart*," she says, exaggerating Isabella's Texan accent. "Do with that as you will." The microwave beeps. She grabs the plate out and brings it over.

"Thank you. For the intel and for reheating this for me."

"You're welcome. Eat fast. The Uber is less than ten minutes out."

I scarf down my food faster than I should, considering my stomach is a little off from how much I drank last night.

"Five minutes!" Riley hollers right as I get in the bathroom.

I flush, wash my hands, splash some water on my face, and gargle, then head for the door. Riley's in her room or something so I shout, "Thanks for letting me hang here, Ms. Riley Collins! Bye!"

"Goodbye, Dion!"

As I reach for my black Vans, I notice the paper sticking out of my shoe. It's a note from Isabella. *Reading material for the ride back,* I think, folding it up and tucking it deep into my pocket.

I'm halfway down the hallway, following exit signs, when the door behind me opens.

"Dion, hold up!" Riley hollers.

I spin around. "What's up?"

The barefoot girl prances over to me, extending her phone to me, a mix between a grimace and a grin on her face. "It's Isabella."

Scowling, I take the phone. "Morning, Isabella."

"Hey, you."

"Why do I get the impression from Riley's face and your tone that this call isn't because you couldn't wait for me to charge my phone to talk to me next."

"Well, I mean... technically I couldn't wait." She lets out a huff of a laugh.

"What's wrong? You okay?"

She sighs hard. "I'm fine."

"Doesn't sound like it."

"It's nothing serious. What are you doing today, hon?"

"Uh, Santa Monica Beach and some sightseeing, unless the boys are too hungover. What's going on?"

"Listen, it's a long story that I'll explain if you do me a *huge* favor."

"Ask away."

"Essentially, I'm dropping out of school and moving out of this town, like, now. If Riley drives you up here, can you help me move? I know it's a crazy thing to ask of you considering you're here on vacation and we've known each other for, like, four hours, but my life's crazy right now and I recently cut a bunch of people off and you're the only guy I can think to call on to help with the heavy lifting. It's not much, I swear."

"Two conditions."

"I'll literally do anything."

"You find me a Samsung charger and you also let me take you out to dinner tonight. Then I'm in."

That gets a little laugh. "Um, shouldn't I be treating you for what I'm asking of you? Buy pizza for movers, that's, like, Moving 101."

"Those are my terms."

"Fine, hon. You got yourself a deal."

"Alright then, I'll see you soon, Raunchy Sauce."

A snicker turns into a giggle. "Thanks, I needed that laugh. And thank you soooo much for coming to help! See you in a bit!"

I hand the phone back to Riley.

"Hey," Riley says, nodding toward her apartment. "Yeah, I'm going to get dressed and we'll leave in five… Yeah… Okay. See ya, girl." She turns to me. "Um, *raunchy sauce*? Should I even ask?"

Smirking, I shake my head. "It's classified."

She rolls her eyes, then twirls around and heads toward her apartment. "So, you're legit going to take time out of your vacation to help a girl you barely know move today."

"Yup."

"I can't tell if you're the nicest guy ever or if you just really want to get laid." She gives me a look as she holds the door open for me.

"Meh, I'm sure I can probably get laid for a lot less work if I leave now and hop in that Uber. But it's not all about that. Isabella's someone worth helping."

Riley smiles. "Well, alrighty then. Just be careful with all that nice guy shit in the future, buddy. It's a good way to get taken advantage of in life." That warning sounds foreboding.

"Trust me. I don't just go out of my way for anyone."

She nods a few times, holding eye contact. "Kay, well, make yourself comfortable. I'm going to get ready quick."

I nod and have a seat on the couch, shifting on my hip to fish out the note from my pocket that Isabella left for me. It reads:

Dion,

I live a pretty eventful/crazy life. Like, epic rooftop parties with celebrities crazy. But I can't remember the last time I had as much fun as we had last night! Thanks for tucking me in and for being so chill and sweet and awesome! I'm SO, SO SORRY I fell asleep on you, hon! And sorry I had to run out without saying goodbye. Didn't wanna wake ya... Guess I may have to clear up some time in my schedule after all so I can make it up to ya...

Text me later!

XOXO—Isabella

A.K.A: Your Raunchy Sauce

P.S. I am now laughing quietly to myself at the above phrase...

Her note has me smiling to myself like an idiot.

"Oh, you've got it bad for Izzy, don't you?" Riley says as she steps out of her room.

"No. Your friend is just a goofball."

"That she is, mister." She grabs her keys from the bowl on the table. "Come on, let's go before traffic gets shittier."

7
Isabella

Monday

RILEY AND DION ARE just getting out of her crossover when I step outside. The second he sees me, he's cheesing, clearly trying his darndest to tone it down while giving me a subtle two-finger wave. That smile of his? It's infectious. So much so that, despite my sour mood, I grin too, waving back in broad passes until he disappears behind the rear passenger door to help Riley fold the Honda CRV's seats down.

I can't believe he actually came…

"Hey, y'all!" I say as Riley leads Dion toward me. "That was quick!"

"No traffic for once," Riley says, hugging me and rubbing my back.

Seeing last night's hookup approach cues up a weed and alcohol-hazed flicker of flashbacks from our last interaction, sending something like excitement tingling throughout my body. "Welcome to San Bernardino, Dion!" I open my arms for a hug.

He embraces me, loosely at first then a bit tighter once I hug him harder. And it's weirdly a bit comforting. "This might be somewhere I would've never got to visit had you not invited me, so thanks!"

"No, thank *you* so much again for coming," I whisper in his ear before pulling away. "You made my night and now you've gone and made my morning. It means a lot. Seriously."

"Don't mention it." He stares deep into my eyes, exuding something that can only be described as adoration. Whatever the classification of his gaze, it quickens my pulse for some reason.

"Oh," Riley says from near the elevator, "I see how it is… He gets a big thanks and a long hug and I just get a regular ol' greeting."

"Um, you're my bestie so you kinda have to be here when I need you. He's basically a stranger giving up precious vacation time for me. I think he deserves a little extra praise."

"Mhm, I'm sure he'll get *a little extra* something after this, all right," she says quietly, smirking after.

"Riley…" I snap through clenched teeth, glaring at her only to glance sidelong at Dion to see his reaction.

He's just looking at the floor, shaking his head as we step into the elevator that has just arrived.

The apartment door was left unlocked and partially closed, so I just shoulder it open and step to the side to hold it for my helpers.

I grab the charger from the counter and extend it to Dion. "Got you a present from the gas station, hon!"

"Thanks! You are a lifesaver!"

"Pssh… no, you're the lifesaver. You're giving up, like, three hours of your life for me. All I did was drive two minutes away and spend nine bucks to hold up my end of the deal."

"Either way, I appreciate it."

I wink at him. "I gotchu." Now I turn to Riley. "While Dion is catching up on texts and letting everyone know that the girl who dragged him out of the bar last night didn't kill him for his organs, can you come help me pack the rest of my clothes?"

"Yup, sure." She starts toward my bedroom.

I turn to Dion. "Feel free to delete the voicemail from me this morning, mm-kay? I was kind of a mess at the time and I'd rather you not hear me freaking out. We'll just talk about everything on the drive back."

"Yeah, no problem, Isabella."

I flash him a smile, then partially shut the door behind me.

Riley is all pouty-faced, waiting with open arms. "I can't believe that creep of a dean made a pass at you," she whispers when we embrace. "Are you okay, Izzy?"

I nod against her head. "Better now that I emailed all the evidence of the harassment to the other conflict resolution administrators, filed a complaint against that bastard, and told IT to compile his browser history to substantiate my claims about Dr. Wentworth being a pervert. Told them that he used intimate knowledge from that cam site as a means to proposition me to keep him quiet so he wouldn't try to get the university to sue me," I whisper back.

"Wait, he said that?"

"No, but it adds fuel to the fire."

"Gawd, I love how vindictive you are!"

"You know me, I'm not one to sit idly by."

"Truth. So, you're sure you still want to drop out?"

I nod. "It was something I've been debating for a while. And after today, I definitely need to start over—especially if me diddling myself while wearing school merch might get me in trouble… Then there's also the possibility that these guys I reported might come looking for revenge or some shit."

"Probably a good idea. Not like you can't just finish up at another college or campus when you're ready."

"Exactly."

She leans in. "So, what's up with you and the tourist?"

Now I'm smiling. "Yeah, sorry for leaving him at your place like that."

"No worries. He's cool and genuinely seems nice. Definitely got good vibes from him. And you know my vibes are never wrong."

"That's true."

"You gonna let him…" She makes a circle with her thumb and pointer then pokes her other pointer in and out of it.

"Had I not passed out last night, I would've."

"And now that you've sobered up?"

I bite down on my lip to restrain the grin coming on.

Footfalls approach the room. Then there's a knock. "Ready for me to get to lifting?" Dion says, appearing in the cracked doorway. A curious look takes hold of his face at our sneaky smiles.

I turn and point at the dresser. "Yeah, we can start with that."

Obviously, Dion rides back with me on the drive to Pasadena. I get to filling him in on how being a victim of revenge porn and what happened today led to me dropping out, excluding the bit about how Zach let my whole family know that I used to be a stripper and how the camgirl work that came to light may get me in trouble. Even though I'll probably never see him again after this week, I'd rather him not see me that way. Because I like the way he looks at me and I'm afraid once he knows the shameless things I've done, that will go away.

"Shit," he sighs, planting a hand on mine. Unlike Dr. Wentworth's unwanted touch, Dion's brings me much-needed comfort. "I'm so sorry you have to go through all that."

"It is what it is, I guess." I glance over at him, squinting. "You won't go googling my name to see if you can find my nudes, will you?"

He looks genuinely offended. "I can't believe you just asked me that… Of course not."

"Practicing delay of gratification until you can see the show in person then?" I say, pushing my tits together and shimmying in my seat.

He snickers and shakes his head. "Raunchy sauce."

Per usual, that makes me giggle. I giggle to the point that I swerve. "You didn't answer the question…"

"The only way I'd ever want to see the *show* is in person. You know, if that's an option."

"Maybe it is. Maybe it isn't." I look over at him again. "Guess it depends on if you can keep from disappointing me from now until the next time we suck face."

"Oh, there's going to be a next time?"

Smiling, I turn back to the road.

"Mind if I ask why you and that ex of yours broke up?"

I sigh. "Let's just say I wasn't the best girlfriend to him."

"Gotcha."

There's a bout of silence. He's probably waiting for me to elaborate while I wait for him to ask an inevitable follow-up question. But he says nothing.

"Thanks for not probing any further," I say.

"Figured by your tone it was still a bit of a sore subject, so I figured I'd leave it alone."

"For the record, I *love* how intuitive you are. You pick up on, like, all my cues, even drunk."

"Told you I'm good at reading people. Some are easier than others."

"Mm-hmm. I'm starting to believe you." I take a deep breath. "So, what's your story? Any crazy exes? Do you have a girlfriend back east?"

"I had a super jealous ex who had it out for my two closest female friends in high school but nothing worth talking about actually happened."

"Why'd you break up?"

"I moved to Pennsylvania for college. She stayed in Orlando."

"Smart. Screw long distance. That shit never works."

"Yup. And no, no girlfriend, currently. When I get back home, I've got a date with a girl named Jessica that I've been crushing on since last semester."

"Are you just saying that because she's actually your girlfriend and you're trying to keep that from ruining your chances with me if I see texts from her? Because you can be honest… I'm not going to feel bad about last night."

His face scrunches up. "Based on some of the questions you ask me, you must have met some shitty dudes in your day."

"Oh, I have. And considering that you are literally the nicest guy I've ever met, it's hard not to be skeptical when something too good to be true comes along."

"Can't say I blame you. Most people are pretty shitty these days."

"Truth. Um, you never answered my question."

"I haven't even kissed Jessica yet. Not even on the cheek."

I smirk. "Oh wow… so after months of crushing on her, me and you further along?"

"Gotta go for what you want while you can, you know?"

I side-eye him for reciting my quote from last night. "Oh, so it's because you only have a week with me and the whole rest of the semester for her?" I tease.

"I get a whole week with you?" He plays at being all excited.

"If you're lucky. Guess it depends on how you answer my question."

He grins. "Honestly? Aside from right now, I haven't thought about her once since I met you."

Warmth spreads across my cheeks. "Guess that means you like me more, huh?" My voice comes out all sultry, and not by choice. I rapidly wiggle my eyebrows when I turn to him.

He looks out the passenger side window. "Something tells me that when I get back, I'm going to have a hard time being interested in her. Or any girl for that matter."

A carnal urge pulses between my legs.

It doesn't take long to unload my crap into my new bedroom. After we're done, I shower quick, get all dolled up, put on something eye-catching, grab a few things, and then drive Dion back to his Airbnb in Beverly Grove so he can shower up too.

"This place is amazing!" I say, gawking at the gorgeous interior and the high-end furniture.

"Right? Too bad I've only spent about two of the last twenty-three hours here." He smirks.

"If you're looking to get your money's worth, I can just leave you here." I flop down on the couch and cross my legs after stretching out.

"Yeah, no thanks. Going out on this date with this amazing girl I met trumps lounging around a fancy house any day."

"Oh, right! Can't pass up on that. Not after the girl spent forty minutes rushing to get ready for him."

"Exactly."

"Where are you and this *amazing* girl going, anyway?"

"Not sure. I was hoping she would continue last night's trend of introducing me to the hidden gems of Los Angeles and I could just treat her."

"And what if she picks something expensive?"

"Doesn't matter. She's great company so, no matter what, it'd be money well spent." He slips into the room and then the bathroom door shuts.

If joining him in the shower didn't mean redoing my makeup and hair, I would totally follow him in there...

For the first time all day, I catch up on social media, emails, and texts. Given I haven't really been on my phone since yesterday, there's too much to respond to and too damn much to read, so I opt instead for replying to what's important before googling spots to take Dion to.

Not long after, he emerges from the room wearing a dark-blue, black, and grey flannel with a black T-shirt underneath, dark-wash jeans, and black Vans. I'm not sure whether or not he tried to match with my black off-the-shoulder long-sleeve and the best pair of ass-hugger jeans I own.

Since he missed out the beach with the boys, that's where I take him. Because I'm thoughtful like that. At least with people worth the effort, anyway.

We start at Venice and walk our way up to Santa Monica, stopping for pictures every five minutes, sharing food, goofing around, chatting about everything and anything. Flirting is rampant. More on my part than his, because a flirt is what I am, especially when I'm attracted to a guy. And it gets worse the fonder I grow of someone. And there is a lot about Dion to be fond of.

My face hurts and my abs are getting sore because his humor is relentless. From conspiracy theories to talk of multiverses to commentary on relationships today and why they fail—conversations with him are deep, probably because he's more intelligent than anyone I know. I've met many guys who could sexually stimulate me, but Dion is the first to ever stimulate my mind.

His game isn't really game. This brand of wooing is more like courtship. When he flirts, it's thoughtful compliments like how he likes the flecks of green in my eyes or how he digs my ability to reason or how I'd look just as good without makeup as I do with it. It's that instead of the sleezy shit I usually get like, "*I love your tits,*" or, "*Nice ass!*" or, "*You're sexy as fuck, girl!*" or, "*Oh, the things I'd do to you!*"

When he looks at me, it's like he *sees* me, not like he's only staring at the parts he likes and trying to imagine what's underneath my clothes while fantasizing about what he wants to do to me later, though I imagine that's still happening to some extent. I mean, I'm definitely doing that.

There's this amazing Mexican restaurant that I frequent when I come down here, so I take him there. While we eat appetizers, I down a margarita and he guzzles two beers. When the waiter comes to clear our plates in preparation for the entrees, Dion looks at his phone and then says to the man, "Can we get the entrees to go?" When the man nods and leaves, Dion turns to me.

"Do you have to go or something?" I ask.

His eyes flick back and forth between mine. "Yeah. I have to go watch the sunset on the beach with you, if you're down."

I lean forward, plant my elbows on the table, and plant my chin in my palm. "Well, aren't you quite the romantic?" I say, batting my lashes. "Sunset on the beach is why I brought you here for dinner. Was gonna take you to the pier. I thought we'd miss it though because of how long it took to get seated and served, so good thinking with the to-go dinner."

After he pays our bill, he grabs the to-go bag and we're beach bound. I keep bumping into him as I walk. Eventually, he takes my hand. That prompts me to interlace my fingers between his. We walk hand-in-hand toward the shore, and then he whips out a beach blanket from his backpack.

I snicker. "I was wondering what you had in that bag."

"Dion Johnson always comes prepared."

"So does Isabella," I say, pulling out weed from my purse. "There's nothing more Californian than getting high and seeing your first sunset over the ocean. It's what I did my first visit here."

We eat. We smoke. We sit shoulder to shoulder talking as the sky goes from cornflower blue to a beautiful blend of neon orange and midnight blue with notes of deep purple toward the horizon. Then we both just take it all in, in silence. That's when his hand finds mine. Dion and I look at one another, smile, then turn back to the sunset.

The scene mixed with the weed and margarita buzz makes me feel at peace. Having him here on top of all that fills me with euphoria. I sigh in awe. "This is the most beautiful thing I've seen in such a long time."

He turns to me. And when I lock eyes with him, he says, "*This* is the most beautiful thing I've ever seen."

My eyes close as I laugh. "God, you're so cheesy." My eyes reopen. "But I really like your flavor of cheesy."

A laugh turns to a smile. The smile fades as he leans in.

With my quivering lips eager to greet his again, I meet him halfway.

Gentle pecks transition to hot and heavy tongue play. Right here and right now—I'd be so down for sex on the beach if there weren't people around. When I drag him down to the blanket and straddle him, I can tell by his already-present bulge that he'd be down for it too. My hips pretty much buck forward on their own to let him know. By the second dry hump, I'm ready to go.

Eventually, I manage to pry myself away and I just take a moment to stare into his eyes.

"You want to get out of here?" he pants.

Slowly, I nod.

"You want to go dancing?"

"Horizontal or vertical?" I flash him a coy smile.

"I meant vertical, Raunchy Sauce…"

I dismount and lay on my side as he's propping himself up. "Seriously?"

He chuckles. "Seriously."

My eyes squint and a confused smile stretches across my face. "Are you the kind that pretends sex isn't what he's after?"

"Oh, any guy who says they aren't after sex is a damn liar. Just because I'm not pushing for it or prioritizing it, doesn't mean I don't want to bed you." He brushes the curls out of my face, his thumb caressing my cheek. His touch excites me.

"Then why aren't you trying to race to get me to the nearest bed? Or car?"

"Because sex isn't all I'm after. That's not my sole goal when I finally find someone that I really enjoy spending time with and enjoy getting to know. And, right now, I want to get to know Isabella the dancer."

After getting lost in his eyes for, like, ten whole seconds, I peck his lips. "Well, I'd love to go dancing." Now I rise. "Hope you're ready to get blown away."

The bus back to Venice comes every twenty minutes, so we manage to catch the 8 P.M. back to my car. There's a chill dance club up in Pasadena that Riley and I frequent that plays a nice mix of Latin music, hip-hop, and slow jams.

We do two shots at the bar, then hit the floor. Dion two-steps and vibes to the Spanish music that's on, moving his feet like he's dabbled in salsa dancing a bit. He's got rhythm, thankfully. I get to shaking my hips and ass, mixing a little bit of belly dancing in between. It makes his jaw drop. Then we grind, and slow dance, kissing as we move. My fingertips dig into his back. His hands caress mine, they grip my hips, and, eventually, wander to my ass, palming both cheeks.

As we slow dance to the R&B song I can't recognize, I kiss him deeply and then bring my mouth close to his ear. "My feet are starting to hurt. How about we go back to my place and... take care of my *box* situation."

He takes my hand. "I helped you pack, so I might as well help you unpack."

"Oh.... The box I'm talking about needs to be *packed*. Stuffed."

Judging by the look on his face, the inuendo clicks.

At the apartment building, we make out in the elevator. We kiss as we blindly navigate through the apartment to my new room, tripping over box after box on the way to the bed. The sexual tension is high and there's an itch that I've needed scratched since last night, so I push him onto the mattress and straddle him, pulling my top off.

"You don't have to pee again, do you?"

Grinning, he shakes his head. "Went before we left this time."

Now I work on unbuckling his belt. "Good boy..."

I help him pull off his shirt. He unhooks my bra and I toss it. Once he fishes out his condom, I pull off his jeans and then he strips me of mine along with my panties in one go. He's awestruck at the sight of me, taking the time to appreciate every inch of bare flesh. Lust isn't what's in his eyes. It's another L-word. Longing maybe.

When I pull off his boxers, his freed dong springs to attention. "Well, I guess it's true what they say..."

He looks confused. "What?"

"Big brain. Big cock."

"I've never heard that one before."

I stroke him, then snatch the condom out of his hand. "Oh, it's a new phrase I just coined today."

The second his sword is sheathed in latex, I rub the tip back and forth through my slick opening a few times before I lower onto him and impale myself.

His entire core spasms.

Excitement surges through me from my cooter up through my spine. A tingling scalp coincides with the scrambling of my thoughts and the rush of euphoria unleashed by his gentle touch across my body. An indescribable wave of bliss and ecstasy quickly overtakes me in a way that I don't think I've ever experienced with any other guy, or alone, for that matter. Maybe this is what it's like having someone inside me who actually values and appreciates me.

As he thrusts up into me, the shiver runs back down my spine and, in seconds, I'm moaning.

8
Dion

Tuesday

SHE'S EVEN PRETTY WHEN she sleeps, I think the second that I open my sleepy eyes. My eyes wander from her face to her perky breasts and the upper half of her abs, which aren't covered by the burgundy satin sheet.

No words can describe last night. When I first saw her outside that bar two nights ago, I thought she was allure incarnate, the embodiment of sexy. Now, I don't believe in any deities, but I'm convinced she might actually also be the goddess of sex itself because, holy shit… The way she moved, that reverse cowgirl, the way she gyrated on me, the energy she exuded… hot damn, none of the four girls I've been with ever screwed like that. It was like what I imagine banging a porn star would be like; if it was an authentic love-making session with the actress and a boyfriend she actually enjoyed practicing her film skills on, that is.

I just hope I didn't disappoint her. Despite all the moaning toward the end and the way she smiled back at me after dismounting and lying beside me, she was seemingly satisfied with my moderately long performance, though I'm sure I failed to get her to where she needed to go. I mean, she's clearly way more experienced than I am.

After some time, she takes a deep breath and peeks at me through one squinty eye. A faint smile stretches across her face as she groans. A yawn follows. "Watching me sleep, weirdo?" she says groggily, rubbing the sleep from her eyes.

I smile back. "Not watching so much as I've just been entranced." My voice is just as rough.

Her closed-mouth giggle is muffled. "Is it weird to say that I like the way you look at me?"

I cock a brow. "And how is it that I look at you?"

"Like you see me… Like I'm not prey or some walking pocket pussy that you just want to stab with your meat lance." She plants her elbow and props up her head on her palm. "Coincidentally, that's a big part of why I wanted to fuck you."

I'm cheesing now. "Well, there's a first."

"Oh, it's a first for me, too, hon." She rolls over and grabs her phone from the end table. "Shit, it's almost nine already."

"Do you have to go to work?"

"I uh… work from home pretty much when I feel like it, so no. But I have to meet up with this dancer I know around noon-ish. I'm just surprised you're still here gawking at me. Don't you have shit to do today?"

I sit up. "Yeah, but I didn't want to disappear on you."

"Oh," she laughs out. "I guess I'm not used to my one-night stands sticking around after scoring."

"Forgive me, I've only had one other one-night stand. Her, I skipped out on."

"Wait, really?"

"Really. I prefer something more meaningful. I'm weird like that."

"You are definitely an anomaly, hon." She smiles.

"Does this even count as a one-night stand if we spent two nights and one whole day together before hooking up?"

"Guess not. Maybe fling is a better word choice."

I shrug. "I guess so. But, uh… I didn't want to skip out on you because I thought we could grab breakfast or something if you don't have to rush to work."

A coy smile creeps onto her face. "Breakfast or something? What's *'or something'* exactly?" She searches my eyes. "Sticking around in hopes of an encore of last night's dance performance?"

I shake my head. "Time with you in any form is what I meant."

She blushes. "Since you're sticking around, I might need your help with one more *problem*. If you don't mind."

"Oh, sure. Ask away, Izzy."

A bulge under the sheet slowly moves toward me as her hand burrows its way toward my leg like a snake slithering under sand. "Sooo… I woke up pretty horny…" Her fingers trace their way up my thigh to the family jewels. Her expression conveys both amusement and surprise when she finds that I'm already standing at attention. Little does she know, I sprung up the second she uttered the word horny, as it triggered a pulse-pounding montage of last night's events. "Ooh… looks like I'm not the only one." Her fingers lightly trace their way up my shaft. "Guess we're both in need of some *'or something'* before breakfast."

I crane my head forward and kiss her, wrapping an arm around her waist and coaxing her to roll over on top of me.

Round two definitely didn't last as long as the first. That's because I went in raw this time around due to a lack of a second condom. Gotta say, that was a first for me as I've been paranoid about catching an STD since sex-ed in ninth grade, so unprotected sex was something I avoided unless I knew my partner well. She promised me that she was clean, as I did her, so hopefully that won't bite me in the ass. Her being on birth control was another good selling point.

With a permanent Joker smile plastered on my face, I whip up eggs and put in a few slices of bread to toast while she preps French press coffee.

"Good morning, Izzy," Riley says as she emerges from her room dressed in a teal sports top and black leggings, her purse over her shoulder and a small gym bag in hand. She looks at me. "Oh, it's you again." She sounds irritated, but she's smiling.

"Good morning to you, too, Riley," I say with a smile.

Riley arches a brow and purses her lips when she looks at Isabella. Then she looks back to me as she opens the fridge. "You're not going to be over here all week, are you, Dion? Because I'm not really looking forward to hearing you two going at it every night and every morning."

"Sounds like someone is jealous," Isabella fires back.

"Psh," Riley blows out as she pours coffee into her thermos. "Please. It's more like I'm not used to hearing someone other than myself moaning in this apartment. My last roommate was basically a nun." She pours a bit of the creamer and then returns it to the fridge. "Well, I'll see you later, Izzy. Dion? If I don't see you again, it was nice meeting you. Don't let the world turn you from a nice guy into an asshole. There's enough fuckboys running around these days."

I nod. "I'll do my best to resist joining the dark side. See ya, Riley."

She waves with curls of her fingers as she exits the apartment.

When the Uber is two minutes away, Isabella walks me outside. "Gotta say, this was quite the experience," she says.

I scowl, a faint smile still present. "You say that like we're never going to see each other again. I've got five days left in town; you know. And you don't have school to keep us from hanging out again."

She shrugs, curling her nose up. "True. But you've got your boys to hang with, places to explore, girls to meet. I still have dance classes, and work, and people I need to see. You never know, you know?"

"I guess. But I want to see you again before I leave, Izzy. I'll make the effort. If you want to hang, that is."

"Yeah, I'd like that for sure. But shit happens, so, just in case." She opens her arms for a hug and we embrace, rocking side to side in silence for a few moments. "In case we don't see each other again, I'm glad we met and I really, *really* enjoyed our time together, Dion." She pulls away.

I nod, getting lost in those alluring weapons of mass seduction she calls eyes. "Yeah. Same."

"And thanks so much again for everything you did for me these last two days. You're awesome."

"Of course. You're welcome."

"I'll forever be in your debt, sunshine."

"You don't owe me anything." The car pulling up in my periphery briefly steals my attention. "Actually, maybe I will collect on that debt. I refuse to say goodbye to you now, so if you want to pay me back, let's hang at least once more before I go back east."

"Deal." She smiles. "See ya later then?"

I smile, then kiss her cheek. "See ya later, Izzy."

Back at the Airbnb, I punch the code into the keypad and stroll all into the house, shutting the door quietly behind me, then listening to see if anyone is awake. I find Stefan, Jeremy, and Tommy lounging around on the couches, staring down at their phones as a movie plays in the background. Sounds like someone is in the kitchen too.

Stefan looks right at me when I step into the living room. "Holy shit! Look who finally decided to come back!" He sets his phone down.

"Well, well, well," Jeremy says dramatically in a deep voice, shaking his head and clasping his hands. "If it isn't Mr. Hoes-Before-Bros…"

Scowling, I tilt my head to the side. "Come on. You would have gone rogue for over a day too if you had the opportunity to kick it with a girl like her."

Jeremy bobbles his head side to side. "No, you're right." He laughs.

Mike emerges from the kitchen entrance. "So? Did you bang her or what? Please tell me you banged her after she got you to help her move… If you didn't, it's been unanimously decided by the council of bros that we're sending your ass back to PA on the next available flight. At your expense."

Han appears beside him, nodding, arms folded.

All eyes are on me.

I hold up two fingers. "Last night and again this morning."

"Hot damn!" Mike begins slow clapping.

The guys all join in, hooting and hollering as they applaud.

Mike pats me hard on the back. "He who practically never closes, closes! On a smoke-show at that!" He's not wrong. Isabella may have been my fifth sexual partner, but she was only my second one-night stand ever. "I am proud, bro. So proud."

"You planning on seeing her again?" Han asks. "If so, does she have equally skanky friends she can introduce us to?"

I nod. "First of all, she's not a skank. Secondly, I will without a doubt see her again."

"Dayum!" Stefan says with a grin. "Was the pussy that good?"

"Grade A, brotha," I say, cheesing. "But it ain't about that. I actually kind of like this girl."

"Bruh…" Stefan drags, rolling his eyes.

"Dude…" Mike sighs. "See, this is why we can't take your Ted Mosby ass anywhere."

"Uh, pretty sure I organized this trip so, technically, I brought you along, Mike," I snap back.

Mike scoffs. "Alright, let's not get technical… The point I'm trying to make is that this was just a fling. Chances are, she won't even hit you back up after today, never mind entertain the idea of a relationship if you end up moving out here."

"I don't know," I say. "There was something there yesterday. And this morning."

"Don't get your hopes up," Mike says. "That's all I'm saying."

The guys all nod in agreement like a damn studio audience watching Steve Harvey.

"Yeah, yeah," I groan, waving them off. "So, what did y'all decide on doing today? We still roaming Hollywood?"

"Yup," Stefan says. "And as soon as your pussy-whipped ass is ready, we'll roll out so we can knock out as much touristy shit as we can before we need to get ready for tonight."

The guys all nod.

"And what's happening tonight?"

Jeremy snaps his fingers. "Oh, that's right, you were absent for almost forty-eight hours. We're going to Malibu to hang with these girls we met yesterday who are also here for spring break."

"Oh really? Dopeness!" I nod, smirking.

Mike nods. "That's right, D. We've been busy meeting a bunch of free-spirited gals with questionable morals so we could set up a wild night for the group. You know, instead of just looking out for our individual *personal* interests."

I shake my head. "You know, it sounds like someone is salty that I hooked up with a girl who's hotter than anything he's ever reeled in."

Mike pats my shoulder. "Just wait until tonight," he says, turning and heading back to the kitchen. "Just wait until tonight."

The Hollywood Walk of Fame, Hollywood Boulevard, the TCL Chinese Theatre—we see it all and take pictures with landmarks and knockoff superheroes. Then we hit a bar before we end up at a food truck thing on Sunset Strip.

Jeremy chomps down onto his taco. "See," he mumbles, munching after. "This is why Pennsylvania sucks. There's no good food there! We need more of this!"

"This is why I kept saying we need to move west!" Han exclaims.

"Oh," Mike says. "And here I thought you were planning on moving here to open up an MMA gym in San Francisco because it's a hotbed for mixed martial arts."

"Yeah, but the food, man," Han says, smacking his lips. "The food is the other half of that equation."

Right as I'm about to bite into the taco the food truck server has finally just handed me, my phone starts vibrating and ringing. I fish out my cell and I'm surprised to see the picture of Isabella that I took at the beach on screen. "Yo, Izzy!" I answer after stepping away from the gang, side-eyeing Mike, who's side-eyeing me.

"Hey, Dion!" she says cheerily. "Whatcha up to?"

"Not much. We're just out here in Hollywood hitting up food trucks. You?"

"Ooh, yum! Um, I just got done dancing at this new studio."

"Oh yeah? How was it?"

"Frickin' great! The instructors are amazing. And the girls here are all really welcoming and supportive. What are your plans for today? And what are you doing tomorrow?"

"Uh… Party in Malibu tonight with some people the guys met. Hitting up San Diego tomorrow? Why, what's up?"

"Oh. Fun, fun… If I were to ask you to go on an adventure with me, would you be interested?"

"Uh, definitely. Unless you're going to Mexico because my passport is back east."

"Nothing that extreme."

"Where are you planning on going?"

She takes a deep breath. "Okay, so, basically, I met this professional dancer named Allyson Reynolds at a party last weekend, right? So, we get to talking and it turns out she's the niece of this really famous choreographer named Cynthia Essex. Like, she's really big. If you watch *So You Think You Can Dance*, you've seen her."

"Yeah, I remember her! The hard-ass with the amazing contemporary routines," I say.

"Yes! Her! Okay, so, Allyson checked out my work and invited me to this studio today. After we finished practicing some choreography and recording a video for her Instagram, she leaves to make a call then comes back and tells me that she forwarded my YouTube dance reel to her aunt and talked to Cynthia about how well I picked up the choreography. Anyway, Cynthia Freaking Essex wants me to do a private solo audition for her! She's in San Francisco working on something for a new tour she's putting on and I need to get there before Thursday!"

"Holy shit! That's incredible! Congratulations, Isabella!"

"Right?! Thanks! Oh, and fun fact: you're actually the first person I told this to!"

"For real?"

"For real!"

I grin. "Consider me flattered."

"Oh, you should be, hon… So, what do you say? Want to take a road trip with me? Please say yes! Riley is the only other person I could ask, but she won't be able to get out of work for it. And I could *really, really* use the moral support."

"Damn, you must kind of like me to invite me along as moral support after barely knowing me two days."

"That might have just dawned on me when your name was the first one I pulled up when I needed to share the news with someone."

"Hmm," I mumble, smiling to myself. "Interesting."

"Oh hush. So… You in or out?"

"A road trip to a city I'd otherwise never visit and another day or two with you? Um, of course I'm in!"

"Fuck yeah! You're the best, Dion! Text me your location and I'll come pick you up and take you back to the house so you can grab your things!"

"Copy that!"

"Oh, one more thing. My *monthly visitor* greeted me a little bit ago so, if you're only coming so you can *come*, fair warning. It'll be a sexless trip."

I sigh. "Yeah, I don't give a shit. I'm tagging along to *be with you* and to cheer you on, not to get laid. Do you still really think that's all I'm after?"

"Can't blame a girl for having doubts."

"Guess I can't."

"If it's any consolation, I think I'm starting to see the light." She clears her throat. "Anyway, I'm going to pack. I'll call you when I'm on the way."

"Sounds good. See ya soon."

"Alright! See ya!"

I slip the phone back into my pocket as I approach the guys, finally biting into my taco.

"Don't tell me that was her," Mike says.

"It was," I mumble.

Jeremy shakes his head. "Don't you dare say you're ditching us again."

I grimace, sucking air through my teeth. "Yeah… Soooo… I'm going on a road trip with her to San Francisco. We're leaving in an hour or so. I'll be back late Wednesday; early Thursday at the latest."

"Bruh," Stefan sighs. "Are you serious right now?"

"Very," I say.

The guys all shake their heads.

Mike palms his face. "What kind of couple's retreat bullshit is that, dude? I thought this trip was supposed to be about us spending one epic week together before we all split up after graduation only to end up probably seeing each other once a year after becoming slaves to the workforce. Your words, Mr. *I'm Leaving PA After Graduation*. Not mine."

I shrug. "Dude, I know. Trust me, I feel shitty about going rogue again, but… this girl is just… something else. I like her. A lot. And I need to see where this goes. Shit, for all I know, she could be wifey."

Jeremy snorts. "Pretty sure you said that same shit about Jessica on the way back from the club on Saturday."

"Who's Jessica?" I say with a grin.

"Oh, it's like that?" Jeremy asks.

"It's like that. Things with Isabella are different."

"Aye," Stefan says, "do what you gotta do, D. You can make it up to us the rest of the trip."

"And the rest of the semester," Mike grumbles. "So don't let her trick you into blowing all your money on her, because you're buying us drinks from now until we graduate."

9
Isabella

Tuesday

ROAD TRIPS ALWAYS SEEM to drag on, but not today. Hills of sand and dirt with sparse patches of greenery blur by, the way they should at 75 miles per hour, but time seems to dissolve quicker than cotton candy in water. I suppose it helps that Dion, being the sweetheart that he is, is the one driving. And it helps that everything out of his mouth for the last three hours is entertaining enough to distract me from continually checking how many miles and hours are left on this never-ending highway that is the I-5. Except for the last few miles. I've been keeping an eye on it for a reason.

Right as we hit the halfway mark, I put on Bon Jovi's "Livin' on a Prayer."

"Holy shit!" Dion shouts out of nowhere.

"Fuck!" I yelp as I jump, my attention snapping to the highway ahead. When I realize there's nothing barreling toward us, I turn to him, confused as hell.

"Geez, you scared me, Izzy."

"*You* scared *me*! What was that extra-loud '*holy shit*' about?"

"Oh," he chuckles. "I was excited because I was about to ask you to play this song! You know, because we're halfway there…"

I go from looking confused to cheesing in an instant. "That's fucking great that you were watching the GPS and had the same idea!" I throw my head back and cackle. "I always need my music to serve as a soundtrack to the movie that is my life. Like, I need rap when I'm in the hood, country when I'm cruising through the desert. Indie shit when I'm in a hipster area."

He turns to me, laughing. "No way! I do the same damn thing! Music just enhances the vibe and the vibe enhances the music—" He stops abruptly.

At the same time, he and I start singing the chorus at the top of our lungs, me planting my hand on his shoulder as we sway side-to-side, almost in perfect sync. The way we vibe, it's like we're old friends. Not just here and now or in the last three hours—it's been like that since that first night. If I didn't feel this comfortable with him, I wouldn't have invited him on this trip.

After I finish screaming the lyrics at the convertible that we've just passed and getting a laugh from the driver with a man bun, I pull my head back through the window and turn to Dion right as he looks over at me. Both of us just smile. Warmth spreads across my cheeks and my heart is a pitter-patter.

This guy… he does something to me. Hooking up with a one-night stand the morning after isn't exactly something I do. But lying there with him today, having him giving me that look while he whispered those sweet nothings—it was like waking up next to an old flame. And, honestly, after we parted earlier, I didn't have the slightest intention of seeing Dion again. Unless there was an itch that I needed scratched in the next few days, and then I probably would have thrown him a booty call instead of Chase. That probably would've happened when Bella made her appearance Friday night.

Other than that, what's the point of hanging out again? Yeah, we had a great time together and had two sessions of surprisingly glorious, albeit kind of short sex, but what else is left? Two memorable days with an amazing guy and a good dicking with someone I don't have to worry about cultivating a relationship with is exactly what I needed. And he *definitely* got what he wanted. It's obvious he likes me a little too much already, it's clear he basically adores me, so spending more time together after that would definitely end with him undoubtedly falling for me. And come Sunday, he's gone for good, so why make that goodbye any harder for him?

Just like with all of my one-night stands, I intended to forget Dion when he got in that Uber. Yet the time we shared together, his face, that smile, his jokes, his surprisingly toned body, the way he looked at me, the way he made me feel in bed and out of bed—when I wasn't dancing or socializing earlier, that was all I kept thinking about. It's like in cognitive psych when the professor tells you not to think about a purple elephant. All you end up thinking about is that elephant. For some reason, he's become that purple elephant for me when no other hookup has.

And when Allyson told me about the audition in San Francisco, I knew exactly who I wanted to ask to accompany me on the trip. It had to be Dion. Because sometimes I'm co-dependent and I need support when I go for auditions. Because he has this way of making me feel like I'm up on a pedestal, not only with his words but also with the way he looks at me, and I dearly need someone to make me feel like I'm more amazing that I actually am for an audition this big. Also, other than Riley, I don't exactly have anyone right now that I could've called on. Considering she can't take off work for this trip and Dion is basically putty in my hands at this point, I figured it wouldn't hurt to see if I could drag him along for the trip. So what if he had to abandon his friends during their last college vacation for me? Coming was his choice.

And choosing me over his friends even though it pissed them off? Tagging along when I told him sex was off the table? That just tells me how much he actually cares.

It's just after 8 P.M. when we pull into the driveway of our Airbnb. I grab my purse, then head to the rear passenger door.

"I got the bags," Dion says as I open the door.

I place a hand on my chest, batting my lashes. "Oh, my, such a gentleman," I say in my best southern belle accent.

I skip gleefully over to the door and punch the four-digit code into the keypad, shaking my hips from one side to the next with each press.

"Someone's happy." He laughs as he comes up behind me.

I am and I don't know why. "Maybe. Or maybe I just like teasing you." I look back at him, leaning against the door and doing a half-assed twerk.

"Holy hell," he says in awe, jaw hanging. "You are something else."

I give him a wink before opening the door.

It's a one-bedroom, one-bathroom house nestled in Noe Valley, San Francisco, seventeen minutes away from the Herbst Theatre—the site of tomorrow's audition. Given the location and how nice this place is, $125 per night seems too cheap. That's probably due mainly to the time of the year. I totally could've paid for it myself, but Dion insisted on Venmo-ing me money for half of it. I didn't fight him over it for long. Taking money from guys is my livelihood after all, though taking money from him makes me feel guilty for some reason. Probably because he's not a creep. Probably because he's the best guy I know.

"All yours!" I announce upon emerging from the bathroom.

He rises from the couch, handing off his phone to me as we pass each other. "There are some good food options around here on Uber Eats. I'm game for whatever you want. As long as it's not sushi."

I flop on the couch and get to scrolling. "What? You don't like sushi?" I shout, shamelessly switching from Uber Eats to text messages. He texted that Jessica girl once since Sunday before we met. Other than that, he's only texted his mom and his boys in a group text.

"Microbiology ruined raw fish for me!" he hollers so I can hear him through the closed door. "I like to minimize the risk of getting food poisoning and parasites! Didn't you hear about that one guy who had worms throughout his body?"

"Aaaaand now I'm scared of un-cooked sushi forever," I proclaim, skimming texts to and from his boys. They complained about him running away with me. He hasn't texted them anything perverted or rude about me. ***This girl is amazing*** is part of one of his responses, and reading it makes me blush. "Thank you very much."

There's a flush, then the sink goes for a bit before he emerges. Swiping back to Uber Eats, I say, "Do you like Thai?"

"I love Thai food!" he says, flopping onto the cushion beside me.

I lean against him. "Perfect! I'll have pad Thai." I hand the phone back to him.

"Drunken noodles for me," he says, thumbing through the options. "Spring rolls?"

"Mmmm… Please." I palm the remote and power on the TV. "Netflix or cable?"

"Netflix."

"Oh, should I check the fridge to see if there's some chill?"

Smirking, he snickers. "Very clever, Raunchy Sauce."

A fit of laughter overtakes me as I click through movie options. "Oh, look, a recommended Netflix series about dancing called *Soundtrack*. Must be a sign."

"Must be… Speaking of which, how are you feeling about tomorrow?"

I turn to him. "Honestly? Nervous as hell. Kind of stressing out."

"I bet. But I've seen some of your dance videos on Instagram and—"

"When did you have time for that?" I interrupt.

"On the Uber ride from your place this morning."

I bite my lip. "Couldn't stop thinking about me, could you?"

"You're worse than the catchiest pop song ever made."

I blush, nibbling at my nail.

His gaze flicks back and forth between my eyes. "Like I was saying… I've seen your videos and you're an amazingly talented dancer. Your lines are sharp. You have crazy good extension. All of the choreography I saw was beautiful." He rests his hand on mine. "You're going to kill this audition without a doubt. I know it."

I take his hand and squeeze it. "Aw, wow… thanks, hon! That was really sweet. I needed to hear that!"

"You are very welcome."

"Where'd you learn all of that lingo, anyway? Did someone Google dance terminology at some point when I wasn't around? Hm?" I cock a brow.

"After years of watching *So You Think You Can Dance*, you pick up a few things." He chuckles.

I giggle. "Gotcha. Well, since it sounds like you kind of know what you're talking about, your praise has definitely eased my mind, but I think I'm just going to be all tense until this is over."

"Have a seat on the floor."

I arch a brow. "Uh, why?"

"Because I'm hoping a massage can help relieve some tension."

"Well, I won't say no to that." I sit on the floor between his legs. "Show me whatcha got, hon."

We watch *Community* while he kneads my shoulders and neck. I end up belly down on the couch and he straddles me, massaging up and down my back.

God this feels good.

By the end of the episode, the food arrives. It's clear how hungry we are by how quickly we devour our dishes.

"I'm paying you back for dinner. And breakfast tomorrow, okay?" I say, dumping our containers in the trash.

"A girl who offers to pay, how refreshing."

I flop back onto the couch beside him. "Oh, but I'm not usually that girl."

"You know, it sounds like you've been making a lot of exceptions for me since we met."

"I'm starting to notice that."

"Any particular reason?"

I sit up and gaze into his eyes. "Because you're ridiculously amazing, and selfless, and because I truly appreciate the shit you've been doing for me since we met. Like, you've been my hero from minute one. And you don't know how much you being here for this means to me. I figure the least I could do is treat you to food for ditching your bros to come on this adventure. You know, since I can't thank you the other way." I run my hand up his thigh, then palm his junk.

His face lights up. "If it's any consolation, Raunchy Sauce, I'd prefer if sex with me was something you desired and not just a thank you."

"And who said I don't have the *desire* to invite you Poundtown again?" I shift onto my knees. "Because I do. For a couple of reasons." Now I straddle him. "Something you should know about me? Affection is how I say thank you." I kiss him. "Thank you for coming, by the way." Another kiss. "Thanks for driving." Our lips meet again, for longer this time. "And thanks for paying for half of this place even though I said you didn't have to."

When I plant my lips on his again, we kiss deeply, our tongues eagerly reaching out to play against each other. My heart pounds in my chest as his fingers caress thoughtfully across my ribs and back. His touch electrifies me. His lips set me ablaze with desire and bliss. Slowly grinding against him is purely reflexive. Through my leggings, the feeling of him between my folds and against my clit has my basement flooding. He's a plumber and I need him to lay down the pipe. Now.

And here I thought I could hold out until bedtime…

I pull away and hold his gaze. "I have a confession."

He looks super concerned. "Um, okay… What is it?"

"I lied to you. I'm not on my period."

Relief appears before a smile dominates his expression. "That's a weird fucking thing to lie about. But alright." He snickers.

"I know. I wanted to test you to see if you'd still go out of your way and come out here with me if sex was off the table. You know, to see if you really were different than other guys."

Laughing, he shakes his head. "You're quite the mastermind, aren't ya, Izzy?"

I squint. "Oh, you have no idea," I say, trying to play at being serious. "The plan was to see if you could make it through the night without trying to get me to give you head or a handy. Too bad I couldn't hold out long enough to see the experiment through."

"If you want some closure, while I would have surely kissed you at some point, you should know that I wouldn't have tried to get you to take care of me if I couldn't return the favor."

I nod. "Considering you came knowing you wouldn't get lucky again, I actually believe you." Now I shake my head in silence for a moment. "My whole post-puberty life, guys only wanted one thing from me. Yet here you are wanting time with me more than anything. How does someone like you exist, Dion?"

He shrugs. "Amazing parents who never fought, a good upbringing, and a strong sense of morals cultivated at a young age?"

"That must be it." I brush his lips with mine, holding them a hair away after, teasing him. Teasing myself. Then I rest my forehead against his, close my eyes, and take a slow, deep breath. "Hey, mind carrying me to the room and taking a *stab* at helping me with this wet panty issue I'm having?"

He's beaming now. "As you wish." Dion rises and lifts me effortlessly, prompting me to wrap my legs around him and plant my lips against his.

Wednesday

After breakfast, we drive around the city, cramming in as many must-see landmarks and internet-recommended stops as possible; that includes eateries for some small plates. For whatever reason, I make him partake in photo-ops every chance we get, like we're a goddamn couple. A picture in front of the place *Full House* was set in was a must for both of us, so I post that one along with a few of the best ones, something I don't typically do with guys I'm not actually dating. And I judge myself with every upload.

Something has been different since embarking on this trip. I noticed it when I picked him up. For some stupid reason, I couldn't stop smiling at him. Then, last night, it took everything to hold off on kissing him until after dinner. One look from him was all it took to make me wet. The sex was way more intimate than the first two times. It was slower. There was more eye contact. Every stroke made my body tingle.

I came three times.

All morning, all afternoon, a passing glance at him has been enough to send my heart into a pitter-patter. Or maybe that's just my nerves from the audition ahead. Making eye contact triggered reflexive smiles from both of us. I'm finding myself unable to keep from touching him. We're holding hands now as we walk down the street, like we have been on and off all day.

I'm not sure when it happened but, at some point, we went from a one-night-stand territory to two friends on a road trip to couple's vacation out of friggin' nowhere.

I'm not sure when it happened, but at some point, I think I caught feelings for this guy who I only met three days ago. This is definitely not something I wanted.

I don't like it.

But I kind of like it.

I like the way I feel when I'm with him. Can't say this is a familiar feeling, either. And that scares the ever-loving shit out of me.

We get to the Herbst Theatre a little before four. A woman at the desk directs us to the theater where Cynthia Essex is. A group of men and woman look to have just finished rehearsing because they're all sweaty and migrating off stage.

"Hey, Cynthia?" I whisper as I approach the woman in a gray tank top and camouflage leggings who has half of her head shaved.

She turns and smiles. "Ah, you must be Isabella!" She extends a hand.

"That's me!" I shake her hand and then turn to my escort. "This is my… amazing friend Dion! Is it okay that he's here? Can he spectate?"

"Yes, it's fine. Of course, he can watch! Thank you for coming all of the way out here!"

I shake my head. "No, thank you for taking the time out of your busy schedule to see me!" I reply before she barely finishes the sentence.

"Allyson spoke very highly of you. And, I must say, my niece has quite the eye for talent. She says you have more passion than anyone she's ever seen, and that's important in our line of work. I dearly enjoyed your dance reel and I truly look forward to seeing you live."

I spring up on my toes. "Wow! Thank you for the kind words!"

"You are very welcome, darlin'." She points at the stage. "If you go backstage, there will be a place for you to change and warm up. Take fifteen minutes or so to get yourself in the zone, then let the folks backstage know when you're ready to dazzle us, okay?"

"Okay, thanks so much!"

"Should I—" Dion starts to whisper until I grab his hand and drag him along.

I take him into the changing room with me. He talks to me about how much he like my song choice while I stretch. He watches as I practice some moves, staring in awe, smiling the whole time, peppering me with compliments with every extension and spin.

I take a deep breath. "Okay." Eyes closed, I exhale slowly. "I'm ready. Don't forget to record it, kay?"

"I won't." He hugs me, rubbing my back as he does. For some reason, it's weirdly calming, soothing. "Listen, you got this. Okay?" he whispers.

I nod rapidly, my mouth unable to move.

"You have the drive and the talent. All you need to do is will this success into existence. I believe in you. So believe in yourself.

Okay?" His words hit with undeniable honesty, sending a wave of comfort washing over me.

My left eye wells up with tears as I give his hands a firm squeeze. "Thank you so much, Dion," I finally manage to choke out. "Fuck, I'm so glad you're here. I'm so grateful that we met." I release him.

He lets one hand go and uses the knuckle of his pointer finger to wipe my tear away. "Oh, me too. And you know I wouldn't want to be anywhere else. This is one of the few times in recent history that I feel like I'm exactly where I'm supposed to be." With his left hand, he caresses my arm. The other gently cups the side of my face and guides me toward him. Then he kisses me nice and slow, with such passion. It sets me on fire. It leaves me breathless, like I just finished my routine. "You don't need luck," he whispers, his lips a hair away from mine, "but I'll be cliché and say break a leg anyway." He pulls away and flashes me a warm, assuring smile. "Now go make your dreams come true, Izzy." He starts walking backwards toward the exit.

With the widest smile possible plastered on my face, I stand there nodding until he pivots around. Then I wipe the next round of tears away before they fuck up my makeup. My body remains frozen in place as I watch him walk out of sight.

The lights bathing the stage are brighter and warmer than they looked from the floor. I take my position and look out to the audience of seven.

There were times these last few days where the sight of Dion made my heart rate speed up, today especially. But seeing him nodding slowly in the row behind Cynthia Essex, her entourage of dancers, and fellow choreographers—it steadies my heart.

The music begins.

Muscle memory kicks in on cue, and my body is in motion.

10
Dion

Wednesday

SHE TWIRLS LIKE A ballerina with perfect form. Or at least what I consider perfect. She prances. She bends to the side and extends her leg straight up into the air. She shakes those hips rhythmically. Her moves become sexy in nature before transitioning back to a graceful display. She bends over backwards, hands going flat against the floor then she flips over backwards effortlessly, displaying acrobatic prowess. She splits, she rolls on the floor and demonstrates her contortion skills. From our bedroom play, I should have known how flexible she was, but her flexibility still surprises me.

It's a contemporary dance that has elements of ballet, flares of slow-motion samba, notes of hip-hop. It's clean, it works, and it blends well.

Her extensions, her lines, they're all exquisitely executed.

Every movement she makes is captivating, mesmerizing. I'm entranced with her right now in a way that differs from the hypnosis her beauty, energy, and personality usually have me under.

To see her express so much passion in her art, to watch her fight so hard for her dreams, it makes me want her so much more than I already do. It makes me wish I had something I was that passionate about.

I'm not the most emotional person in the world, but I feel what her dance conveys. Pain. Sorrow. Joy. Frustration. It's like a story about losing something, seduction, finding fleeting joy only to lose it. I don't know, that's my interpretation anyway. It helps that her face is incredibly expressive the whole time. *She might be an actress after all.*

Isabella spins and spins and spins, descending onto her knees during the last go-around, then she throws her head back and reaches up to the ceiling right as the song ends.

Cynthia claps, and so do the rest of her people. I keep recording until Isabella bows. When she looks over at me, her smile matches mine and I nod and pump a fist. Holding her hand over her mouth, she stands there for a moment before hurrying toward the edge of the stage.

"Isabella," Cynthia begins, "that was absolutely beautiful!"

"It really was," some effeminate dude with a man bun says.

There's more agreement from the others.

Isabella does a partial bow. "Thank you all so much!"

"You can come on down now," Cynthia says.

Isabella races down the steps, my cue to stop filming.

"May I ask who choreographed that?" Cynthia asks as Isabella approaches the front row.

"I did," Isabella replies, breathlessly, looking apprehensive after. "Why, did it suck?"

Cynthia shakes her head. "No! The opposite actually! It was wonderfully put together and well executed. Perfect for the song choice."

Isabella grins. "Wow, really?"

"Really. And the way you show all of your emotions on your face… bravo!"

The others nod, as do I.

Cynthia briefly glances down her phone. "You are very talented and, with a little work, I think you have the protentional to be something great indeed."

"So, does that mean…" Isabella says hesitantly. The worry on her face is evident.

Cynthia holds up a hand. "It means I am not going to throw you into one of my ongoing shows or dance groups. *Yet.* But, from what I saw here today, I think you can cut it as a professional dancer. So what I am going to do is make some calls to see about getting you repped by my friend Dacha over at Rhythmetrics Talent Agency in Hollywood."

Isabella's eyes go wide as she cups her hands over her mouth. "Oh my gawd, are you serious right now?" She looks from Cynthia to me then back to Cynthia. "Are you actually serious?"

Cynthia nods. "Oh, *very* serious, dear. That'd be a horrible thing to lie about." She laughs. "RTA is going to want to see how well you can pick up choreography, so as long as you pass their trial-by-dance, you're in. You should hear something from Dacha before the end of the week."

Isabella hops up and down, hands near her face, arms shaking. "Oh my God! Thank you so very, very much! I will not disappoint!" She extends a hand.

Cynthia shakes it. "I know you won't, Isabella."

The scrawny guy beside Cynthia nods toward the door.

"Alright," Cynthia says, "we've got to go to an event, so if you want to go on ahead and freshen up, I'll let security know you'll be here for a bit longer."

"Alright! No problem!" Isabella squeals. "Thank you again so, so very much for allowing me this opportunity and for your referral to RTA! You don't know how much that means to me!"

"You are very welcome. All truly passionate artists deserve a chance, especially the humble ones who demonstrate real talent. It has been a pleasure, Isabella." Cynthia leads the pack of dance professionals toward the exit.

As I'm rounding my way to the first row with Isabella's gym bag, she runs on her toes toward me and then leaps at me. I catch her and hug her sweaty body tightly, spinning her around. "Holy hell, Izzy!" I say as I set her down. "That was fucking amazing! You were incredible!"

Still holding on, she pulls away a bit, fingers still digging into my back. It's only now that I notice the trembling in her hands. "Thanks, hon!" She buries her head in my chest for a moment and exhales. "Shit... I can't believe I just did that and didn't fuck up!"

"I mean, I've only seen your recent dance routines, but I don't think it's the least bit surprising that you killed it just now."

"See, but you haven't seen my previous *auditions*... I typically never do that well with an audience, especially when it's high stakes. I usually get all in my head and the pressure gets the better of me."

"I guess that means you've done some growing up here." I tap my pointer against my temple. "So now your confidence matches your skill, you know?"

She shrugs. "Maybe... But truth be told, I feel like I only did that well because you were here with me."

I grin. "Pretty sure you would have done great without me."

She shakes her head. "Yeah, for some reason, I don't think so."

"Really? And how exactly does me being here make a difference?"

"It just does." She gazes deep into my eyes. With a smile, she turns away shyly, shaking her head. Then she clears her throat. "Alright, I feel disgusting. I should probably hurry and freshen up before we get kicked out and I'm left smelling like red onions the rest of the day." She starts toward the door leading backstage, tugging my shirt like it's a leash.

That makes me snicker. "Red onion, huh? Figured you were more of a scallion kind of gal."

She cracks up. "Is that better or worse?"

"Considering I love the smell of scallions, definitely better."

"Well thanks for the weird-ass compliment, darlin'." Another laugh. "Speaking of food ingredients, while I'm washing up, how about you peruse the web and find us San Francisco's best restaurant to celebrate?"

"You talk like I hadn't anticipated your success and already bookmarked a few places while you were getting ready earlier."

She looks back at me, smiling. "Oh, excuse me, mister! I guess I'm not used to being with someone so confident in me. Or someone who plans so far ahead, for that matter."

Isabella picks this highly rated, Mexica-Asian fusion restaurant called Bajakyo (Ba-ha-kyo). That was actually my first choice too because there's nothing like that back in Pennsylvania. As we near the end of the second round of drinks, she grabs the beverage menu and debates getting drink three. Considering I'm driving us back to LA after this, me having another drink isn't a good idea. Besides, being with her makes me feel plenty intoxicated as it is.

Isabella finishes drink two a second after I finish mine. "Is there anything you'd like to see or do in San Fran before we leave?"

I shrug. "Not really… You?"

"Nope!"

"You know what I would like?"

She leans forward, smiling. "What? Tell me! Tell me!"

"If it wasn't going to take eight hours, I would love to drive the Pacific Coast Highway back to LA."

"Um, no way! I always wanted to do that!"

"Really?"

"Yassss! Ever since I saw it on the travel channel when I was in high school! Do you want to? Because I really want to! And I'd like to do that with you." She's half-pouting, half-smiling.

"If we drive through the night, we'll miss all the scenery."

"That's why we'll stop at a hotel before sunset, smart guy." She unlocks her phone and starts tapping at the screen.

"You okay with getting back home on Thursday?"

"Honestly, I'm not ready for this adventure of ours to end yet." Biting her lip, she brushes her hair back. "What about you? I get it if you don't want to. Taking Route 1 means another day abandoning your bros."

"Hm, let's see… Rushing back to LA to hang with the guys I'll have the rest of the semester with or another day with *you* on a once-in-a-lifetime adventure. Yeah, I think I'm going to choose you." *I'd choose you every time* seems like it may be too much to say.

She blushes. "Pssh, it'd be silly not to…"

"Very silly." I get lost in her eyes.

The longer her stare lingers, the wider her smile becomes. She breaks eye contact first, looking back to her phone. "Well, we can probably make it to, like, Monterey before sunset if we leave now." She pinches out on the screen. "Oooh, there's a hotel called Monterey Tides right on the beach!"

"Romantic."

She looks up at me, smiling coyly as she makes her eyebrows dance up and down. Then she looks back down at her screen.

I lean forward. "Book it, Izzy. I'll get the check."

The drive south is just like the drive up. When we're not singing, we're talking. Or laughing. There's never a lull with us. The way we connect is unlike anything I've ever experienced with another person. Since we embarked on this trip, I've become as comfortable with her as I am with my oldest, best friends, and as smitten with her as if I'd been longing for her since high school. Hell, it feels like we've been dating for months or years. Given the way she's been looking at me since we got to San Francisco, given how she can't keep her hands off of me, I think she might just feel as strongly for me as I do for her. I hope she does, anyway.

Something like what my parents have is what I've been on the lookout for since starting college. They met on a blind date, hit it off immediately, fell in love in less than a month, got married a year later, then had me. Now it's been twenty-two years of marriage and they're still best friends who have still never fought. Two halves of the same being. I want that and nothing less. The thing is, what my parents found is a rare twist of fate that I doubted would ever occur during this age of ghosting and dating apps. This thing between Isabella and me has me second-guessing that for the first time.

It takes almost three hours to get to Monterey. The extra forty minutes were spent on frequent stops to take pictures on the beaches. Her social media is flooded with solo pics of her along with pictures of us sprinkled throughout. Mine is full of *us,* and I don't care what that means for this potential thing with me and Jessica. Because Isabella is who I want.

It's taking everything in me not to tell her that I want this fling to become something more. I mean, it's only been four days… The last thing I want to do is scare her off by coming on too strong like I sometimes do.

After picking up a celebratory bottle of Jack at the liquor store, we check into our hotel and head out to our room's balcony, where we sit shoulder-to-shoulder to watch the sunset.

I pour a double shot in her glass, then mine. "To your success, and to this dope-ass extended adventure of ours," I say, raising my glass.

"Yasss!" With a nod, she extends her glass toward mine. "And here's to you coming into my life at the perfect time—for continuously coming through for me and encouraging me, for venturing out here with me when it counted the most."

"Cheers," we say in unison, clinking our glasses together and then throwing back our shots.

She immediately gets to pouring us another round.

"If you ever need me again, I'll show up."

She side-eyes me, smiling. "I'll hold you to that. I may need you to come back for this choreography test or whatever. And maybe to my first performance." She giggles.

I chuckle. "Seriously though, did me being here really help that much?"

She locks eyes with me and nods subtly. "Having you out there being all smiley and looking all proud and shit, knowing I had you out there supporting me... It really made all the difference this time around."

"*Really?*"

"Really." She smiles, placing her hand on mine.

I'd be blushing if my skin wasn't brown. "Is there any particular reason why?" I say, interlacing my fingers with hers. *Is it because you like me? Come on, say it...*

There's a moment of silence. Suddenly, she throws the next shot back, gulping hard afterwards. "This is going to sound cheesy, but..." She takes a deep breath, setting her scotch glass down. "When you look at me, it always feels like I'm the only girl in the world. It's been that way since we met. And today, when I was up there on stage, it felt like there wasn't anyone else in the seats watching but you. The second I started dancing I didn't feel any pressure because it was like I was just up there dancing for you."

My grin stretches wide. "Shit, for real?"

"For real … That's why it was so easy this time around. You… relaxed me."

"Wow."

"Yeah, wow is right, hon." She leans against me, resting her head against my cheek.

"Something tells me that's a first for you."

"Oh, it is."

"Why do you suppose that is?"

She shrugs. "Maybe because no one's ever cared about me the way you do. Which says a lot considering we've known each other less than a week." She lifts her head and locks eyes with me.

"At least you know," I whisper, leaning closer.

"Know what?" she whispers back, also leaning in.

"Just how much I care," I say even quieter.

We kiss.

The way her lips press into mine evolves each time we kiss. That first night, it was wild, eager. On the beach and right before we first had sex, it was a bit tame, but still feisty and full of lust. Yesterday, it was more passionate, there was more desire behind each peck and each play of her tongue against mine. Today before her show, I felt something different when she kissed me back. That something different is present now as she's clawing at my arms and back. It's like a yearning, intense affection.

In under thirty seconds, we go from making out to her mounting me and ripping off my shirt. Her top's gone next. Pants come off. She guides me inside of her slip-and-slide tunnel, then we're going at it on the balcony like two newlyweds who've been abstaining for months just for this moment.

She quivers with each exhale, making her breath uneven like she's suffering from hypothermia. In minutes, she's moaning in a way she hasn't the last few times we were intimate. Her vaginal walls contract rhythmically around me. She cries out in sweet bliss, so loudly that the family of four walking along the shore looks in our direction. If she was faking it before, she's definitely not now.

Please let us finish before someone calls the front desk with a complaint…

11
Dion

Thursday

WARM WAVES WASH PAST our feet as we walk along Morro Rock Beach, my arm over her shoulder, her arm around my waist. Her honey-brown curls tickle my face and neck as the cool breeze blows her locks my way.

Our post-lunch walk is a warmer, sunnier recreation of the one we took three hours ago following our complimentary breakfast, with the exception of not having hot coffees in hand this time around.

We stop 300 or so feet away from Morro Rock for our photo op before meandering back to shore.

I let out a heavy sigh.

"What's wrong?" Isabella asks, examining the seashell she just picked up.

"I can't believe this little getaway of ours is three hours from being over."

"I know, right?" She plays with the shell for a moment. "I imagine things will be pretty damn dull after we get back to LA. And I can't imagine what shit'll be like after you head back home." She kind of pouts.

"What, are you going to miss me or something?"

"Or something," she says flatly.

"Geez, you're so cold," I say, giving her a playful shove.

She giggles and pushes me back. "Yes! I will miss you, okay? How can I not?" She looks at me, smiling and biting her bottom lip. "You're amazing, and fun, and sweet, you stimulate me mentally… and sexually. Our time together has been… pretty fucking magical."

I grin. "Magical might be the only way to describe it."

"It's not over yet, you know. We've got three hours left of the trip. Maybe I'll come hang with you at your Airbnb tonight. And then Friday you and your *bros* can come with me to that party I told you about last night, if you want. If not, then Saturday we can spend the day together. And the night together." She winks, fondling my junk.

"Remember a few days ago, when it seemed like you didn't want to see me after you got the D?"

"Eh, what can I say? Things change." She and I stand there, staring out at the horizon in silence.

"Whenever I think about California, I always think about earthquakes."

"Wow, what a pleasantly random thought, hon," she says with heavy sarcasm.

I smirk. "If the San Andreas fault and the Cascadia subduction zone quaked right now and a tsunami was hurdling toward us, what do you do? Who do you call?"

"Oh geez… Um. I'd definitely call my mom and tell her I love her, then I'd grab on to you and get one last kiss in before we got smashed by the water wall. Oooh! Or maybe I'd have you ravish me on the sand so we could *go* and *come* at the same time." She laughs.

I lose it. "I would be very okay with that, Raunchy Sauce!"

She's laughing so hard that no sound is coming out. Eventually, she settles down. "What about you?"

"I'd call my parents for sure. Then I'd turn to you after you got done with your call—you know, before the kissing and the finale fuck—and I'd take your hands and tell you that meeting you and spending this week with you was the best thing that's ever happened to me."

Isabella brushes her hair back behind her ear. "That's probably when I'd interrupt your sappy speech and say *samesies!*" she squeaks.

I smile. "Then I'd tell you that I wish we had more time together and then something like how I didn't think it was possible to be so into someone I've known barely five days."

Her head hangs. "It is crazy isn't it? Feeling something so strong for someone you just met?"

"Wait, is this a critique about my feelings or are you saying you're as crazy about me as I am about you?"

She sighs. "If I tell you…"

"You'll have to kiss me?"

She brushes her hair back as she turns to me, revealing her reddening cheeks. "I told myself I wouldn't say this out loud, but… I like you too, Dion, okay?" She rolls her eyes. "A lot more than I should. Way more than I wanted to."

Grinning, I lean in for a kiss.

She meets me halfway with a peck on the lips. Another follows.

I pull away, just a bit. "So, hypothetically speaking," I say, my mouth hovering a few centimeters from hers. "If I uh… was a Los Angeles resident, I'd be someone you'd date, right?"

She pulls away even further. "If you're going to slyly segue into saying that you're going to move out here for me, don't, okay?"

"I told you that I was looking for a reason to move out west."

"Dion, you can't make me the deciding factor for you wanting to uproot your life and move, like, 3,000 miles across the country. You barely know me."

I scowl. "Just because I don't know your past, that doesn't mean I don't know what kind of person you are. Trust me, I know you."

"You know the best parts of me because that's what you have a habit of bringing out, but you don't *know* me, you know? If you did, you'd realize pretty quickly I'm not the kind of girl you'd want to get mixed up with or bring home to meet the parents."

"Um, I'm pretty sure I would feel the same way no matter how many skeletons you have in your closet."

She sighs. "What if I told you that I was a stripper for a semester last year? Would you see me differently?"

"Of course not," I reply without hesitation.

"Okay, remember that amazing work from home job that I'm always going on about? The one that was helping me pay for school and that allows me the income to buy whatever I want and afford spur of the moment trips like this?"

"Yeah…"

"It's not, like, online customer service or something… I'm a camgirl." She searches my eyes and face for a reaction, something like embarrassment or shame or vulnerability creeping up on her face.

"That's a bit of a shock, but it's no biggie."

"I'm talking box of sex toys, putting on dildo swallowing and riding shows and taking kinky requests for tips kind of camgirl."

That explains why she told me she doesn't have a gag reflex…

"Isabella, I don't give a shit. It doesn't change how I see you or who you are."

"Really? You don't care that there are thousands of guys probably jerking it to my pictures and videos as we speak? You don't care that I flirt with the hundreds of guys who frequent my inbox and send them private content for money and gifts?"

"No. I don't."

She scoffs. "Oh, bullshit."

"Like I said the night we met, it'd take some getting used to but, for you, that's something I can accept."

Her jaw hangs. "So, what, you'd be the kind of boyfriend who'd help me film scenes to help his fellow men get off?"

"If you wanted me to, sure. So long as you're not screwing them or have feelings for them, what do I care? It's not like it'll last forever. You'll be a pro dancer soon."

"What if I kept it up while I danced? What if getting faceless strangers off gets me off?"

"Then you keep on doing what makes you happy. It'd be shitty of me to ask you to stop."

She snickers and shakes her head as she looks up to the cloudless sky. "You're unbelievable. There's no way…"

"If it were anyone else, I'd probably have a different answer."

"And what makes me so special?"

"You're worth any potential hurdles I might otherwise avoid."

She stares out to the horizon in silence. The silence is heavy, heavy enough to weigh on my thoughts to the point that it's hindering a segue. "Dion," she finally says.

"Yeah?"

"What's the worst thing you've ever done?"

That gives me pause. "Uh… I guess… Um… That girl I told you I broke up with before I graduated high school? I hooked up with another girl before we *officially* broke things off.

"Oh, hon." She snickers. "That's nothing. You guys were already going to break up, right?"

"Yeah, I mean, we talked about it. But still. It was kind of shitty of me."

"I guess, but you were planning on splitting up, not making it work so…" She looks back out to the ocean. "Zach? The guy who leaked those nudes and nuked my social life? I loved him. At least,

I think I did. He loved me, that's for sure. Way more than I did him. Zach was the nicest guy I'd ever met. Not as nice or sweet as you, but he was good to me, decent to others. He went out of his way for people he shouldn't have. There was a point three months in where I thought, *wow, here's someone I could maybe see myself marrying...* It was a fleeting thought, but it was enough to make me want to really try with him instead of going back to being happily single and promiscuous. And then do you know what happened?" She turns to me.

"What?"

"I fucked it all up." She looks back to the ocean. "There was this well-connected, super-talented choreographer named Christian Collins who I met at an audition. He was this tall, bronze Adonis that someone would probably cast to play lead man in a dance flick. Actually, I think I saw on Insta that he was on set recently... Anyway, the second I got my chance, I flirted with him. I threw myself at him because I wanted to, because I was attracted to him. But I also had an agenda. I thought if I could get him to fuck me, that might improve my odds of landing a spot on his company. So, I went out with him and I let him screw my brains out. And he promised me that he'd put me on the team when the time was right. But guess what?"

"The time was never right."

She nods. "I messed around with him behind Zach's back for a month and he picked several other girls over me. And then some jealous bitch from the dance class I took with Christian private messaged Zach and told him everything. He went from nice guy to a life-ruining asshole like that." She snaps her fingers.

"Damn."

"Yeah, *damn*... Oh, and the week before Zach confronted me, this DJ named TyDie noticed me giving him fuck-me eyes at a concert and called me on stage. The minute after his set was over, I was blowing him in a bathroom backstage. The weekend after, maybe hours before Zach found out about the choreographer, I let TyDie plow me in his penthouse. I did that not just because I wanted to but because that's how badly I wanted him to take me to exclusive parties so I could meet someone who could help me *make it*. And guess what? Hoeing around kind of paid off. Because that's how I met Allyson and got this audition with Cynthia Essex." She looks at me, shame in her eyes. "So, tell me… am I still someone you'd consider moving across the country for?"

"Without a doubt," I answer without pause.

"Why? I'm clearly not someone who should ever be in a relationship. Shit, I'm not even sure a relationship is something I even want at this point in my life."

I wrap my arms around her and hold her close. "If you don't want a relationship, that's fine. But, one way or another, I want you in my life. You know, if you want me in yours."

"I mean, would life be better if you were around? Sure. But I don't want you here waiting for me to decide that I'm ready to be monogamous. Like, who knows when that will be? If that'll be. All I want is to be single and have fun. The last thing I want to do is string you along. I've strung along tons of guys since high school all so I can always have a backup or someone to use when I needed something. I won't do that to you, Dion… I can't."

"What makes me so special?"

She shrugs against me. "You're the best person I know." Her body finally relaxes and she buries her head in my chest. "And you're willing to accept all of me without judgement. My super-religious mom wouldn't even do that after she found out about the whole stripping thing, and parents are supposed to love you unconditionally."

"I'm sorry." I kiss the top of her head.

"It is what it is."

I take a deep breath and then sigh. "To your claim that you're not someone who should be in a relationship, you're wrong."

"How so?"

"Sure, you screwed up, but who doesn't? Especially at this age. Making a few bad decisions doesn't mean you're a horrible human being. It just means you weren't ready to be tied down in a serious relationship."

"I guess."

"I mean, you said it yourself, Zach felt more for you than you did for him. Sounds like you just didn't want to be in it for the long haul with him."

"You're not wrong about that. I was having doubts toward the end."

"See? And if you're willing to confess all of that to me, what does that say about where you are now in your life?"

"Maybe it doesn't say anything. I still kind of just want to be single right now, you know? Maybe me being all honest is me trying to scare you off so I don't end up breaking your heart and turning you into another savage," she says with a muffled voice.

"Well, I appreciate you being open with me. So, thanks for that."

She pulls away and meets my gaze. "You're actually the first person I told any of this to, aside from Riley... Zach didn't even know about me being a camgirl. Thank gawd," she says softly.

I search her eyes for a moment. "My gut's telling me that you trying to scare me off isn't the only reason you confessed all of that to me."

"Oh yeah? Why else would I tell you how big of a skank I am?"

"You're not a skank. And, I don't know... maybe because you wanted to see how I'd react to seeing all of you?"

"Or maybe I just really care about you and I don't want you making any rash decisions without knowing *exactly* where I'm at in life."

I nod. A moment of silence follows as I get lost in her sad eyes. "For the record, I still like what I see. A lot. And I'd still take a chance on you, if you wanted the same thing I did."

"Good to know." She leans in close and kisses me. "Now can we drop this? Let's just enjoy the rest of our time together. No more heavy shit. Let's just live in the present. Okay?"

I nod again, faster this time. *Fine, but that doesn't mean I'm giving up on winning you over,* is what I think. "Yeah, you got it," is what I say.

"Good." She takes my hand and leads me in the direction we parked in. "Since I haven't *worked* in a few days, and now that you know what I do, maybe I can enlist your help in filming some kinky shit in my car." She smiles naughtily. "There's a reward in it for you. The non-monetary kind, that is."

I couldn't grin any harder if I tried. "Tell me what you want me to do."

Isabella drives back the way we came, down Cabrillo Highway, bound for a spot she picked out on Google Maps. Once we get there, she makes a U-turn and then pulls over on the shoulder. From where we are, there's a clear line of sight to the beach.

She opens her door. "Switch seats with me, hon."

"Alright." I climb out of the car and walk around the front end as cars blow past us. As we pass each other, she hands me her high-end 4k camera.

She slams her door a beat after I do. "Make sure you get the beach in the background."

I snicker for some reason. "You got it."

All of the sudden, she pulls a blond wig out of her bag. "To conceal my identity. You know, because sunglasses aren't enough."

Smiling, I nod.

She gives me the thumbs up, my cue to start filming.

In a very sultry voice, Isabella does a bit about getting horny in the middle of her road trip and not being able to drive off until she gets off. She then slips her hands into her jean shorts. It doesn't take long for her to pull them off and toss them my way, angling herself toward me and spreading her legs. Now she pulls her panties to the side and rubs her clit for a while before slipping her middle finger inside. A few moments later, she worms her way out of her panties and fingers away. The whole time, she's staring at me, biting the right side of her bottom lip.

For twenty minutes she goes at it before her body trembles and her toes curl. Moaning and panting, she tells me she's about ready to wrap up, and signals me to stop recording.

"Did you enjoy that?" she pants, pulling her panties back on.

I smirk. "I was barely keeping it together over here."

"Good, because I did. Thought of you the whole time." She smiles. "Gotta say, thinking of you, having you watch? It helped me finish faster than usual."

"Glad I could be of service."

"Now let me be of service to you." Isabella tosses her wig in the back seat, sets her glasses on the dash, and then reaches over and grabs my belt.

"You don't want to go somewhere more... secluded?"

With my belt undone, she unzips my shorts and yanks them down just below my ass. "Nope," she says, stroking me. "The risk of getting caught makes it that much more exciting, don't you think?"

"Guess there's only one way to find out."

"Are you ready?"

"For?"

"Remember when we met and I mentioned the Gluck-Gluck 9000?"

"Oh yeah, how could I forget?"

She strokes a little faster. "After all the times we had sex this week, I can't believe you didn't ask about it."

"I guess mutual pleasure was enough."

"Get ready to have your life changed." Her mouth engulfs my tip.

Her tongue plays against my shaft as she bobs her head, taking me deeper and deeper with each descent, looking up at me the whole time. Her lips hit the base of my shaft and I can feel the back of her throat. She goes at it a little faster. The longer it goes on, the sloppier it gets. There's slurping, and glurping, glucking sounds with every bob and it's driving me absolutely insane.

I get why it's called Gluck-Gluck 9000 now. The 9,000 probably comes from how many hours it takes off of your life.

My body becomes putty. My thoughts are scrambled like I've been drugged. Every muscle is twitching. I'm grunting, groaning, and panting like a wounded ape. I try to hold out a little longer, but it's futile.

Her mouth work slows down and becomes shallower and more delicate as she cleans me off with thoughtful and thorough tongue-work. Each slither makes me twitch.

Her lips smack as she lifts her head away. A gulp follows. "So?" she says breathlessly.

"I think you left me quadriplegic." A tired laugh follows.

She wipes the corners of her mouth, then her chin. "That means I did it right."

"Oh, *right* would be an understatement! You get a hundred out of ten," I say, finally mustering the strength to pull my shorts up.

"Goodie!" She claps her hands. "Yours was the first real dong I tried that on. It's been dildos up to this point."

"Well, thank you very much for sharing that with me." I grin.

With a smile, she winks, reaching for her shorts.

I stop her. "Nuh-uh, leave those off. Let me take care of you now."

She arches a brow. "I thought you said you'd never gone down on anyone before."

"Yeah, but I never said I wouldn't," I say, slowly sliding my hand up her thigh as she shifts back against the door, maneuvering her legs over the center console after. "And I would cross any line for you." I caress her underwear-covered cooch, then pull her panties aside. "Now, tell me exactly what you like and I'll do my best to deliver."

The instant I give her an Australian kiss, she throws her head back and her core spasms as she bucks her hips forward, like my lips and tongue just tased her kitty.

"That," she pants. "More of that!"

12
Isabella

Thursday

FOR SOMEONE WHO HAS never chowed down on punani, his tongue work was absolutely stellar. Or maybe he displayed average technique and my mind and body just responded really well to him. That's probably it considering everything he says seems to set me on fire lately. Every touch, every act of pleasure, every sweet nothing he speaks—it all sends electricity coursing through me.

His oral worship of my sacred love tunnel has left me with a blissful post-orgasm high that persists through the first hour of our drive, and the second. Well, maybe at that point it was just elation from his company. Because just being around him has a way of making me happy in a way I haven't been in… years.

When the third hour rolls around, I get behind the wheel at our final gas stop. Driving helps me divert my thoughts from the feelings I'm trying to make sense of, and it's sobering.

As the mile count between us and Los Angeles dwindles, my stomach starts getting all flippy as a bout of anxiousness strikes. Something like melancholy washes over me soon after.

I glance over at Dion, who's been quietly staring off out the passenger window for the last mile or so. As though he feels my eyes on him, he turns to me and his tired, expressionless look quickly morphs into a smile that demands my mirror neurons to do the same. Even after telling him about being a camgirl and a stripper and how I cheated on Zach, he still looks at me the same way he used to, like I'm this magical, wonderful thing that brings him pure joy. A sight to cherish. A person he cherishes. His feelings for me, they're… unconditional.

I don't want this trip to end.

"Whatcha thinking about?" he asks.

Oh, you know, wondering what it'd be like to spend more than just a week with you. It's a scramble to think of something to say other than what's actually on my mind while also focusing on the road. "I was just thinking about… how surreal this whole audition thing has been for me and how it finally feels like I'm close to making my dreams come true, and it just dawned on me that I don't know your dreams. Like, I know your *goals* of wanting to work in biopharm and becoming a homeowner before thirty, but is there that one thing you want to achieve before you're too old to?"

He shrugs. "The reason I got into science in the first place was to be the guy who discovered a method to stop aging so I wouldn't have to get old in the first place." He laughs. "Or, at the very least, I wanted to make a world-changing discovery. You know, cure cancer or Alzheimer's or something."

"So go to grad school and make it happen, smart guy!"

He chuckles. "To be honest, the idea of grad school doesn't sound all that exciting to me after chatting with some grad students about their research and workloads. Especially when walking that path means I'd be broke for years to come. Sounds like financial suicide considering the amount of debt I'll have after graduation."

"I totally get that. It's probably best to start working your way up the corporate ladder, as godawful as that sounds." I pretend to gag.

He gags too. "Trust me, the idea of working for someone else pains me."

"I've spent a lot of time around influencers and content creators these last few months. If dummies like Chase can make a living online, you should have no problem, hon. All you need to do is find something you're super passionate about and find out how to make money off of it." I turn to him. "So, what's the one thing you're most passionate about. Other than gaming."

He grins. "Right now? You."

With a laugh, I shake my head. "Funny... But seriously, though, what's the one thing you would do if you could do anything?"

He shrugs. "Honestly, I have no idea. That's part of the reason I've been feeling so lost lately. My greatest fear is living a life of mediocrity, so I know that I don't want to be a laboratory bench-monkey for the rest of my life, but I'm not sure of how I can to turn what I've learned into a business."

I reach over and hold his hand. "Hey, don't stress. You're still young. You may not be sure of what you want to do now, but you'll figure it out. I know you will."

"There's only one thing in my life that I'm sure of right now."

"And what's that?"

He gives me this longing look and a heart-melting smile.

I scrunch my face to stifle a smile and quickly avert my gaze to the road.

Traffic worsens the second we enter Los Angeles. While I didn't want this trip to end, being stuck in traffic with dumb-fucks wasn't what I had in mind.

This isn't what I meant when I said I wasn't ready for this trip to end. Be careful what you wish for, I guess.

It takes forty minutes longer than intended, but we finally make it to the residential area of Beverly Grove.

"Well," I say as I pull into the driveway of his Airbnb, "here we are."

He sighs. "Here we are." His solemn eyes flick back and forth between mine, working hard to take this entire moment in. "Even though I'm tired as all hell, I'm not ready for it to be over."

"Same." I open my car door. "But it's not *over,* over, right? I mean, who knows what the next few days will hold," I say as I emerge and stretch my stiff body.

"Yeah," he says, climbing out and doing the same. "But I can't imagine it's going to be another spontaneous and memorable trip filled with straight-up Dion-Isabella time." He shrugs. "But maybe that's a good thing. I'm sure you're tired of me by now." He flashes a faint smile, hoisting his bag out of the back seat.

I smile shyly. "You know, after, like, five days of collecting data, I don't think it's possible to get tired of you, Dion Johnson."

He's cheesing now. "Likewise."

I look through the window of the lifeless house as I stroll beside him to the door. "You sure you don't want me to drive you over to where your boys are getting dinner?"

"Nah, I need to nap before they make me stay up drinking until sunrise as punishment."

"Good call," I say, nodding. "If I don't go all comatose when I get home, maybe I'll crash the party tonight and whisk you away to bed to save you from drinking your liver into oblivion."

"Um, you'd be my hero for that."

"Hey, it's the least I could do for the guy who's been saving me all week and potentially changed my life by going rogue with me for this audition."

"Shit, I would've went to North Korea with you if you wanted, Izzy." He grins.

I can't help but cackle. "Alright, that's a little extreme, but I get what you're saying."

Silence follows the laughter as we get lost in each other's gazes.

I open my arms and then he embraces me, squeezing me half as hard as I'm squeezing him. We rock side to side and then pull away, locking eyes before simultaneously leaning in for a kiss. A peck turns into something more passionate. That then becomes a make-out session that sends tingling down my spine and has me buzzing all over my body.

Sparks. That's what kissing him sends surging across my being... I think there have been sparks for a while now.

Dion is current. I am a filament. His kiss lights me up, and I can't get enough of him. It's obvious he can't get enough of me either.

It's just a fling. It's just a fling. It's just a fling.

I pull away before things get any hotter than they already are, my chest heaving. "I'll see ya later?"

The look in his eyes is filled with more longing than usual. "Yeah. See you later."

I run my fingers from triceps to forearm to hand as I backstep away from him. Our arms are extended out to each as my fingers run across his, and it feels like a live *The Creation of Adam* fresco painting. Right as I'm almost out of his reach, he leans forward and his hand clasps mine. Then he pulls me back in. For some reason, I get all giggly as he takes my other hand and brings me in for one last kiss. This one is longer, more thoughtful. It means something. I try to convey the same feeling with the puckering of my lips and the caress of the back of his neck.

I laugh into his mouth as I pull away. "Okay, bye!" I shout, unable to stop grinning.

"Later, Izzy."

"Hey, Iz—" Riley says from the couch when I walk in, stopping abruptly as she squints. "Wow! I think I need my sunglasses because you're glowing!"

A wheeze of a laugh escapes me. "Shut up, Ri."

She rises. "Seriously! Like, what the eff happened from Tuesday until now with you and Dion that has you looking like you're on uppers?"

I roll my eyes. My shoulders shrug. "Nothing... I mean, we just went at it like bonobos for three days and just had a good time hanging out together. That's it."

"That's it, my ass." She greets me with a hug. "Does your butt hurt?"

Scowling, I bring my chin to my neck as I flop onto the couch at the same time she does. "No butt stuff happened. And if it did, I'm not sure I'd be all smiles about that."

Riley giggles. "No, I meant does your butt hurt from falling, because I'm guessing Mr. East Coast swept you off your feet."

A snort precedes my laugh. "What's that? You want to see the video of my audition, you say?" I unlock my phone and start tapping my way to my camera roll. "Great, here it is!"

Riley shakes her head and snatches the iPhone from me. "Don't think you're getting out of telling me all about your romantic tryst."

Riley showers me with praise when the video's done, then I start to spill the tea about the entire trip, sparing no details. Actually, I leave out confessing the feelings that I may have caught but I do include every dirty detail about what went down sexually.

"So... You love him, don't you?" She smirks deviously.

"Psh! What did I say that gave you the inclination that I *love* him?"

Riley shakes her head. "It's not what you said, it's how you said it. It's the look on your face when you talk about him or say his name." She waves her hand around me like a damn psychic. "It's the energy you're giving off."

"Riley, I've known the guy five days. Come on."

"Izzy, I legit have never seen you like this before."

Leaning my head back, I look up to the ceiling. "Do I like the guy?" I sigh. "Yes… I *like* the guy, okay? I like him a lot. It's impossible not to like him. I mean, we have this incredible chemistry together. He's fucking amazing. Handsome. And hilarious. And intelligent. And sweet. And thoughtful. And really good in bed. And it's un-fucking-deniable how much he cares about me. And I guess I care about him too because I didn't use him once… But I didn't, like, fall for him or some shit."

"Are you lying to me or are you lying to yourself?"

That question hits me like a cup of cold water to the face. It gives me pause.

Riley arches a brow and turns her palm to the ceiling, fingers slightly curled.

"I didn't fall for him," I repeat.

"Mm-hm," she says, tilting her head with each syllable.

"Alright, I'm done being interrogated. I need a nap in case I decide to go out later."

"Wait, you just got back from a freaking road trip! Where the hell are you going now?"

"Dion's boys are throwing a thing at their place tonight," I say apprehensively as I walk to my room.

Grinning, Riley shakes her head. "Oh, okay, I get it," she says knowingly. "I've got nothing to do tonight, so maybe I'll tag along and see if any of his friends are as amazing as he is so I can fall in love too."

"Ha. Ha. Funny." I shut the door.

To say I'm exhausted would be an understatement, but after twenty minutes, I can't fall asleep for the life of me. My mind is racing with thoughts of *him* and memories of the moments we shared since meeting. I'm mad he's leaving Sunday. I'm happy he's leaving this weekend. It makes me kind of sad that I may never see him again after Saturday.

"Ugh." *I hope I never see him again after Saturday.*

But I need to see him again before he leaves… Maybe a few more times.

Overdose myself on him until I can't stand him anymore, then get sober.

Or maybe I just cut myself off cold turkey now so I can get it over with…

13
Dion

Thursday

"WAKE YOUR BITCH-ASS up, Dion!" a bassy voice thunders, jarring me from my nap. Tommy. It's definitely Tommy.

Lights flick on, forcing me to shut the one eye I just opened.

"Get up! Get up! Get up!" a cacophony of manly voices chants.

The familiar *snap-pop-hiss* of a can of beer opening follows.

Groggy as hell, I roll over and squint. The blurry image of my best friends gradually clears up, only to vanish behind a can with blue mountains that Jeremy holds up to my face.

"The fuck?" I groan.

"Chug this shit," Jeremy demands, "grab another, chug that, and get ready!" It's evident by his voice that he's drunk as shit. Makes sense considering they texted me at 4 P.M. saying they were getting started with the pre-pre-game.

"We got a bunch of honeys coming over in an hour!" Mike adds. Judging by the look on his face and those around him, they're all buzzing hard. "You need to catch up and get ready to get some strange so you can get over this fucking gold-digging dancer that stole you away all week."

I gulp down the mouthful of beer. "She never once asked me for money, so I don't think she qualifies as a gold-digger." I put the can back to my mouth.

"But I bet you still paid for shit," Mike retorts, arching a brow.

I scowl as I gulp down a third of the beer. "You want to see the Venmo transactions of her paying me back for some of the meals?"

Stefan looks taken aback. "Oh, dayum. That's some couple shit then."

I shrug.

Mike shakes his head. "Either way, we have three nights left. It's time for you to go spelunking into some new damp caves. And I have the perfect girl for you. Spent all yesterday talking you up, buddy."

"Yeah... Isabella might come through tonight so thanks, but no thanks."

"Ahhhhh!" the guys all groan in harmony.

"No!" Mike says, throwing his head back and shaking his fists at the ceiling. "Dude, tell her ass to stay home! You two live on opposite coasts for fuck's sake! The minute you leave, she'll forget all about you, then you'll be moping around and shit because you screwed up and caught feelings... Having her around any longer isn't doing you any favors, broski."

"He ain't lying," Stefan chimes in.

Jeremy and the others nod in agreement.

"If she wants to come, she's going to come," I declare.

Han grins and nods. "Yeah, she is," he says, giving a pound to Jeremy, who's laughing along with him about the inuendo.

The others join in with disjointed chuckles once it clicks.

Smirking, I shake my head. "Listen, *when* she gets here, be nice or I'll kick all your asses. Alright?"

Mike snorts. "I'd like to see you scrap against five of us." He laughs.

"Ummm," Stefan hums, "don't forget Dion's been doing martial arts since he was seven."

"Yo, remember when he sparred against two guys at once in high school and won?" Jeremy adds.

"Shit was wild!" Stefan chuckles.

"I mean, I could definitely take you guys. Not Tommy though," I say, sizing up the towering heavyweight. "But I won't have to put anyone in their place since Isabella's a bit of a savage. She won't take you guys' bullshit without verbally kicking your asses in return."

Mike raises his hands in surrender. "Fine, whatever… But please don't be lame tonight just because she's here, okay?"

I pat his shoulder. "Oh, you don't have to worry about me acting any different when she's around. I have nothing to hide from her."

Once I'm showered up and dressed, I stroll into the living room just as Han is taking the order of 100 wings, three pizzas, and curly fries from the delivery guy, passing them off to Jeremy.

With plates of wings and fries in hand, we sit around the living room catching each other up on the last few days. Of course, it starts with them interrogating me.

"Did you at least get laid the entire time you were gone, or did she just make you drive her up there?" is how Mike begins.

I tell them about the drive up and down, the audition, what San Francisco was like, cool shit I saw, the banging food I had.

"Yeah, but did you smash in between all that?" Jeremy interjects.

"What do you think?" I reply with a smirk, scanning the faces staring back at me.

"Well," Jeremy says, "you look sprung as hell any time you talk about her so…"

"There's your answer then," I say. And I leave it at that. How frequently we did it, the way she worked her body, getting my life force drained by the Gluck-Gluck—those are things I'll reveal when we're back east and they don't have the chance to say anything stupid, like they might if she shows up tonight.

"So, you really like this chick, huh?" Stefan asks.

"I do," I say with a heavy breath. "A lot. No lie, I'd move here for her." I guzzle down beer three.

"Well, damn, dude," Han says. "You sound like Mike at the strip club last night after that lap dance from Holli."

Mike grins. "Dude, Holli was an Amazonian goddess! I can save her from this stripper lifestyle, I know it!"

That kicks off the recap of what I missed since Tuesday. Mike goes on about getting Holli's number after getting a free handy in the champagne room. "I'm going to get her to come over tonight with some stripper friends if these girls tonight end up being lame. Either her or the Malibu girls."

They talk about Tuesday and the epicness that was the party in Malibu. From the pictures and Instagram and Snapchat stories, they aren't exaggerating. All the girls were hot, the bros there were chill, and the weed was strong. Han brought along Emma, the food-truck girl from Sunday, and they got really high on edibles and screwed on the private beach behind the house.

Somehow Jeremy ended up doing Molly—the drug, not a girl—and then he hooked up with this girl who was also rolling on MDMA. From the picture of her that he shows me, she looks like she was dressed for Coachella that night. I'm talking gold metallic temporary tattoos down her arms and on her face, a mesh top with a yellow bra underneath, and booty shorts that showed more ass cheek than shorts typically allow. It makes sense that she was the one handing out drugs.

Mike goes on at length about getting lucky with a rich girl named Bethany who paid for her group's Malibu spring break trip with daddy's trust fund money. That was his second hookup after

Alexia on Sunday. Stefan made out with Bethany's friend but didn't seal the deal like he did with Winona.

Part of me feels bad that I missed out on the epic tale they're spinning. But I wouldn't trade the last few days with Isabella, even to be a part of my group's craziest collection of stories to date.

Mike gets to talking about the girls coming tonight. They're locals, college girls from University of California that they met Monday at Santa Monica Beach. Mike's been texting with the one girl named Nancy all week and they had dinner and drinks with her and some friends last night before the strip club.

Mike's phone chimes. "Nancy and friends will be here in five!" he announces.

"Woot wooooot!" Jeremy cheers.

As Mike is going on about the plan for entertaining tonight, my phone buzzes against my leg. Seeing her name in the preview makes me smile instantly.

Isabella: **Hayyy! Whatchu up to?**

Me: **Sup, Izzy! Hope your nap was better than mine. And I'm just pregaming with the guys. You?**

Her response comes fast. Isabella: **Aw, why couldn't you sleep? Not the same without me snuggled up to you, huh?**

Isabella again: **I slept like an overworked thirty-year-old so I'm well-rested. Eating with Riley now.**

Me: **Not having my cuddle buddy may have been why it took me a while to pass out... My bros storming into my room like a SWAT team yelling at me to get up is why I didn't stay asleep...**

Isabella: **HAHAHAHA! I mean, you can't really blame them... You were MIA for a week, hon... No rest for the wicked.**

Me: **You're not wrong...**

Me: **You still thinking of coming tonight?**

Isabella: **Debating it. I'd rather not see the interior of a car for a while if I'm being honest.**

Me: **Right there with you haha. No worries if you don't want to come. Maybe we'll do something tomorrow.**

Isabella: **Yeah! Let's plan on tomorrow! Thanks for being understanding.**

Isabella again: **Maybe we all go out to dinner before the shindig tomorrow night?**

Me: **I like the sound of that!**

Isabella: **Sweet!**

Isabella again: **BTW, I expect drunk texts from you tonight.**

Me: **Good. Because it's probably going to happen. Apologies in advance.**

The guys and I grab a round of cold ones, then gather around the kitchen island for shots. That's when the doorbell rings.

There are four of them in total. Our girl-to-guy ratio is going to be off if Emma doesn't show up for Han.

Nancy is a stunning blond bombshell. The rest of her friends are pretty attractive as well, especially the Latina girl with brown roots that transition into crimson locks.

"Mikayla," Mike says to the Latina, "this is my best bro Dion that I was telling you about." Now that she's up close, I realize she favors my friend Karla from back at Penn State. By that I mean, she too is caramel-skinned with the face of an angel and the body of a sinner.

She giggles. "Nice to finally meet you, Dion."

"Nice to meet you too," I say, shaking her hand.

"Mikayla here is also a biology nerd like you," Mike says with a grin. "And she might be more hardcore into Marvel movies than you are!"

She bats her lashes. "You say that like it's a bad thing, Michael. Nerds and geeks reign supreme these days!"

"Preach on!" I cheer.

We loiter in the kitchen, mingling and drinking, me chatting it up with Mikayla about major-related topics and MCU. While we chat, I record a clip of the festivities and add it to my Snap and Instagram stories—bait to coax Isabella over. Not long after, she texts me.

Isabella: **Drunk yet?**

Me: **3 beers and one shot. Not even close haha.**

Isabella: **Haha good. It's too early to be obliterated already. How's the partay?**

Me: **It's chill. Something's missing though…**

Isabella: **Weird… My night is missing something too…**

Me: **Hm that is weird… Might help for you to come over so we can put our heads together and figure out what's throwing our night off.**

Isabella: **That's kind of what I was thinking…**

Isabella again: **I guess since I'm wired from my nap and dressed to go out, I might as well, huh?**

Me: **See you in 20?**

Isabella: **19.**

Isabella again: **Lol.**

Isabella again: **Riley is looking to get out tonight. Cool if she comes?**

Me: **Of course.**

Isabella: **Perf because we're getting in the car now.**

I snap my fingers to get the guys' attention. "Yo, Izzy is coming with her friend Riley."

Mike curls his lips into his mouth, shaking his head subtly.

Mikayla notices his reaction and then looks at me.

"Oh, so we finally get to meet her, huh?" Jeremy blurts out. Sloppy. He's getting sloppy.

I nod.

"Who's *Izzy*?" Mikayla asks, looking from Mike's sour face to my cheery one.

"Dion's future wife!" Jeremy almost shouts.

Mikayla sticks her bottom lip out a bit, tilts her head, and then downs some of her beer.

Time was going fast up until Isabella said she was on the way. Now I'm staring at my phone every few seconds, calculating how much longer I have to wait until she gets here.

Two minutes after the ETA, I get a text.

Isabella: **Open up, buttercup!**

I hurry to the door, sliding to a stop just before the doormat. My palm finds the knob right as the doorbell rings. I'm smiling before I even open the door, like I haven't seen her in weeks.

Her face lights up at the sight of me. "Long time no see."

"Tell me about it," I say coolly, getting lost in her hazel pools of allure.

"Oh, yeah, it's fine," Riley says, scowling. "I'm not here at all. Pay no mind to me."

"Hey there, Riley," I say, finally looking away from Isabella.

She smiles knowingly. "Hi, Romeo."

Isabella spins around and pushes her shoulder. Then she reaches into her bag and pulls out a baggie. "I brought weed and edibles!"

I step to the side, letting them enter. "Um, you're the best."

"Um, I'm aware," Isabella says in a valley girl accent, tickling my chest as she passes. "Well, you guys look kind of familiar!"

The gang turns to Isabella and they're all grinning.

Jeremy claps. "Well, there she is!"

"The girl who stole our bro!" Stefan says, also clapping.

"Gosh, it feels like we already know you!" Mike says, walking up to her with a hand out. "Dion's been going on and on about you all week!"

"All good things, I hope," Isabella says, looking back at me with a smile as she shakes his hand.

I smirk back.

"Yeah, it was a whole lot of, *oh she's beautiful!*" Mike says in a mocking voice. "*Dude, she's smart too! You should see her dance! This chick is hilarious!*" His eyes snap to me after.

I nod subtly. *Thanks, wingman.*

"I'm not as perfect as he makes me sound," she says.

Mike shrugs. "Dion ain't much of a liar."

"And he's never been known to exaggerate," Stefan chimes in.

She turns to me and grabs a fistful of my shirt. "Well, thanks for talking me up, hon."

"Don't act like you haven't been talking up Dion too, Izzy," Riley pipes up.

Isabella rolls her eyes. "Have you guys been introduced to my roommate Riley yet? You know, the girl who also ate all your food on Sunday." She curtseys to the guys. "Thanks for that, by the way."

"Yeah, thanks for your generosity," Riley says with a curtsey.

The guys glare at me before looking back to Isabella.

"Oh, Dion is who you should thank for that," Mike grumbles.

Isabella pulls out the bag of gummies and cookies. "Riley and I brought y'all a tribute for your unwanted sacrifice. Feel good snacks. Strong ones."

Mike picks up a baggie. "You are both as generous as you are gorgeous."

Edibles are ingested. Drinks are downed. The group migrates to the living room to play some games. Riley and Isabella mesh well with my group, both of those feisty sass-queens taking shots at the guys every chance they get. The girls Mike invited seem to be a bit salty about the duo stealing all the spotlight. It doesn't help that Mike can't shift his focus off of Riley for the life of him.

Isabella is beside me the entire night. She leans against me readily. Her hand finds mine on the couch, our fingers playing against each other's. Two hours in, her hand lands on my lap, her nails scratching me lightly like she's trying to get me all riled up.

By this point, everyone is pretty sloshed, with the exception of Isabella and me, who took it easy on beer to enjoy the THC ride. Everyone else is too drunk and high to function, never mind play games. They opt instead to turn on some music to just vibe out and talk.

Isabella's hand slides into mine and she tickles my palm. When I look at her, she nods toward the room.

I bobble my head eagerly.

She squeezes my hand and rises, leading me to my room.

The gang and our guests are too messed up to notice our departure.

"I realized what was missing," she whispers, pushing me against the door I just shut.

"Oh yeah?" I whisper back. "I did, too."

She kisses me, gripping my shirt and pulling me along as she walks backward toward the bed. When her legs hit the mattress, I grab her behind her thighs and lift her up. Her legs wrap around me and she giggles, mushing her lips back into mine after.

Being high and slightly buzzed makes it a struggle to strip each other out of our clothes. With every fumble and flub, we giggle uncontrollably. But we manage, eventually.

Sex with a body high is a different ball game. And since lovemaking with her is already a heightened experience, every touch and thrust feels amazing.

My perception of time is too wonky to keep track. Maybe it's been an hour, maybe it's been fifteen minutes. Either way, when we finish, she doesn't look or sound disappointed.

She and I lay there naked, chatting about random shit, meaningful things, more life plans. And when we talk about the future, it triggers a thought that's been rattling around in my head the last few days.

"Hey, I know you don't want a relationship and you don't want me to move out here for you. But—"

"Dion," she whines in a groggy groan.

"Can I say this, please?"

"Nope!"

"Please?"

"Fine," she relents.

"Thank you… I just want you to know, that this wasn't ever about hooking up. I didn't give up nachos and go out of my way for you day after day all for a week-long fling. I did what I did because you are worth my time and energy. Not many people are. And I know you're somewhere different in life, but I need you to know that I want you for keeps."

"Dion…" She sighs.

"If or when you change your mind about relationships or about me… call me. Text me. Tell me you're ready. If I'm with someone, I'll dump her ass if it means I'll have a chance to see where this goes."

Her face scrunches up. "You're so full of shit." A snicker follows.

"I swear on my life. Even if I'm engaged." I laugh to soften the admission, but I'm serious as all hell.

There's a bout of silence. "You can't promise some shit like that."

"I can. And I am."

She sighs. "You saying all this? It just complicates things. You know that, right?"

I nod. "Sorry, but… I had to get that off my chest. Not saying how I feel when I should is a problem for me. I get in my head about coming off too strong, I worry about the consequences and then I end up not speaking my mind. That's how I missed out on the girl I crushed on all through high school—not the one I ended up with either. Same for a few girls in college. It's not even the fact that we may never see each other again that's compelling me."

"Don't you dare say you love me."

"Relax, I'm not that sprung." *Or maybe I am*, I think during the brief pause. "But this thing between us is unlike anything I've ever felt. And you're unlike any other girl I've ever met… Not telling you how I feel even if nothing comes of it? That'd be something I'd live to regret the rest of my life. And I don't want to live with regret. It's draining."

"I regret letting you finish this sappy-ass speech."

"It's okay to not be so guarded, you know."

She sits up. "Sorry, but I'm not some mushy romantic. Even with Zach. The last thing in the world that I wanted was to catch feelings for someone, then *you* came along and fucked that up for me!" She plays at being angry but she's smiling.

Her admission makes me grin. "You act like I ventured out here looking for this. All I wanted was to visit a place where no one knows me and come out of my shell a little bit—you know, mingle, have meaningless sex maybe with a few girls that I'd never see again like my bros got to. But here we are, Isabella."

She laughs quietly through her nose in rapid puffs, the way one does when reading a hilarious text in public. "Funny how meeting someone can be *so* good for you and yet *so* bad at the same time, huh?"

"Yeah, it's hilarious, alright."

There's a bout of silence.

Her sigh breaks the prolonged hush. "If it makes you feel any better... *this* isn't going to be easy for me either."

"What isn't?"

"Saying goodbye." Her words come off so heavy.

"Good thing there are these fun things called smartphones with internet, texting, calling, and video chatting capabilities that'll let us stay in touch!"

She smacks her lips three times and scrunches her face like she just tasted something bitter. "Wow, you went a little heavy with the sarcasm, hon."

I laugh. "You just make parting ways sound so final, is all."

"I'm not the best at staying in touch."

"If someone matters, you'll make the effort."

"No, you're right."

"I'll make the effort, even if you won't."

She caresses my abdomen. "I will."

"Good. Because I want to hear all about all the success coming your way. And I'd rather not just find out from Instagram posts."

"I suppose I owe you that much."

"You don't owe me shit. I just want you to want to keep in touch."

She sighs, running her finger up from my abdomen to my pectorals. "I do. Want to," she says softly, caressing my cheek.

"Good." I cup the side of her neck and guide her in. Then I kiss her.

Her lips don't move at first but then, very hesitantly, she kisses me back. Her apprehension to be intimate is evident but it melts away as she embraces me and we kiss each other deeper.

Though she won't admit it, I think she's feeling as strongly as I am. I feel it. The way she's gone from holding herself back to pressing her fingers firmly into me, nibbling at my lip, squeezing me, clawing my skin with her nails makes it clear she's frustrated. Conflicted. Scared to let go like I am. Scared to give in.

I feel it. Because we're on the same vibe.

We kiss and caress and roll around for what feels like forever. Then we just hold each other in silence.

She falls asleep on my chest.

I lay there stroking her head, trying to stay up as long as I can to hold onto this moment. Then the edibles make my eyelids feel like steel curtains.

14

Isabella

Friday

"I WANT YOU FOR keeps." His words have been rattling around in my head since Riley and I left after breakfast at Dion and friends' place.

"Tell me you're ready. If I'm with someone, I'll dump her ass if it means I'll have a chance to see where this goes."

"Like, who says shit like that?" I whisper to myself as I tend to my makeup in the mirror. Talking to myself? Yeah, that isn't exactly a normal occurrence for me.

When he said all that, it just went and made everything so goddamn serious.

I rub my temples with my middle finger and thumb. *I should've stayed home yesterday.*

I tried to resist the urge to go see him last night. I tried so damn hard. But I ached for him. I ached between my legs. Every inch of flesh yearned for his touch. Not seeing him was ironically akin to ocular strain. Like how looking away from the screen you've been staring at for hours and then looking at something in the distance relieves the strain, seeing him is what I needed. Sitting on the couch with Riley, staring at his pictures on my phone... it wasn't enough.

To want to be with someone I just saw four hours before, someone I already spent almost four full, amazing days with...

Never have I ever craved a guy like that.

Three nights. That's how long I had left to get my fix.

So I got ready, going as far as to skip out on glamming up. Because what's the point? Then I saw his Insta story with all those random bitches. I texted him in case he didn't want me over anymore. Because the last thing I wanted was to show up and find him sucking face with some skank. If that happened, he'd be just like every other guy. And him turning out like just another fuckboy? That'd break my heart. Because that'd mean there is no hope in the world to find a decent man. Not when he's the best I've ever come across. Not when he might be the best that I'd probably ever get the chance to meet…

He gave me the green light so I rushed on over there. Then after incredibly euphoric, weed-enhanced sex and a deep conversation, he opened his stupid mouth and made this amazing, easy thing we had going all serious and shit. Okay, maybe that's not true. It's kind of felt serious since that first night in San Fran, though I'd prefer not to admit that to myself. But vocalizing his feelings the way he did, it gave the *seriousness* form. It made me acknowledge these ridiculous feelings. Then the walls that I put up years and years ago began losing structural integrity.

When I awoke all snuggled up to him, I wanted to slip out of bed, get Riley, race home, and cut things off cold turkey like I planned. Except I ended up watching him sleep… Then, when he got up, we lay there talking, caressing and touching each other, slowly mapping every inch of each other's bodies like our fingertips were scanners. Gentle touches led to giggling. It quickly led to arousal. Light pecks became something more. His fingers ended up in me. His meat stick ended up in my hand. Fingers were replaced by his tongue. When I pulled his head up, his tongue was replaced by dick.

One last time. It's goodbye after this, I thought as I rode him. That was a failed promise I'd made last night…

We took it slow. Held eye contact. Kissed often. Held hands whenever the position allowed. I pleasured him with every trick I knew. He lasted longer than ever, giving it to me the way he'd learned I liked it, like no guy ever has. It was more intimate than it's ever been. I let him finish inside me. Again. Like last night. And at the hotel in Monterey.

Post-coital clarity told me to run, but when he offered to make us breakfast, that *"Yeah, I'll stay"* leapt out of my mouth reflexively.

Twenty more minutes, I thought.

Another failed promise because I sat around talking for ten minutes longer than intended.

When he walked me out the door, I kissed him with everything I had, like a wife saying goodbye to her husband who was shipping out to a war he likely would never come back from.

Goodbye. Goodbye, Dion. I thought it hard, like he'd somehow hear it if I did. I thought that and one other secret thing he could never hear out loud. Our make-out session went on for almost a full minute. It took everything in me to part from him.

"Wowzah," shouted Riley from the passenger seat, fanning herself. "Watching that made me hot!"

Mike, who was leaning against my car, chatting with Riley, just slow clapped.

When I pulled away, helpless against smiling after finally being able to breathe, he gave me this meaningful look. A knowing one. Not sure which of the two meanings behind my kiss he picked up on—the *"this is goodbye to the amazing thing we shared this week"* or the *"I like you way more than I could ever admit."* One more peck, then I got in the car and waved goodbye.

I look at myself in the mirror, pleased at the artwork I just pulled off in the face of ADHD levels of distraction. Yet seeing myself in the mirror makes me shake my head in disdain for ending up swooning like this over some guy I *just* freaking met.

"Damn you, Dion Johnson," I whisper. My phone buzzes across the counter. It's a text. "Speak of the devil."

Dion: **Hey, Izzy. We still doing dinner?**

"Izzy!" Rylie calls out from what sounds like her room.

"Yeah?"

"Mike just texted me," she says, her voice growing closer. "He asked if we're all going to dinner. Says he's buying." She smiles. "For me, of course. But I'm sure Dion will take care of you."

I smirk. "Someone looks eager to see Mike again. Was the D that good last night?"

Riley grins. "I mean..."

I roll my eyes.

"So, are we meeting up with them or not?"

"I don't know... I feel like I need a break."

"Wait, why? You and Dion seemed so into each other this morning. That fucking chemistry between you two. The passion. My god. Award for best kiss goes to you two!"

"Yeah, that's the problem."

"Izzy," she says in that stern mom voice she does when I'm being irrational.

"What?" I snap.

"Don't screw this up."

"Don't screw what up? There's nothing to screw up. It's just a fling, Ri. That's it."

She scowls. "Wow... You are hella defensive right now."

"Sorry... I'm just—"

"Head-over-heels for a guy who's leaving in two days and you don't know how to deal?"

"No."

"Did he text you *I love you* or some shit? Is that why you're freaking out?"

"No… I just need a little more time to myself."

"Did you forget they're coming to the party that *you* invited them to in, like, four hours?" She cocks a brow. "Wait, are you uninviting them to the party too?"

"No, they're still invited."

"So why don't you want to get dinner with Dion?"

"I just feel like the less time I spend with his smitten ass, the easier it'll be for him."

"Mm-hm." She scans my face intensely. "You're mispronouncing *me* like *him,* right?"

"I need a little more time to sort my thoughts. Okay, Riley?" I snap. "Can we drop it? Please?"

"Sheesh, fine." She rubs her hands together dramatically, like they're coated with Cheeto crumbs. "Done." She heads for the living room. "Bee-tee-dubs, you owe me dinner for getting in the way of my free meal."

"Fine. Dinner is on me tonight."

Riley grins then twirls around, exiting my room in a prance.

I pick up my phone to respond to Dion.

Me: **Hey! Um, actually, can you just meet us at the party?**

I copy and paste the address from Allyson's message, then hit send.

Me again: **Get there around 10.**

Dion: **Alrighty! Text ya when we're close.**

Me: **K! See ya then!**

Why did I have to invite him to this? Why?

Girls' night out is just what I needed. Dinner with Riley. Cocktails. Girl talk. Dance talk. It's simple. The stress and anxiety stirred up from last night fades the more I drink. And I down two knock-you-on-your-ass drinks before the grilled chicken and baked potato arrives. I guzzle the third before the check comes. By the time we get to the Uber, I'm buzzing. Hard.

I told Dion to get to the party at ten, but we arrive at nine. That extra hour should be enough time to wind down and mingle before he starts buzzing around me like a fly around a buffet all night.

"There's the soon-to-be professional dancer, ladies and gentlemen!" Allyson announces from behind a wall of people before she parts the crowd like a stunning, long-legged female Moses.

A very tall, very handsome man with disheveled brown hair and a square, chiseled, scruffy jaw appears from behind her, instantly locking eyes with me, smiling at me. I recognize him but I can't recall from where. All I know is he's important. I'm compelled to talk to him.

"Eeek!" I squeal, running at Allyson with open arms. "And there's the girl I owe everything to!" I embrace her like I'm trying to turn her bones to dust. "Thank you! Thank you! Thank you!" I say as we rock side-to-side while jumping up and down.

"Auntie Cyn spoke very highly of you!"

My smile seems permanent. "Oh my gawd, your aunt is just freaking amazing!"

"She is the best auntie ever!" She lets out a short giggle. "Rumor is I might be seeing you around at RTA next week…"

"Yup! I got a call this afternoon about the choreography thing. Choreography practice, then an audition Friday. Anything I should prepare for?"

"Prepare to be tired," she says grimly. "Carb up. Rest up. Stretch. Caffeinate. Meditate. Do all that and you should be good."

"Excellent. I will do just that!" I turn to Riley. "This is my bestie, Riley!"

Allyson flashes her a friendly smile and hugs her. "Nice to meet you, Riley. So I hear you're a dancer too?"

"Yes indeed. I teach at a studio in Pasadena!"

"Very cool!" Allyson cheers. "We all need to get together and do something for my YouTube one day!"

"I'd be very down for that," Riley says with a perky hop.

Allyson looks around. "Didn't you say you had more friends coming?"

I nod. "Yeah, they should be here around ten-ish."

"The one guy on your Insta, the one that my aunt said came to the audition, is he one of the ones joining us? Is he your boyfriend?"

I hesitate. "Oh, he's not my boyfriend…"

"Really? You two looked hella happy in all those posts."

Riley shoots me a look.

I nod. I shrug. "We're just… like, hooking up or whatever. He's not from around here."

Allyson giggles. "Oh, I see."

"He's visiting from Penn State," Riley interjects. "That sweetheart abandoned his friends to accompany Izzy to San Francisco just to cheer her on."

"Sounds like a keeper to me," Allyson says, waving at someone in the distance. "We'll, I have some more guests to greet. Meet by the bar in a bit for shots, and I'll introduce you to some other dancers and friends of mine. K?" She trots off.

Riley grabs some drinks, then I go say hi to a few people before settling near the bar, where I see people from TyDie's crew. After doing shots with them, we do a lap around the bar.

Guys ogle me as we float around the venue, something I haven't noticed while I've been running around with Dion. Because his gaze is the only one that mattered when we were together. I felt like I was the only girl in the world when he looked at me, but I didn't realize until now that my eyes haven't been wandering all week.

Guys come up to us, hitting on both Riley and me. It feels like a normal Friday night on the town with my bestie. Exactly what I needed after pretty much being tied down for a week.

Then I see Mr. Tall-Handsome-and-Shaggy. He's eyeing me from the bar, tempting me with his stare. I return the look, downing my drink and strutting over to the bar without looking over at him at all.

The buzz is hitting harder. *I'm in bad-decision territory now.*

I lean against the bar and signal the bartender, who holds up a finger in response.

"As a photographer, I'm trained to fixate on the most beautiful thing in sight," a man's voice says to my right. "So forgive me for staring."

I turn to him, biting my lip. Then I look around dramatically. "Oh, did you mean me?"

He laughs confidently. "Connor Braddock." He extends his large hand to me.

"Like, Connor Braddock the photographer with, like, one-point-five million followers and a gallery in New York?"

"Perhaps."

I'm cheesing now. "Isabella Monroe."

"The model?" He smirks a devilish smile.

I cock a brow. "Uh, not in the profession sense of the word."

"Oh, looking at you, I had just assumed. You really should be professionally shot."

"Are you offering to photograph me, Connor?"

"It would be my pleasure, Isabella."

Connor and I chat. And flirt. It doesn't take long for his hand to find my shoulder, my hand, my hip. He's commanding. Suave.

My phone chimes and rings. I peek at it and of course it's Dion. *If he's here, he'll find me,* I think, slipping the phone back into my clutch.

Flirting with a handsome, well-connected stranger. This feels right. This is Bella free in her natural habitat. This is how it should be.

Connor looks up and I follow his gaze to the group approaching us. Riley is leading Mike, Dion, and the guys our way. The second I see him, I'm conflicted. I want him near me yet I also want him as far away as possible all at once.

Mr. Observant sizes up Connor and then eyes me curiously, his mind connecting dots.

"Excuse me a moment," I say to Connor, walking toward them.

"Haaay!" I sing, walking right for the dapperly dressed Dion.

"Hey, Izzy," he says coolly, an even smile on his face.

I open my arms for a hug and when he goes in to kiss me, I lean away and let his lips find my cheek. Because Bella can be a savage sometimes. "If you guys didn't pregame, it's an open bar so feel free to get shit-faced."

"Seems like we have some catching up to do," Dion says, searching my eyes, working to probe my mind. I can tell by the look on his face that he knows I'm being weird.

"Seems like it!" I grab him by the wrist. "Come on, let's get you guys some shots. Yeah?" I lead him to the other side of the bar, away from Connor.

A round of shots for us all and a round of beers for the guys. Martinis for me and Riley. Everyone clinks their shot glasses together, throws them back, and then chases the whisky with their primary drinks. Then we all get to talking about how obliterated everyone got last night. Dion and I exchange looks on and off throughout the conversation.

"Hey," he says, leaning in. "Is everything alright?"

I act confused. "Yeah! Why wouldn't it be?"

He shrugs. "I don't know... You seem kind of... off."

"Replace *off* with drunk, hon." I smile.

His head bobbles. "Maybe that's it." He looks around, his sights stopping on something behind me. "So, where's Allyson?"

I tippy-toe and look around. "She's around here somewhere. She asked about you earlier, actually. I guess her aunt mentioned you attending my audition so she figured you'd be here."

"So if a random girl comes up to me, I'll know who it is."

"If she's tall with auburn hair, that's her. If not, it's some rando girl trying to get your milk chocolate candy bar." I smirk.

"There's only one girl here who'd I share that with." He smiles back, looking at me like I'm the last girl on Earth. I hate it. I love it.

"I want you for keeps..." His voice echoes in my head.

A wave of anxiousness attacks every muscle in my body and makes my gut gurgle.

I sip my martini. "Hey, I'll be back, okay? I'm going to run to the bathroom quick." I hold out my glass to him. "Watch this for me? Make sure no one roofies it?"

"Of course."

"Thanks, hon!" I hurry to the house.

After I potty, I stare at myself in the mirror while I wash my hands, then I head back outside, taking slow, deep breaths.

As I approach the bar, there's a camera flash from my right. "You. Are. A. Natural," a manly voice says.

My sights rest on Connor, fancy camera in hand. "What, do you moonlight as paparazzi for people who aren't famous as a side gig?"

He strolls up to me. "No. Not that it matters if one is famous. Nature, architecture, people—if I see something breathtaking, I do my best to capture it." He holds my gaze and licks his lips in the way someone very full of themselves does. Then he turns his camera's screen to me. "See, look how this dazzling specimen of a woman stands against a wall of mundane. Breathtaking."

It's a shot of me in the perfectly fitting, ass-accentuating midnight-blue dress, while I'm nervously looking out for Dion. I don't look as drunk as I do sad. "That is quite the picture," I say, looking up into his emerald eyes, which are shining with desire. It's not the longing, adoring look that I've grown accustomed to. My sights wander to his recently moistened lips. The thoughts running through my head right now send an unexpected pang of guilt through my stomach. Because I want to be bad tonight after being uncharacteristically sweet all week. I want to lash out in defiance against this *thing* that has had me acting like a good, loyal girl since those goddamn loaded nachos and bacon cheese fries got knocked over.

I'm in bad-decision territory…

<u>15</u>
Dion

Friday

EXPERIENCE ENOUGH PATTERNS OF human behavior, analyze them and find the correlations, and then anyone's motives and their objectives can become predictable, within reason. For a hyper-observant, over-analytical type like myself, it's second nature. Instinct.

A change in texting frequency, canceling dinner, avoiding eye contact, dodging my kiss after a passionate lovemaking round and a heart-throttling make-out session this morning, disappearing on me for ten minutes—it all hints that what I said last night and how heartfelt this morning was left her shook. Avoidance tactics I've experienced many times before after pouring my heart out to some girl.

The first time was eighth grade. I told the girl I had been crushing on since fifth grade that I loved her, over instant messenger. The memory still makes me cringe until this day. Then, after she became distant the following week, I told her I was just kidding. She yelled at me for playing with her emotions.

In tenth grade, this girl I used to always hang with gave me a handy while we watched some crappy horror movie, then I texted her something stupid the next morning like "**Next time we hang, maybe we should talk about a relationship.**" She acted like I had the plague for the next few weeks. And rightly so.

By senior year, I got the hang of it, playing it cool and wooing this Colombian girl that I went on to date the last half of the year. I chose her over my female best friend because I felt too strongly about her and knew I'd screw it up.

Play it cool. Don't come on too strong. Sensor your feelings until they're mutual. That's what worked from senior year onward. If there was someone I felt too strongly about, like my friend Karla back at Penn State, I just avoided going there at all costs. With Isabella, I thought I felt a mutual intensity in her feelings. Hell, I literally felt the difference in how she kissed and how she screwed me as the days went on. I shared my feelings and thought I did a good job toning it down this time.

Clearly, I was wrong.

As I lead Mike and Riley through clusters of hipsters and flower children in search of Isabella, I spot her then stop dead in my tracks, Riley and Mike forming up around me like this is the place I chose to settle at. She's over by the jacuzzi with that tall douchey-looking dude I saw her with when we first got here. She slaps his chest over something he said, she leans into him when she laughs, brushes her hair back and bats her eyelashes. Her eyes linger on him with drunken lust. It's the way she looked at me when we first met.

Riley wanders off to talk to someone and Mike gawks as she walks off. That's when Isabella scans the yard and locks eye with me. Then she looks back at the douche like I'm just some stranger.

Mike shakes his head. "Ice cold." His hand falls on my shoulder. "Told you she'd forget about you eventually."

I chug my beer in silence.

"Want me to run interference for you so you can steal her away?" Mike says, cracking his knuckles.

I shake my head. "Maybe inaction might be the right move."

"Maybe you need a couple more shots to ease the hurt, brosiff."

Heels clop up from the left. "Did you find her yet?" asks Riley.

Mike points. "Yeah, over there flirting with that hipster fucker. What's up with your friend?"

Riley shrugs. "That's just Bella being Bella."

"Did something happen after you guys left today?" I ask. "Did she complain about something I did?"

"Go get your bro a beer, would ya?" she says to Mike, patting him on the arm.

With a nod, Mike charges forward with the urgency of someone rushing to get an EpiPen.

Riley steps in front of me, obscuring my view of the girl deliberately torturing me. "She's been weird all day, but she wouldn't tell me why."

"It's probably what I said last night," I sigh.

"And what'd you say?"

"Basically, that a fling isn't what I wanted and that I wanted her for keeps. And that I'd dump whoever I was with if she ever wanted to try."

Riley grimaces.

"We were talking about the future and I was high as shit. Couldn't stop the words from coming out."

"Yeah," Riley drags. "I mean, that's really sweet and all, but Isabella… is a commitment-phobe. And even though she won't admit it to me, or herself for that matter, I think she feels very strongly about you and I'm guessing she doesn't know how to deal with it. You didn't hear that from me."

"Hear what?" I smirk.

"Good boy," she says with a smile. "The way she is with you… she wasn't that way with Zach at first. Or during. I think that she's scared shitless after what you said and how she felt after that romantic-ass newlyweds kiss this morning. Like, she was legit in a daze the whole drive back home. And the fact that you're heading back east in a few days has her all flustered. Again, you didn't hear any of that from me."

"I mean, I kind of figured some of that."

"Figured you did."

"So, what do I do? Just let her put on a show with that asshole so she can make a point that she doesn't want to be tied down? Because I know that already. I don't need a reminder."

Riley whips out her phone and rapidly types up a text. **Stop being an asshole, betch** is what it reads. Isabella is who it's addressed to. "Uh, if I were you?" she finally says. "Act like you don't give a shit. Go flirt with another girl. Make sure she sees it."

"Yeah, that's not my style."

"Of course it's not, you boy scout."

I scowl at her, lips curled into my mouth.

"Listen, you wanted the advice of someone who knows her best? That's my advice. She doesn't want to feel like she's tied down. Especially not when she's drunk. Bella loves to flirt. And Isabella is rebellious by nature. I'm sure you've heard about her protesting days."

I nod.

"Yeah... So, when she's in Rebel Bella mode, she's going to do her thing to make her statement. Give her space and she won't feel like she needs to throw herself at some hunk that she'll never talk to again." She grabs my shirt. "Come on, let's get out of sight so she doesn't see you looking like a lost little boy."

"Alright." I walk alongside her, stealing one last glance at Isabella.

She glances at me at the same time, only to look away shamefully a second later.

"Thanks for uh… your help, Riley," I say loud enough for her to hear me as we pass by the chest-vibrating speakers.

She turns and gives me a warm smile. "Don't mention it, Dion. I like you and your whole vibe. And you clearly care about my Izzy. And you make her happy as hell. You're exactly what she needs in her life. She just doesn't want to admit it. Or accept it."

Riley and I rejoin the group right as Mike pops out from a nearby clearing at the bar. I stand there silently, guzzling down beer every ten seconds like it's a nervous habit. Drinking was never the way I chose to solve my troubles, but tonight, I desperately need to stop thinking. The second this bottle is done, I grab another.

"Be right back," I shout to the crew. "Bathroom."

Riley shoots me a stern look as I walk off.

I put my beer to my mouth and look away. I slip into the house, dodging drunks left and right. Some girl points me to the bathroom and thankfully it's open.

As I wash my hands, I imagine Isabella leaving with this random guy and the thought makes me sick to my stomach. Or maybe it's the volume of alcohol at work.

I splash my face with water, dry my face with paper towel, then stare at myself for a long while, holding my own gaze as I contemplate what to do while I ignore the dude knocking on the door saying, "Hello? *Ocupado?*" in a shitty accent.

Listen to Riley, I tell myself.

I guzzle the beer I brough with me. "Fuck that. Go talk to her," I whisper.

I leave the bathroom with conviction and navigate my way back outside like a man on a mission. She's not where I last saw her. A quick surveying of the bustling backyard leads to me spotting her on the other side of the bar with that guy. His hand is on her hip and he's leaning unnecessarily close to speak to her. My heart is throttling now, it's vibrating. The increased blood pressure makes me dizzy as I approach them.

"Izzy," I say when I'm maybe five feet away. I don't look at the guy once.

Isabella looks over with a smile that snaps into shock, like she forgot I was here. "Oh, hey, Dion! Connor, this is my friend Dion. Dion, this is Connor freaking Braddock! He's a super talented, famous photographer!"

His hand leaves her hip and reaches out to me.

I nod at him. "Cool, nice to meet you," I say flatly, turning back to her. "Can I talk to you for a second?"

"Uhh," she hums, turning to him. She turns back to me. "Yeah." To him she says, "Excuse me for a moment."

Connor nods, then smirks at me as I'm turning away.

"What's up?"

"What's up with you?" I almost snap.

"What?"

"Can we go somewhere a little quieter?"

She looks confused. "Yeah, this way." She leads me around the side of the house near the driveway. "So, what's up, hon?" she says, folding her arms.

"What's up with you? You having *fun*?"

She squints a bit. "Um, yeah. Having a great time, actually. You?"

"No. Not really."

"Uh, how can you not be having fun? You're at an exclusive LA party with a bunch of important people, probably some famous celebs. You're drinking free booze and snacking on fancy hors d'oeuvres."

"You know I don't care about any of this shit."

"Um, okay… then why are you here?"

"Why do you think? You invited me here to hang with you and then, the minute I got here, you ran away."

"I didn't invite you here *just* for us to spend *more* time together. I invited you so you could get the full LA experience! A rich guy's mansion party in the hills is the most LA experience you can get. You should be doing crazy shit with your friends so you can have an epic story to tell when you get back."

"Oh, fuck an epic story," I snap.

"Excuse me for getting you all on the list to make up for stealing you away all week."

"Yeah, that's why you invited me and the guys here."

She scowls. "Why are you being a dick right now?

"I'm being a dick?"

"Yeah. What, are you implying that I am?"

Eyes wide, I nod with a mocking smirk.

"How?"

"You're out here flirting with this guy right in front of me and you've barely acknowledged me since I've been here."

She rolls her eyes. "This is how I network... I'm a flirt. I told you that. I told you what I do when I come to these parties. And news flash, hon—we're not together."

"Oh, I'm well aware we're not together."

"Good! I'm glad! Now don't act like I can do whatever the hell I want."

"I never said you can't do whatever you want. You can do whatever it is that makes you happy."

"Then why are you acting like a jealous fucking boyfriend?"

"Because you're about to get everything you've ever wanted as far as your dance career goes. You don't have to *network* like this anymore."

"I don't have to. But I want to."

"You know how I feel about you."

"Yep. You made your feelings clear," she says snottily.

"Then why are you deliberately flirting with him in front of me? Why bother inviting me if this is what you planned on doing the second you found some potential career-changing douche?"

"No one told you to watch. You could've gone and mingled until I was ready to come find you. Because I planned on coming to find you and Riley after I was all done working him. Maybe I wanted to have fun and flirt with him and whoever else I wanted after before deciding that you are who I wanted to go home with. But now that you're tripping, maybe I'll just go home alone. Or maybe I'll just go home with Connor!"

I shut my eyes for a moment. "It's when you say shit like that, that I know you're deliberately trying to hurt me."

She looks away.

"You're something else, Isabella."

"I am… I really am."

"Alright, if this is how you're going to act all because I told you how I felt, maybe I should just go. You clearly don't want me here for any other reason than to torture me. Mission accomplished."

Her face is neutral. "If you want to go, go."

I shake my head. "Don't worry. I am." I start back toward the backyard. Then I stop abruptly, spinning back around to the pouty girl. "For the record, if the roles were reversed and you were as crazy about me as I was about you and I showed you an amazing time only to ignore you while I hit on another girl right in front of you at a party that I brought you to, you'd label me as *just another asshole* or say that I was *just like every other guy.*' Hell, you tested me several times to make sure I wasn't, then you went ahead and chose to be shitty to me anyway. If I did something to deserve this, I'd understand. But I was nothing but good to you and the only thing I'm guilty of is telling you how I felt… Sit on that for a while." I walk off without looking back.

16
Isabella

Saturday

MY FIRST THOUGHT WHEN I wake up, other than *holy shit my head* and *bleh… my stomach*, is of the look on Dion's face last night. For some unexplained reason, a wave of nauseating guilt hits as I think back to letting Connor bore me from behind against the washer in the laundry room that I dragged him into not long after Dion left the party without his boys.

There was this movie called *White Fang* that I watched with my dad one summer. In that movie, Ethan Hawke's character was moving to a city or something, so he had to let the wolfdog he'd bonded with and tamed go back to the wild, where he belonged. He yelled at White Fang and chased the dog off with a stick into the woods to be free. I think that's what I was going for last night. Set Dion free by making him see me as something he wouldn't like. Rid myself of attachment by severing ties. That's what was best for us both.

That scene made me cry. So did witnessing Dion sulking off, looking all hurt.

I wanted to feel good. I wanted to get over him. Connor was the obvious remedy. But Dion was that purple elephant again that I couldn't stop thinking about. Not even while I made out with Connor. Not even while I was being finger blasted or railed by the stud that I used to piss him off. It killed the mood. So much so that

I made Connor stop, like, not even a minute after he got the condom on, and I fled the laundry room with tears pooling in my eyes, ducking into the first bathroom I came across. Then I cried so hard I threw up.

Or maybe I puked because I drank way more than I should've, per usual, and I was getting the spins.

I felt guilty when I kissed Connor. While I let him screw me. I feel even guiltier now that I'm sober. Like, why the fuck do I feel so crappy about hooking up with a handsome stranger? I'm single, for fuck's sake!

Probably because I was shittier to Dion than I needed to be, I think, squinting against my phone's bright screen to see if he texted me. I was expecting to see over a dozen paragraph-length drunk texts damning me. But nothing.

The next thing I know, I'm thumbing away a message to him.

Me: **Hey... I was an asshole last night. Sorry...**

I delete the draft, then return my phone to the nightstand.

You got what you wanted, I tell myself. *Don't give him false hope. Leave it alone. Things will go back to normal eventually.*

"Bella the Savage," Riley announces when I finally emerge from my room after noon. "She lives."

"Really? My bestie is the last person I need to be catching attitude from right now."

"You didn't have to do all that last night, you know."

"I know." I grab a gallon of water out of the fridge as well as a loaf of bread.

"You tortured the nicest guy in all of America just for liking you."

"He liked me *too* much," I say, filling up my cup. "It was just too much for me. I did him a favor. Showed him who I am before

he left to scare him off for good. Now he can get on with his life."
I sip the water slow, just in case my stomach rebels against it.

Riley shakes her head. "As your best friend, I say this with love… But maybe you need to see someone about your intimacy issues."

"I don't need a shrink. I just don't need…" I whirl my hand around as if I'm trying to bring the word up to the surface.

"Love?"

"Anything serious," I snap, retrieving the Advil from the drawer containing a random assortment of pills, ketchup packets, and other miscellaneous condiments.

Raunchy Sauce, I think, eyeing a ranch sauce packet. My heart starts thudding in my chest, my head bumping along with every beat.

"You make it seem like him coming on too strong is what's ticking you off, but you wouldn't have been acting all defensive and snappy or done what you did last night if you weren't feeling something that scared the shit out you."

I drink the rest of my water in silence.

"Don't ruin the poor boy, Izzy. Please. You'll give him a complex that'll jack him up for the rest of his life. Text him. Tell him why you were a dick. Apologize. Okay?"

I shuffle my feet, a plate of plain bread in hand. "Maybe when my head stops pounding, I'll think up the right words to say. Okay?" I shut the door behind me.

17
Dion

Sunday

THE LAST TEXT I sent to Isabella read: **Hey, can we meet up & talk now that we're both sober? I'd rather not leave LA on a bad note with each other.** Sent at 4:05 P.M.

That was what I sent yesterday after waiting half the day for her to apologize or just say "hey" or something. It's 8:05 A.M. now, and she hasn't responded.

Now I'm sitting here on the edge of my bed next to the bags I just finished packing, staring at that last message, debating whether or not to just text her something passive-aggressive like: *Well, my flight leaves in 5 hrs. It's been fun, the last 2 days aside. I hope you achieve everything you've ever wanted. Peace.* But I decide against it. Nothingness seems like a more powerful message because I know she's expecting me to reach out again. Ghosting dudes and waiting for them to keep texting her until she *feels* like responding is probably her game. And I won't play it. She doesn't deserve the satisfaction of knowing that I still want her in my life.

Forget her. Move on. Focus on that date with Jessica this Friday, I think, backing out of the message.

"Yo," Jeremy says, poking his head into my room, "we're leaving."

I check my phone again like I didn't just see the time. "We don't have to be at the airport for another two hours."

Jeremy nods in an exaggerated manner. "Yeah but, you know, LA traffic and shit!"

Mike appears next to him, leaning against the door frame. "There's construction or something on the 405, broski. It was up to me to check since you're not doing your usual duties." His knuckles rap on the wooden frame. "Let's roll!"

Usually, I'm the one rallying the group and making sure we leave on time for things. Not today though. I just don't care. "Alright, whatever." I grab my bag and follow them out of the room.

Mike drives. I ride shotgun, staring out the window in a daze like I just received devastating news. It's bad enough that I was absent all week, but all day yesterday I was far from present. I was just as zoned out as I am now, unable to enjoy my last day hanging at the beach and hitting the bar scene for one last hurrah with the crew. Thursday night, I told myself I wouldn't have traded any of my time with Isabella for forging memories with these guys who have become brothers to me over the years. Now that all of this has happened, I'm wishing I didn't confiscate our appetizers as the perfect gesture to win her interest. Because hurting like this? It sucks.

The scene passing me by triggers me to snap out of it. "Uh… Did you miss a turn or something?" I ask, pulling out my phone to check Google Maps since the GPS on the dash is angled more toward him. "We should have been on the 405 a while ago."

"We're making a stop," Mike says.

"We're going west… where the hell are we stopping? I thought there was construction on the highway. I'm not seeing any."

Mike turns to me with a troll grin. "We're taking your ass to Pasadena."

"Um, why?"

"Because we want our bro back," Jeremy blurts out from the seat behind me.

"And if you don't get closure, you're going to be all mopey and shit for weeks," Stefan chimes in next.

Mike glances at me. "So me and Riley coordinated a little run-in for you two. She and Isabella are out for a run right now. They should be just getting back when we get there."

I cock a brow. "Weren't you all bitching at me all week for being sprung over this girl? Now you of all people are trying to play matchmaker, Mike?"

He shrugs. "I was pissed you went rogue on us. We all were. But I was just salty because you've become a brother to me and I didn't want our last big adventure before we all go our separate ways to get ruined over some chick. Because maybe I feel like there's no way we'll all stay in touch after we graduate. I did join the group a little later than the rest of the guys, so I feel like I'd be the one who'd just become someone you'd remember to message on birthdays and New Year's."

"That ain't true," I protest.

"You said it yourself. You stay in touch with maybe four or five people from every stage of your life. That's the norm for most people, I feel like." He punches my arm. "But I can tell you're crazy about her and feel like I've been giving you shit all week, so I want to make sure you get your closure. And Riley wants Isabella to get a reality check."

I shrug. "I appreciate it, Mike. But I really don't want to see her."

"Too bad. Because we're doing this."

As Mike pulls up to Riley's apartment, the girls are just walking up to their building's entrance, their faces, arms, and toned abs glistening with sweat in the early-morning sun. Riley is in a green sports top, Isabella in burgundy. Both girls are in black leggings that accentuate their dancer legs with sneakers that match their respective tops. It's only now that I realize how in-shape Riley's lengthy form is, but that's not where my eyes linger.

"Ooof," Mike blows, leaning against the steering wheel. "Yeah, I might have to come back to visit Riley one day… You were onto something chasing after dancers, D. Fit. Flexible. Sexy as all hell. And feisty in the best way possible."

"Mm-hm," I groan, making a mental note to maybe avoid dancers in the future.

Maybe fifteen feet from our vehicle, Riley looks right at us and Isabella follows her gaze right to me. Shock hits her as she turns to her best friend.

Mike shoves my shoulder. "Go. Clock's ticking."

"God damnit," I mutter, opening my car door. My heart is thumping so hard in my chest that my vision is pulsing.

"Did you have something to do with this?" I hear Isabella say as I open my car door.

Riley nods and responds with something inaudible that ends with, "because you need to learn how to act toward decent humans." Riley waves at me and the guys before jogging up the steps.

Isabella folds her arms and curls her lips into her mouth as I emerge, slamming the door behind me.

I tilt my chin up to her as a greeting.

She returns the gesture, then hangs her head.

"For the record, coming here wasn't my idea," I say as I walk up to her, unable to stop myself from admiring that body I've come to know so well.

"Yeah," she says quietly. "Riley told me she had Mike drag you here." She glances up at me.

"I just wanted to get on the plane and forget about all of this. But I'm here, so if you wanted to talk about things and clear the air. Let's talk."

She looks to the ground, tapping the toe of her shoe on the pavement. "Not sure what to say…"

I say nothing during the silence that follows.

"Sometimes I do fucked-up things when I'm drunk," she says, ashamed.

Oh, you were just drunk! Wow, what a great excuse! "So, canceling dinner Friday wasn't related to that show you put on?"

"We had spent all week together, Dion… I just needed a little more time apart after how intense things got. You know?"

"And avoiding me at the party and being all over that guy in front of me, knowing how I felt about you? Was that just because you were drunk, or were you trying to send me a message?"

She looks up at me, mouth twisted to the side, chewing on the inside of her lip. Nervous. "What I did was shitty, I know. Maybe I wouldn't have done that if I wasn't so trashed. But last night? That was me… I told you that you wouldn't want me once you saw the real me. I warned you."

"Who said I don't still want you?"

Her whole face scrunches up as she scowls, locking eyes with me. "How? How could you?"

I shrug. "Not really sure myself."

"What if I told you I fucked Connor as soon as you left? Would you still want me so badly?"

My guts feel like they're being sucked into a tiny black hole. A half-laugh, half-scoff escapes me. "Why would you—why would you ask me that?" I stutter. "Or tell me that, for that matter."

"Because I did. Fuck him. Right after I watched you leave. I'm being candid so I can figure out how much abuse you're willing to take before you write me off. I'm waiting for you to get mad like a normal human being and admit I'm no good for you." She averts her gaze. She can't look at me for more than five seconds. Her arms are still crossed. She's been hanging her head since I walked up to her. All indicators of guilt.

"Am I more upset now that I know you did? Of course. It fucking hurts. But I'm not mad at you for living your life. You're single. You can do whatever you want to do. I have no place to judge you for that. What I'm mad about is that you're acting like you don't care."

Her eyes are glassy now. "I never said I didn't care."

"It's not about what you said or didn't say. Actions. That's what matters."

"I don't know what to tell you. I am who I am. When I get overwhelmed emotionally, sometimes I get sloppy drunk and lash out and do heartless shit."

"Okay, but you *chose* to act like that, though… You don't have an addiction or mental disorder. You didn't blow me off only to fuck around with Connor to prove something to me. You did that to prove something to yourself. And, judging by how guilty you're coming off, you didn't find the answer you went looking for."

She shuts her eyes and rubs her face from brow to chin.

"Answer me this—did this week mean anything to you? Because I know it did. You can't tell me it didn't."

"It did mean something," she whispers like she doesn't want me to hear it. "But that's the problem. I don't want something meaningful in my life. This *thing* between us was overwhelming as hell and I wanted no part of it. And, honestly, feeling like I'm the only thing you'd ever want was just too much pressure on me."

"Here's the thing. I didn't ask you for anything. I didn't ask you to be my girl. I didn't ask if we could move in together. I didn't say I was *absolutely* moving here for you or that I'd never date anyone until you were ready. I didn't profess my love."

"But… it's just… I don't know that the pressure I felt wouldn't have gone anywhere unless I straight-up fucked things up. I think that's why I was such a bitch to you. I wanted to make sure you didn't move here in hopes that I'd come around. I didn't want you holding out hope or pining over me. I just want to be single and do scandalous shit and hook up and have fun while I focus on building my career!"

"Here's what I don't get. All I did was tell you how much I liked you," I continue, keeping my voice calm. "I told you what I'd do if you wanted to try and I was unavailable. I expected nothing in return from you except for us to remain friends and to stay in touch. That's it, Isabella. And what did you do? You used some guy to put on a show just to rub my nose in the fact that you were free and you could bang anyone you wanted, like I was some asshole you caught cheating on you. Shit was *very* unnecessary."

"It was."

"No one has ever gone so far to hurt me like that before. Especially not someone I was on good terms with." I search her face. "One thing is clear now, though. What you did wasn't about me. That was about you. You couldn't handle the fact that we had this amazing connection. You couldn't handle the fact that you caught feelings. So you went and blew it all up to make this whole situation easier for *you*."

Her eyes are squeezed shut, her hand covering her mouth.

"Yo," Mike calls from the Pathfinder, his head sticking out of the window. He slaps the outside of the door. "We need to get moving."

When I turn around, Isabella's head is turned away and she's wiping her arm across her eyes. It's taking everything in me not to console her. "You know what your problem is?"

"What?" she chokes out, sounding slightly annoyed.

"You're strung out on hopeium."

She sniffles. "*Hopeium?*"

"Yeah, it's a mashup of hope and opium—something my psych professor taught us about. She defined it as a clinging to unreasonable hopes or desperately holding onto hopes without having any foundation for believing they'll actually pan out. And it's addictive as opium. Because people always feel so damn good about things that will come from the future that they don't worry about the present."

"Okay," she says, uncertainly.

"You live your life doing shitty things in the present, living in hopes that everything will work out for you one day. You hope that only by being alone you can live your best life and make your dreams come true."

She looks away.

"You hope that when you achieve everything you're working toward and when you're done having your *fun*, something amazing like what we had this week will just come into your life when you're *finally* ready to settle. You probably hope you'll find another me when the *time is right*. Or maybe you'll reach out to me when you finally realize what we shared is something rare. It's a pipe dream. And it's a mistake to destroy something amazing that comes around once in a lifetime just because you may have another shot in the future. Life's too short for that."

She finally looks back up at me, face pouty, eyes watery, lips curled into her mouth.

I search her eyes. Her lips twitch like she has something to say, but seconds pass and her mouth doesn't move. "I got a plane to catch," I finally sigh out, backstepping towards the SUV. "Bye, Isabella. Good luck with the choreography audition Friday. I hope you get everything you want. I really do."

She untucks a hand from under her armpit and gives me a half-hearted wave. "Thanks," she says with a strained voice. "Goodbye, Dion," she almost whispers.

I turn away, walking slowly to the Pathfinder, waiting for her to call my name, then apologize and kiss me goodbye. But she doesn't.

Guess I'm high on hopeium, too, I think, palming the door handle.

When I climb into the passenger seat, the door closing behind her as she hurries inside is the last thing that I see.

18
Isabella

Sunday

FLIRTING WITH CONNOR IN *front of Dion, confessing to him that we screwed, that was about me,* I think, slumping against the wall opposite the elevator's button panel and burying my face in my palms. The sad part is that didn't dawn on me until he said it. *He was right. Everything he said was right.*

The hurt in his eyes just now... *oof.* It made my heart ache. I knew he liked me. It was undeniable that he cared. But I didn't really know how badly he did until just now. Hurting him like that? The guilt of that weighs down on me more than what I did to Zach, which doesn't make any sense at all to me. And as soon as the elevator doors close, my emotions flow.

I wipe my eyes with my forearm, snort, and try to get my shit together before reaching our apartment.

Riley's in the kitchen working on breakfast when I walk in. She stops what she's doing and turns right to me, grimacing. "Geez, you're a mess."

"Oh, really? And whose fault is that?" I snap.

She raises her hands in surrender. "Sheesh, I was just trying to help. Forgive me for trying to give you a chance to salvage this wonderful thing that had you happier than I'd ever seen you."

"Yes, because being ambushed by the amazing guy who didn't deserve what drunk me did last night is exactly what your embarrassed and guilty best friend needed the *day* before choreography intensives begin tomorrow."

"Sorry, Iz. I legit thought this whole *Parent Trap* thing me and Mike cooked up would end with you two kissing and making up."

"Well, it didn't."

"Did he go off on you or something?"

I sigh. "He ranted, but didn't go off at all."

"Doesn't surprise me. So, what—did he just not accept your apology then?"

My lips reflexively curl into my mouth as I avert eye contact. I'm only a good liar in front of authority figures. Around people who know me, I don't bother trying. Avoidance tactics are my jam.

"Wait… don't tell me you didn't apologize, Isabella…"

"Fine. I won't."

"Why the hell not?"

"I don't know! Maybe I'm just a heartless bitch."

"We both know you're not… For once, maybe try being honest about what it is you're feeling."

I sigh out the deep breath I just took. "Maybe because I didn't apologize because I think his life will be better without me in it." Great, now I'm tearing up again.

"Is that *really* the only reason?"

I shrug. "Maybe royally screwing things up with him was the only way I could let him go. Because, you know what, I actually like having him around and I really want to see him again. And I'm afraid what would happen if he were to come out here for the summer like he said he would. It's just easier to get over him and avoid something potentially coming out of this if I know he hates me."

"And there it is," Riley says, nodding. She embraces me and my core jumps against her as I sob silently. "Doesn't it feel good to speak the truth?"

"No."

"Stop lying to yourself. Now, how about you call him before he boards his plane and tell him that. And say you're sorry after."

I sniffle. "Nuh uh." I pull away. "Riley, it's over. Okay? The last thing I need is to get my apology rejected by him." The pace at which I walk to my room is somewhere between *gotta pee* and storming off. "Can we just let this go? All I'd like to do is shower and take a nap and get my mind right in preparation for the week ahead." One hand on the doorframe, another on the doorknob, I stare back at her. "Okay?"

She nods slowly and dramatically. "Whatever you want. Just don't come complaining to me when you find yourself regretting not listening to me."

"Yeah, yeah," I say, slamming my door like a hormonal teen.

A good shower crying session ends with me in my PJs curled up in fetal position in bed with my body pillow, music playing softly. Every song that comes on sounds like it's about him, even the ones that aren't sad or about love or sex.

What is wrong with me?

Our first night together, our first kiss, helping me move, the beach, our first time together, our road trip, all of our sweet moments—it all keeps replaying in my head. And the second I stop reminiscing and pining over the past I can't have back, cutscenes of his reaction from two nights ago and today tail each remembrance, tainting them with guilt. I suppose that's my psyche's way of saying, *'See, Dion was good to you, he made you happy. Your actions were unwarranted, so now you should always feel horrible even when you reflect on memories that should be fond.'*

"Ugh, why did I do that?" I say with my mouth mushed against my pillow.

What is wrong with me?

That seems to be a question I end up asking myself a lot lately. Sometimes I feel like I'm broken… Like I'm incapable of functioning like a normal human being when it comes to relationships. Or anything really.

My dad was my best friend. My hero. He was always so proud of his little dancer. After he died, I'd never felt so alone. Yeah, I had my mom and my sister, but I was closer with him than anyone. Then when he died, I vied for my mother's approval. I wanted her to be proud of me, the way Dad was. But she was always hard on me and it never seemed like anything I did was good enough for her. Ever. Not my dance performances. Not my cheering, which she never even came to. Not the surprisingly high GPA that I somehow maintained.

Criticism was all I ever got. Whether it was getting in trouble for smoking weed on campus in high school, skipping class, or getting caught hooking up with my boyfriend in my room sophomore year of high school—somehow, I always found a way to disappoint her. Any time she expressed that disappointment, I rebelled.

Even though I knew she loved me, I never felt loved. It never felt unconditional.

My first big fuck-you to Mom was when I was fourteen, not long after Dad died. While she was working late, I snuck this football player into my house so we could lose our virginities to each other. That was when I made the association that sex could not only be fun and pleasurable, but it could also be a coping mechanism that temporarily alleviates troubles. I fucked to forget.

And just when she was *finally* praising me for doing well in college and paying my bills on my own since she couldn't afford to help, Zach outed me as a stripper and a promiscuous girl, and now my mom barely talks to me.

It's not just my relationship with my mom that I can't get right. My sister Kirsten and I have never really been super close. I was always kind of mean to her since Mom always favored her over me, so that's on me. I also have a long history of ruining things with the friends who didn't end up ruining things with me. I stopped talking to my best friends from middle school after I had to change high schools. The girls that took me in at the new school, I abandoned for the weed heads I rolled with. My guy best friend I ghosted after he confessed his feelings to me. Guys in high school used me to hook up, then tossed me aside after getting what they wanted. The one guy that I dated senior year who didn't treat me like crap, I ended up cheating on. Openly, I might add.

And then there was college… All the sexually manipulative things I've done come back to me in a hazy wave of alcohol-blurred memories. My second semester of college, I drunkenly hooked up with a friend's boyfriend just because I was lonely and I knew he was into me. Our friendship ended when she found out a few weeks later. Then there were those two really nice guys that I'd always tease by sitting on their laps and giving them over-the-pants rubs at parties just to keep them lusting after me—to keep them buying me coffee and food.

More often than not, I blamed alcohol for my promiscuous, immoral, unfaithful behavior. But the truth is, 90 percent of the time, I left the house with the intent to do all those crappy things because I love sex and I have fun doing scandalous shit sometimes. And maybe I think monogamy is outdated. Getting sloppy drunk beforehand was just a cop-out to shift the blame to my boozed-up alter ego Bella, because that was easier than admitting to myself that I wasn't the good girl society said I had to be. What a shitty way to make myself comfortable with embracing my own sexuality.

The way I've always seen it, either I'm always going to disappoint the people who matter most, or the people I want in my life are going to disappoint me. Because of that belief, I've learned to lash out before I got hurt, or White Fang someone before they got hurt worse later. So, yeah, I guess I planned on hurting Dion the second I ignored his first text on Friday. Emotionally wounding him was all so I could protect him from me, and to protect me from building something with him.

But, now that I'm being honest with myself, this was the first time that that the thought of potentially being with someone who I could actually see myself with, and the feeling that things between us could actually work, scared me more than anything. That and the undeniable, magnetic, universal pull between us. And those are shit reasons to do what I did to someone so goddamn incredible.

Laying in the dark while reflecting on my life, cataloging the reasons why I am damaged goods, wondering why I'm so messed up—that's something I tend to do after my actions significantly damage my life. It's what I did after my roommate found out that I slept with her boyfriend and screamed at me to leave. It's what I did after Zach called me out for cheating. It's what I did after Mom called me a disgrace for being a stripper and told me that Dad would be so disappointed in me if he were alive. Of all the shameful things I've done, this is the first time that my actions have left me feeling sick to my stomach—left me feeling maybe equally as hurt as the person who didn't deserve the pain I inflicted.

This is the first time that it's dawned on me that I need to change.

I pull the covers over my head. *Maybe Riley's right… Maybe I do need a therapist or something.*

19
Dion

Friday

DIM AMBER LIGHTING TO set the mood, a live pianist, a classier and tamer crowd than what we'd typically find roaming the bars in downtown State College on a Friday night—Ale House seemed like the best choice for a first date. Delicious, moderately priced food that won't hurt my recently hemorrhagic bank account was also a major deciding factor. That and the fact that Jessica has never been here before.

Jessica sips her peach lambic beer to wash down the last bit of her burger. "So," she says, locking eyes with me, resuming the innocent smile she suppressed so she could drink, "would you move to California now that you've visited?"

I shrug, looking from those hazel eyes to the glass I'm slowly twirling on the table. "Not sure if California is for me..." *I need to be as far away from Isabella as possible,* is what goes through my head. "I think I'm going to just apply to jobs around the York-Harrisburg-Lancaster area, then maybe save up and travel until I decide where I want to go."

"Sounds like a smart move to me. It'd be easier to save if you're living with your parents for a while."

"True that. Especially if I'm sticking around Pennsylvania. The jobs I've been looking at don't pay well at all. I'd have to get a job in big pharm to make a salary I can live comfortably on. The only problem is *entry-level* positions require two to three years' experience."

"That's so lame," she says, shaking her head. "That basically means you're screwed if you don't have any connections. Because that's what it's *all* about these days."

"Yup. The only friend I have in pharm is my friend Carmela, and she's up in Boston."

"Ooh! Boston's nice! My parent and I went up there a few times to visit family. It's a pretty cool city!"

"Yeah?"

"Yeah! I love it there. Maybe add that to your list of places to check out. If you like it, maybe your friend can hook you up, then you can make the big bucks!"

I chuckle. "Yeah, maybe I will! I hear Boston is pretty much the hub of biopharmaceutical companies, so at least there I'll have more than, like, five options."

"See, there ya go!" Jessica says with a bright smile.

That sweet smile of hers is infectious as hell, which makes it impossible to drink until my smirk subsides. When it finally fades, I gulp down some beer. This is my second beer of the night, and it's not enough to get me out of this fog of misery that I've been powering through all night. Or should I say all week? I've pretty much been in a funk since last Friday, and it's taken everything in me not to pound a sixer of beer every day after class to numb this pain. Or maybe I should have drunk before class. Maybe then I would have been able to focus in my lectures and possibly get through the day a little better without being so... sad.

Sad isn't something I do. Not since my grandmother died when I was eight. After that, sorrow was always just converted to anger in my brain. It was just easier for me to process things with anger, like when cancer took my uncle in high school. Because then, I could take it out on my punching dummy and feel better.

Being all mopey and depressed seemed like such a foreign thing to me. Yet here I am. Mopey and depressed over a girl for the first time in my life. *Heartbroken* over a girl I'd barely known a week.

Pathetic...

"What about you, Jessica?" I finally say. "Is it back to Warrenton, Virginia for you after you graduate?"

Her mouth twists to the side. "Um, probably. But, hopefully, not for long. I love my parents, but I'd honestly prefer to stay a few states away from them so they don't try to take over every facet of my life again." A cute giggle follows.

I half-smile, half-grimace. "Considering what you shared with me about your life at home, I completely understand that." If I was homeschooled and grew up as a very sheltered kid with overly religious parents who tried to control every single thing I did, I probably wouldn't be eager to move back home either after tasting four years of freedom.

"Mm-hm." She takes another elegant sip that ends up turning into a chug when she realizes there's not much left. "I'd like to maybe get a job at the physical therapy clinic I'm interning at so I can stick around here for a while and gain some experience until I figure out what to do next."

"Ooh, I like the sound of that plan! Then I'd still have a reason to visit Happy Valley." I smirk.

Jessica smiles shyly. "And who said I was going to invite you up here, mister?"

Grinning, I shrug. "Considering we spent almost three hours talking the last time we saw each other and over four hours together tonight, I had assumed you enjoyed my company."

She squints. "Hasn't anyone ever told you that you shouldn't assume?"

"I only assume when I'm when I'm confident in the information I've gathered."

She cheeses. "Okay, okay… If it makes you feel better, you assumed correctly."

"Good, I'm glad. It'd suck to not be able to hang out with you anymore after this semester ends."

"Yeah, I second that."

"Okie dokie," the waitress says as she approaches. The lanky woman lays the card-check-holder before me after I subtly signal her to. "I'll take that when you're ready."

"Thanks," I say with a nod and a smile, snatching up the check before Jessica does. When I open it, I try not to cringe. Four drinks, calamari, and two burgers totals up to $71. Not terrible, but it reminds me that I shouldn't have spent so much money in California.

I'm going to have to be really frugal between now and finals.

Jessica leans forward to sneak a peek at the bill as I calculate the gratuity on my phone. "You want to go splitsies?"

I look up at her, flashing her a reassuring smile. "No, it's fine. I got this. Thanks for asking though!"

"Yeah. For sure!" She rummages through her clutch. "I can pay tip if you want. I have cash."

I laugh. "Jess, it's fine. Really."

"Alright then. Well, thank you so much for dinner, Dion!"

"You are very welcome. Thanks for coming out with me!" As I'm transcribing the number from the calculator app, my phone buzzes in my hand. The text preview shows: **Isabella Monroe: Hey…** Jessica is saying something but this message has siphoned away all of my focus.

Seeing a text from Isabella makes my heart race. It makes me happy and pissed at the same time, which sucks because I was close to finding my chill. Two more messages come in and I'm scared to open them. Her contacting me makes me wish she was here now. It compels me to consider scrubbing all traces of her from my phone and blocking her. But I can't do that. I can't imagine losing touch with her forever, even if seeing a picture of her on my feed makes the pain of what she did a week ago come bubbling back to the surface.

Curiosity drives me to drag down the notification bar and tap on the messages immediately.

Jessica's foot kicks mine under the table. "Everything alright, Dion? You just, like, zoned out there."

"Yeah, I'm fine… Sorry…" I drift off again as I skim the texts.

"Having trouble calculating the tip? I'm no math whiz, but I can probably figure it out for ya," she teases.

I smirk, rolling my eyes. "No, I already calculated tip. Thanks." I jot down the total and then scribble my signature, sliding the bill to the edge of the table. "I just got a text that surprised me, that's all. Mind if I reply to it quick?"

She shakes her head. "Not at all! Go on ahead." She grabs her phone just as I'm looking back down.

Isabella: **Hey…**

Isabella message two: **I know you probably still hate me (as you should) but I just got done with the choreography audition & I wanted to update you on how it all went. Just in case you were curious. Even if you aren't, I just felt I had to tell you.**

Isabella message three: **This week was brutal physically (and mentally because I've been beating myself up over how shitty I was to you, and I am so sorry for that). But I channeled my emotions into my dance, remembered your words of encouragement and pictured you in the crowd of spectators and…**

Isabella message four comes in as I'm finishing the last one: **I. FREAKING. CRUSHED. IT! RTA is taking me on!**

That tiny part of me that can be petty at times wants to ghost her, but I'm not the kind of person to ignore a text from someone who I don't want to cut ties with. Especially not when I'm holding out hope that I might one day forgive her. And I don't want to ruin her happiness by waiting until tomorrow to text her back so she can sweat a little from the uncertainty that I may never respond like I want to. So, after staring at the message for a few moments, I start thumbing a reply.

Me: **Holy crap! Congrats! I'm very happy for you. Truly, Isabella. Never doubted for a second! Best of luck with everything moving forward.**

Me part-two: **And I don't hate you... I don't know that I can. But that doesn't mean I'm still not bitter as hell.**

Her response comes fast. Isabella: **Bitter as hell is something I can live with. Sorry again for being an asshole... And thanks, Dion! I wish you were here to celebrate with me...**

That message, I don't reply to. I just lock my phone.

"Everything good?" Jessica asks, searching my eyes.

When I realize my facial expression probably conveys something like, *guess who just found out their dog ran away*? I muster up some elation. "Yup. Things are good. You ready to go?"

"I'm ready if you are!" she says cheerily.

I gesture to the exit. "Then let's roll!"

We grab our jackets and slide out of the booth.

As we walk to the exit, I stare sidelong at her and she looks back at me with that doe-eyed gaze she always seems to have and that childlike smile of hers. I smile back, unable to feel what I used to feel before I went out west.

Jessica is sweet. Weirdly innocent. Reserved. Nothing like Isabella. Exactly what I need but also somehow not. She doesn't excite me like she used to. Not that she ever electrified me the way Isabella did. But I'll learn to look past all of that. Because I did like

Jessica a lot before meeting Isabella, and it wasn't just because she's the fit, pretty, intelligent type that I go for. Our chemistry aside, there was something good and worthwhile in her that was really attractive to me pre-Izzy.

I just have to find those feelings again. That's the only way to get over Isabella.

"So," I say, holding the door open for her, taking a deep breath of cool evening air as it breezes past us. "Would you like me to take you home, or would you maybe want to keep the night going?"

She turns to me as we walk to my Jeep Liberty. "It is pretty early… And I did nap before you picked me up so I'm game to hang… What did you have in mind? Downtown?"

"I was thinking something more chill. Maybe a movie and drinks at my place?"

Jessica smiles that shy smile of hers. "Something chill sounds wonderful, so long as I get to pick what we watch."

"Deal."

Two Months Later

20
Dion

Friday

THE PERK OF NOT immediately finding a job after spring graduation is that there's still one last summer vacation left to enjoy before student loan debt servitude becomes a lifelong issue. That means maybe a month or two of these spur-of-the-moment, long weekend trips with my girlfriend and my squad without worrying about work denying PTO requests.

Jessica and I are on the porch of our Ocean City, Maryland beach house with Jeremy and Jessica's bestie and my former crush, Karla—the one who introduced us to each other—pregaming with some mixed drinks while recapping the nonsense that was our first night here. The four of us cheer at the sight of Mike, who's rounding the corner with three boxes of pizza, and Abby Snyder, who's got the bag with the wings.

"We eating outside?" Jeremy asks.

"Damn right!" I say. "It's too nice out to be indoors."

"Cool, I'll get us some plates!" Jeremy says as he rises from his chair. "Tommy! Chaz! Food's here!" he announces to those inside.

"Time to eat up, so we can drink up!" Mike sings to no particular tune, dancing his way down the walkway, bumping Abby with his hip as he approaches the porch.

Abby shakes her head, falling back a bit to escape his nonsense. The shy ginger has been with our crew since sophomore year, and Mike has been trying to hook up with her since the minute I introduced them to each other, to no avail. Player isn't her type. Neither is extreme extrovert. Pretty much everything he does seems to annoy her, kind of like Karla with Jeremy.

I place my palm on Jessica's thigh and give her a rub. "I'm grabbing a beer. You want another drink?"

"Yes, please!" Jessica cheers, smiling with a squint.

"And one for me, too!" Karla squeals.

I grab their cups and head inside. "Beer me, Chaz!" I say to the bearded ginger who's rummaging through the fridge. He's Mike's best friend since high school, who's been routinely coming up from Towson to party with us for the last two years.

"I got you, bro-bro!" he says, grabbing a Yuengling and setting it on the island for me.

I slide the bottle into my shorts pocket, then work on refilling the girls' jungle juice from the cooler in the middle of the island. As I do, my cell chimes and buzzes in my pocket. With one cup filled, I fish out my phone to check the text. **Isabella Monroe** is what's displayed on the preview. Even after officially being with Jessica for a month and four days, seeing her name shamefully still excites me.

This is the second time that she's texted me this month. The last one was a few weeks ago—she asked me to talk. I was studying for finals so I texted her that I'd hit her back up on the weekend, but never did. Before that, I hadn't heard from her since she got into RTA.

I whistle to get Jeremy's attention just as he's heading out with the plates. "Guess who just texted me," I whisper.

He squints like he can't think if his eyes are open. "Isabella?" he whispers back.

I nod slowly.

He shakes his head. "Dude, just reply saying, *'What do you want? I'm taken. You missed out.'* Then don't reply after she responds."

"That might be a little harsh," I say, unlocking my phone and opening the text.

Isabella: **Hey there… Can you please call me when you get a chance? It's important. Like, I missed a few periods kind of important…**

My heart skips a beat and my gut gurgles as I think back to the two times a few months ago where she rode me into blissful oblivion without a condom…

Oh, and that last time when we were high and I kept stroking after she begged me not to stop with her legs hooked around me…

"Chaz?" I say in a daze. "Do you mind taking these drinks to the girls for me please?"

He points a finger gun at me. "No problemo!"

I lock eyes with Jess as she's drunkenly chomping into a slice of pepperoni pizza. "I'll be right back. Got to make a call," I say, dialing up Isabella.

Judging by her smile, it's evident she's blissfully unaware that I probably look like someone who just learned their whole life might be flipping upside down just before it's about to begin. "Alright, babe!"

With the phone to my ear, I descend the porch steps, turn left and then head for the end of the block for some privacy.

"Hey, you!" Isabella answers apprehensively as I'm passing the neighboring house. "That was fast." The sound of her voice makes me smile and cringe at the same time. Hearing her makes it impossible to not picture her face, her body, the things we did together, how it felt being around her. It reminds me how she wrecked me psychologically…

"Hey, Isabella. Of course I'm calling you right away. Your text sounded… pretty damn *urgent*."

"You sound like you're in shock, hon."

I look over my shoulder to make sure Jess or my friends didn't tail me. "Well, I mean… if you're pregnant, how can I not be?" The thought makes me sweat, and it's not even that hot for a July afternoon.

"Whoa there, buddy, I never said I was pregnant," she drags. I can tell by her voice that she's smiling.

"Did you or did you not say '*a few missed periods kind of important*' in your text?"

"Oh, yeah, no," she giggles. "You can relax, I'm not pregnant. That's why I said *kind of.*"

"Wow."

"I just really needed to talk to you and I figured the only way to get you to call me was to make it seem super urgent!"

I sigh hard like I'm deflating. "God damn it, Isabella! Why the hell would you scare me like that?"

"Sorry! Please don't hang up, Dion! Pregnancy scare just seemed like the best analogy to convey just how much I was freaking out about needing to talk with you! And I figured you'd take it literally and call the second you saw it. It's not like you would have if I just said '*call me please.*' And if I called you, you probably wouldn't have picked up."

"I would've called you… Eventually."

"*Really*, though?"

"Yeah. Right after I got back from my vacation."

"Oh, wait, you're on another vacation?"

"Yup."

"Ooh, where at?" She almost sounds hopeful.

"Ocean City, Maryland. Our usual summer getaway since it's cheap and close to home."

"Nice! Looks like I'm still really good at interrupting your vacations, huh?"

"It's uncanny." I laugh. "So, what's up? Are you okay? Is everything alright?"

"Yes, yes. I'm okay. And everything is fine. I just..." She takes a deep breath. "I just think I'd feel a lot better if we could talk. So I could apologize."

"Pretty sure you already apologized."

"Yeah, but that was over text. Also, I didn't really explain myself and I kind of feel like I owe you an explanation. And... it's not like you really ever accepted my apology."

"Alright, well I'm all ears whenever you're ready."

"Okay... well... Um, I guess what I wanted to say was that what you said the last time we saw each other was right. The part about how me being shitty to you was about me. Because it was. I *was* scared of our connection. I was scared that you knocked down these walls that I've had up my whole life and made me feel all of these feelings. I'm not used to that kind of shit and it made me want to lash out to protect myself from being so vulnerable."

"That makes sense."

"Yeah... And in being vulnerable, I legitimately started feeling undeserving of your feelings toward me. Because I'm notoriously good at letting people down and hurting them. For some twisted reason, I truly thought ruining things sooner rather than later was the best way to save you from one or the other. You know, after months or years of me stringing you along and giving you false hope that might have made you miss out on someone more deserving of all that you have to offer... Before you fell any further for me or whatever." She sighs.

I sigh too.

"So," she continues, "I got drunk to make exacting unnecessary cruelty against you easier to carry out. I realize how insanely fucked up that is and I wish that I didn't do it. I wish I could go back and undo it and convince past-me to handle things like a normal person instead of—"

"Instead of pulling a *White Fang* on me?"

"Oh my gawd!" She laughs that goofy cackle that I miss so much. "I was *literally* about to say that! It makes me so happy that you just called it that!"

I snicker even though I don't want to. *Damn you, alcohol.* "Don't tell me that's what inspired you."

"I'd be lying if I said it wasn't."

"Well, then I wish you never saw *White Fang.*"

"I can't promise that purposely showing my true colors to scare you off wouldn't have still happened. Being me is the best way to drive people away, after all."

Hearing her say that makes me wish I could teleport across the country and hold her. "Come on, that's not true…"

"You say that, but it keeps happening…"

"Did you ever think that it's maybe more about *what* you're doing to people and less about who you are?"

"That may have dawned on me when you refused to hate me even after everything." There's some rustling in the background during the following silence. "That's why I'm trying to be better… And I feel like I can't be better until I amend things with the person that I hurt the most. So, from the bottom of my heart, I am so very sorry for what I did to you, Dion. I hope that you can one day forgive me."

I take a deep breath and let it out slowly. "One day? No." I pause for dramatic effect and I swear I hear her gulp hard. *Yeah, that's right, sweat a little bit. Freak out for a few seconds.* "Consider your apology accepted right now, Izzy."

She deflates now. "Ugh, thank you!" She lets out something like a mix between a laugh and a sob. "You don't know how happy that makes me!"

"Tell me something... Why now? Why wait two months to reach out and apologize?"

"Well, it would've been more like a month and a half if you got back to me a few weeks ago when I reached out."

"Alright, smart ass."

She giggles and it makes me smile because I can picture the way she squints and scrunches up her nose when she does.

"Why'd you wait a month and a half then?" I say.

"I don't know... After what I did, I figured you needed time to get over it, you know? To cool down or whatever. I didn't want to apologize while you were still pissed, only to get rejected. And I guess I was hoping you'd move on with that girl you told me you had a date lined up with. Which you did... A month or so with *what's her face* felt like enough time for you to get over me and maybe make you more willing to accept my apology and... maybe be friends? If you want. Because I want that. I don't want to go through life without you in it. As a friend."

Her words make my heart race. "So, you know Jess and I have been together for over a month, but you act like you don't know her name?" I smirk.

"Ugh, that's what you're taking away from that?"

"Mm-hm."

"Yeah, I've been keeping tabs on you. So what? Had to make sure I didn't break you. Making sure you were able to find happiness after the unnecessary psychological warfare I unleashed on you."

"How sweet."

She giggles. "Um, don't act like you aren't creeping on me, too. I've seen you liking all my dance-related posts. Every one of them. You liked those and not one of my racy bikini or lingerie pictures... or sexy solo ass-shaking videos."

"Wow, sounds like you were looking out for my likes and running a cross analysis?"

"No—didn't have to. It was *super* fucking obvious."

"Guess it was. I mean, I had to let you know that I was still rooting for you and supporting you without seeming thirsty."

"Figured that was your game... Bee-tee-dubs, it was comforting knowing you didn't completely hate me and that you were kind of still rooting for me."

"Again, I couldn't hate you if I tried. And, for the sake of being open, I did really try to hate you those first two weeks after I got back."

"I don't blame you. Part of the reason I *White Fanged* you the way I did was because I was hoping you'd turn into an asshole like Zach so I had a reason to hate you too. Of course, you had to go and be a gentleman about the whole thing."

"Oh, I am very capable of being a savage asshole to people who deserve it. Despite kicking my heart's ass, you didn't deserve my wrath."

"Why?"

"Because I know you... Despite what you think about yourself, you're good to your core, and you deserve to be killed with kindness and hard truths instead."

"You really are too good for your own good."

"Only when it comes to someone who matters." *That, I shouldn't have said,* I think, clearing my throat afterward as though that would somehow cover up the words she's already heard.

"Hmm..." By the sign of that hum, I can tell she's smiling. "So... like I was saying before, can we maybe be—"

"Friends?" I interrupt. "Yeah. Of course. You're not someone I want to go without having in my life either. Even if I'm in a relationship."

She lets out a slow breath. "Words cannot describe the level of relief I'm feeling right now. In less than a week, you made a profound difference in my life, and I don't think I can grow without you around in some capacity. Especially since no one has ever really cared about me like you did. Except my dad." She snickers.

"Hey, you can count on me to be your support system and your friend. But, given our... history, we need rules."

"Fine, I'll preemptively take sending you nudes off the docket."

"Yeah. Please do. And no raunchy comments like that, okay?"

"That's a big ask... Raunchy is my first language, after all."

"Oh, I'm aware. Just like I'm aware your second language is sarcasm. But you're going to have to try and tone it down for me."

"I'll try my darndest, hon. If I cross the line, just say raunchy sauce, okay? That'll be our *safe word*," she says in that sultry voice of hers, giggling after.

I chuckle. "I like that. But I'm going to call raunchy sauce on your tone of voice just now."

"Ugh, this is going to be so *hard*," she basically moans.

"I'm confident you'll manage," I say through clenched teeth.

"So, is that it?"

"If I think of more, I'll text you."

"Oh, I know you will." She falls silent.

I take a deep breath. "So... I should probably get back to the beach house before all the food is devoured."

"Yeah. Shit. I'm sorry for keeping you so long. Your girlfriend is probably wondering where you disappeared to."

"Honestly, she's probably too buzzed and too busy satisfying her drunk munchies to notice."

Isabella laughs. "Are you happy? With her?"

I have to think about that. "I am."

"You paused."

"I am happy."

"Good."

"Are you... seeing anyone?"

"Nope. Taking a break from dating for a bit. Working on me. Focusing on dance."

"And how is the professional dancer life so far? Everything you ever hoped for?"

"Yes! It is a-mazing! I'm learning a lot. Landed a gig in an indie music video, but you probably knew that."

"If you mean the one with you in a leotard dancing on the beach, then yup!" Sometimes I watch it once if not twice a day, because she was amazing in it, and it's a good song. And I love watching her dance.

"That's the one! What else... Um, I have a show in Vegas next month that'll run for a week."

"Wow! That's awesome! I'm proud of you."

"I still think I owe it all to you."

"You owe it to yourself."

"If you say so... What about you? Did you find a job yet?"

"Nope. Still looking. I have an interview next month at a pharmaceutical testing lab over in Amish land so we'll see how that goes."

"Ooh. I'm sure you'll kill it."

"I hope so. I'll miss all of this free time, but income would be nice. Especially if my spending during this trip carries on like it did last night..."

"Need me to send you some money, hon? Call it reparations for the pain and suffering I put you through." She cackles.

I chuckle. "No, thanks. I'll survive. But I appreciate the offer."

"You sure? I still have a nice nest egg from my old side gig."

"Wait, you quit the... *online* work?"

"Mm-hm… I actually quit the day RTA signed me on! I even went as far as to contact the site and begged them to take everything down. Didn't want anything jeopardizing my dance career, you know?"

"Smart call. Makes perfect sense."

"Mm-hm. And I guess I'm trying to exercise a little self-respect and hopefully discover some self-worth."

"Sounds like something worth trying."

"Oh, and FYI, I never even uploaded that video you filmed for me."

"Oh," is all I can get myself to say as I think back to what happened on the roadside in that car while playing cameraman. Blood immediately rushes south.

"Yeah… didn't feel right sharing that with the world. It's yours if you want it for those nights *Jess-ica* isn't around."

"Raunchy sauce."

"What? It beats prowling free sites on the web like I do."

"Raunchy sauce."

She lets out a menacing laugh. "Sorry. Couldn't help myself, hon." A cackle follows.

I sigh. "On that note."

"Yeah, I've kept you long enough. Thanks for chatting! And thanks for forgiving me."

"You're welcome. Thank *you* for tricking me into calling you… And for apologizing again. I didn't know how much I needed to hear your apology until today."

"Yeah, I bet."

"Mm-hm. And, so you know, I'll get you back for tricking me like that."

"I'm sure you will, hon. Take care. Good luck on your interview. And stay in touch, please. I'll make the effort, even if you won't." There's weight to the words that she's quoting from our last night in bed together. *You're someone who matters* is what it feels like she's finally admitting.

"Hmph," is how I stifle my laugh. "I will make the effort too."

"Good," she says, relieved. "You better… Well, enjoy the rest of your vacation! It was really great talking to you!"

"Thanks! It was good talking to you too. Later, Izzy."

"Later, hon."

Four Months Later

21
Dion

Friday

CONSIDERING THAT WORK THIS week has pretty much consisted of me training under the more experienced analysts and not doing any real labor, and given the weekend ahead isn't going to be very eventful, I shouldn't be so eager to want to get the hell out of here. But I am. Because there's something after work that I'm looking forward to.

One of the things that pisses me off the most about corporate jobs is that, even if you've finished all of your work for the day and no one is going to need you, you're still expected to sit at your desk until your eight hours is up. I mean, I probably shouldn't complain when I'm getting paid $18 per hour to sit at my desk while I listen to a business and marketing podcast that I'd probably be playing even if I was home now, but it would be nice if I could've left when I finished my tasks for the day two hours ago. At least then I could beat traffic and take a nap.

To kill some time, I take a walk to the furthest possible bathroom. On the way out of my department's hallway, I pass the lab where my buddy Cory is running a UV protein concentration analysis, misery plastered all over his face as he loads his next sample. Watching the clearly frustrated guy work stirs up the dread I have for the day when I'll be fully trained like him. My manager is super chill, my coworkers are great, the hours are flexible, and the friends I've made here are pretty dope, but it was made clear very early on in my almost three months here that this job is going to suck.

Characterization of chemotherapeutic antibodies and purity tests sounds more interesting than it really is. In reality, biopharmaceutical testing is whole lot of prepping solutions and putting them on instruments according to strict procedures. It's a lot of long hours slaving away in the lab and analyzing data to meet unrealistic client deadlines. And if you mess up a little bit, you have to re-prep and retest your samples. Repetition? It's the most maddening to me. I hate it with a passion. Every screwup in GMP testing comes with an internal investigation and a strike against you that affects raises and promotions. Everyone here, including management, is miserable. From veteran employees of twenty years to those a year or less in, all of the people I've talked to so far all feel unfulfilled, underpaid, and dissatisfied.

I'm already sick of working here and I haven't even started carrying out my duties as an analyst yet. I'm grateful to have work in my field so soon after college when many don't, but I'm already planning to flee this line of work ASAP. Hence the six-plus hours of business and marketing podcasts I consume per week.

Having flexible hours means that I can come in early and leave early, so long as I don't have lab work to finish up. For me, early is getting to work by 6:30 A.M. and leaving by 2:30. While I'm nowhere close to being a morning person, I'm less ticked off on a day when I don't have to deal with the rush hour traffic that would be an issue if I stuck to the default first shift hours of 8 to 4. So, when the clock hits 2:28 P.M., I start packing up. By the time I put on my coat, it's time to submit my timecard. After a quick goodbye to my cubicle mates and neighboring friends, I'm out the door.

The brisk November air feels good after having been cooped up in that stuffy-ass building all day. I take a moment to take a few deep breaths and appreciate the outdoors before I pull out my phone to text Jessica.

Me: **Hey! Is there anything you need me to grab while I'm out? Wine?** Since she moved to Lancaster for the physical therapy technician job that Mike hooked her up with, that's the kind of text I usually send her before I head over there.

My phone buzzes right as I palm my Jeep's door handle. When I see who it's from, smiling is an automatic reflex.

The fact that it's payday Friday is not why I was so excited to get the hell out of work today. It's not the fact that Jessica and I are going out to dinner at our new favorite restaurant tonight and spending the weekend together like we do almost every week. The "phone date" that Isabella and I scheduled is what I've been looking forward to all day.

Isabella: **I'm done with practice early! You still getting out on time today?**

I text back before even starting my engine.

Me: **Yup! Just got to the Jeep! You can call early if you want.**

After reconnecting in July, she called me that third Friday of August to see how my first week of work went. In September, we talked after one of her Vegas shows and then again two weeks later after I texted her that Jess and I told each other "*I love you*" for the first time. She didn't sound as happy about it as she pretended to be. In October, we had two more biweekly chats for no particular reason other than wanting to talk. If our chats are scheduled on days that I'm staying at my parents' house, she calls in the evening. Whenever I'm spending nights with the girlfriend and she wants to talk, we schedule something before Jessica gets home around 5 P.M.

The shitty part about this thing that we have going on is not the fact that Isabella and I talk often. Because we're friends, and we keep each other up to date. There's no flirting. Nothing romantic or sexual at all. There's hardly any reminiscing of our intimate moments. The shitty thing about the situation is that my talks with her are what I look forward to the most in any given week.

I look forward to calls with Isabella more than I look forward to a long weekend. I look forward to a few hours of talking and laughing with her more than I look forward to spending a weekend with my girlfriend. I'd rather chat with her all night than party with my best friends on those rare nights when the whole gang is in town. Whether it's a random text or a response to an ongoing conversation, receiving a text or a Snapchat from her is somehow always the best part of my day. I love sleep, but if it comes down to getting rest or a conversation with her, I'd pick her every time.

Feeling that way about her... it's eating me up inside.

Frequently checking her social media and looking at old pictures of her on my phone just to see her? Feeling slightly bitter when she tells me that she's going on a date? Checking Instagram to see which guys appear the most? Sending her funny memes or a dumb joke every chance I get? Texting her more than I text my girlfriend throughout the day? Sometimes thinking about her and the things we did together while I'm making love to Jessica?

Guilty on all counts.

I'm guilty and I hate myself for letting her hold this special category in my life. I hate that, despite being in a serious relationship with an amazing girl, Isabella's still the thing that lights up my life. And I didn't realize how dark my existence was before her. Actually, it wasn't until recently that I realized *existing* was all I was doing before we met. The first time in my life I truly felt alive was when I was with her. And, now, whenever we're not connecting, I feel dead inside...

No matter how many times I tell myself that our connection and our platonic relationship isn't cheating, interacting with her, thinking about her—it all feels so wrong. I don't know what to do about any of this. I do love my girlfriend. Dearly. But dialing things back with Isabella? Cutting her off? That's out of the question.

As I pull out onto the main road, my phone rings. The picture of her comes up and now I'm smiling to myself like an idiot, shaking my head at myself, disappointed about how excited I am anticipating the sound of her voice. I tell myself I no longer feel the way about her that I used to, but I believe that less and less as the days go by.

Remember what she did to you. Remember how she stopped sleeping around and started dating five months after she said that she didn't want a relationship. That's what I remind myself to keep my feelings in check.

"Hey, hey!" I answer.

"Dion! Hi!" Isabella says cheerily. "How's my favorite person?"

"Second favorite person," Riley shouts in the background.

A door shuts on her end. "Tell me all about your *mentally stimulating* week at work, hon!" Isabella continues with heavy sarcasm.

"Ha… Ha…. Yeah, how about we skip the part where I drone on about lab training and you tell me about your week instead? I'd rather not bore you with the mundane details of my *dream* career."

She giggles. "Fine, if I need something to help me fall asleep tonight, I'll call you up and you can give me the day-by-day breakdown. Or hour-by-hour if I'm still struggling to pass out."

"Just so you know, I'm giving you the finger."

"Oh, you love it when I give you shit. Why else would you keep putting up with me?"

"Maybe because I like being tortured."

"Please, your life would be dull without me."

You have no idea. "Keep telling yourself that."

"Mmm-hm… So, how was your week?"

"It wasn't bad. Basically got paid to do things I've done in college biochem lab."

"See? It's like you're back in college again, except you're not going further into debt!"

"When the real work starts, it'll feel more like slave labor and less like a learning experience."

"Ah, quit bitching! You're making money, you're not working in a grocery store, and you're entry level with fifteen days of vacation time."

I sigh. "You're right... I shouldn't complain."

"No. You shouldn't. But what you *should* do is start putting some money aside so you can break up the monotony by using some of that time off to fly out to Vegas and see my next show in March! You can bring the boys and make it a guy's trip! Hell, maybe I can get Riley to come out so we can have a little reunion! With my club and casino connections, you know it'll be a crazy good time!"

"That does sound pretty epic. And you will be twenty-one by then."

"Mm-hm... Speaking of which, I better find a gift from you in my mailbox before November thirtieth rolls around, or else."

"It should be there by Wednesday."

"Wait, you actually got me something?"

"It's nothing special, so don't get too excited." It's a box full of dance movies.

"Eek!" she squeals. There's clapping in the background. "Your birthday is in less than a month... Should I get you a plane ticket to Vegas for your gift? It'll come with as many free tickets to the show as you want. And I can probably get you a pretty good hotel discount too, if that'll turn a maybe into a yes."

It's probably best for our friendship if we keep at least 2,400 miles apart at all times. "Let's play it by ear. Jessica is talking about taking all of these trips next year, so I'll have to save some PTO."

"Ugh… then make it a weekend trip. You don't need PTO for that."

"You know me, if I'm traveling that far, I'd prefer to be there for more than two nights."

"Well, cancel one of your lame couples' trips so you can spend, like, four nights somewhere memorable."

"How about you call up Jessica and work that our with her for me?"

"Fine. What's her number?"

I snicker. "Never mind."

"I can just message her on Instagram, you know."

"If I didn't know any better, Izzy, I'd think you were trying to get me in trouble."

"If that's what it takes to get one of the most important people in my life to finally come and watch me perform," she says with attitude.

"It'll happen eventually, so there's no need to stir up trouble."

"Promise?"

"I promise." *That was a lie, and I'm sorry,* I think, shaking my head as I pull into the Wine & Spirits parking lot. *Until I purge whatever lingering feelings I may or may not still have, I can't be around you again.*

Nine Months Later

22
Isabella

Friday

THERE'S AN AUDIENCE OF nearly 2,000 people here in Philadelphia's Merriam Theater waiting for our show to begin. Four-thousand eyes are here to watch us dance but when the blue and white lights brighten and the music begins, it feels like there's only one set of eyes on me.

After a year of dancing in music videos, doing shows in Vegas and LA, and being on tour for the last three weeks with the Beat Slave cast, some nervousness still comes over me when it's time to go execute a routine live. But briefly locking eyes with *him* in the front row, seeing him looking all smiley and proud, makes my heart knock so hard and fast against my chest that it feels like my torso is caging a startled hummingbird. Realizing the seat beside him is empty makes the corners of my mouth turn up even though *serious* is what I'm supposed to be conveying.

A reassuring smile and a subtle nod from him brings me ease right before I twirl toward center stage past one of my crew-mates. Beat Slave's *Audiophoria* show begins with an upbeat number to San Holo's "The Future." Then we dance to Sorcha Richardson's "Walking Life" and we end with Claire Laffut's "Vérité." Each piece has been beautifully choreographed by none other than Trevor Wahl, my favorite choreographer, who won *So You Think You Can Dance* years ago and who pretty much inspired me to want to make dance into a career with his success. When word came in that he was casting RTA dancers for this show, I begged Allyson and Cynthia Essex to throw my name out there. I cried when I got the yes. And I got the yes based on talent and merit instead of having to sleep with or blow anyone. Because I don't do that anymore. Because I know my worth now.

The audience erupts into applause when the music ends, and we prance to line up at the front of the stage to hold hands and take our bows. I'm cheesing at the sight of him, making the phone gesture with my hand and pointing at it. He stops clapping, pulls out his phone, and nods. Now our cast turns and hurries backstage.

Trevor Wahl high-fives each of us as we run past him. "Amazing work, everyone! Absolutely beautiful per usual!" he says in that effeminate way of his.

I race to my locker, grab my phone, and text him directions where to go. Then I hurry my ass out to him.

The audience is filing out through the foyer, but my special guest is off to the side, thumbing away at his cell.

"Get your head out of your phone!" I shout to him.

"There she is!" he says, beaming.

I'm basically skipping toward him now, smiling just as hard, giggling like a mischievous schoolgirl. As soon as I'm in range, I leap at him. And he catches me, embracing my sweaty, scantily-clad body. I squeeze him tightly, laughing as he twirls me around. "Holy shit, Dion! Fuck! I'm so glad you came!"

He sets me down. "Come on, you know I couldn't miss your first tour! Especially when it's only an hour and thirty minutes from my job! It was great, by the way! And you were fucking amazing, of course."

With a curtsey, I say, "Why, thank you!" in a stupid accent that I immediately regret. I find myself unable to stop smiling or looking over every inch of his face. It happens long enough for him to be perplexed by my gawking. Eventually, I get myself to grab him by the wrist and drag him along. "Let me show you where you can wait while I freshen up."

"Is it just me, or are you catching a case of déjà vu too?"

"Oh, it's not just you, hon!"

I shower as fast as I can, making sure to hit all the parts that count. Then I apply some lipstick and slap on the bare minimum of makeup before grabbing my shit and hurrying out to him.

"Sorry for the wait!" I shout as I'm barreling through the door.

"Hey, no worries!" he says, rising from the armchair across from the wall of fame.

"You didn't eat before the show, did you? Because I haven't eaten since, like, two."

He nods. "Same here. It was about two o'clock when I stopped at Chick-fil-A so I need all of the food right now!"

"Perfect! Because I got a restaurant recommendation from the stage guy that's walking distance from here and the hotel."

"You sure you're up for a walk after killing on stage for as long as you did?"

I shrug. "Not sure. Between the lack of calories and the wobbling legs, you might have to carry me," I say, wiggling my eyebrows up and down.

He side-eyes me. "If that's what it takes for us to make it to the restaurant," he says dryly.

"So, what was your favorite part of the show?"

"All of it, really!"

"Specifics, please."

He rattles off his favorite parts as we step out into the humid August night air, raving in detail about the highlights with critic-level detail, as though he's been studying dance. He glances at me while he talks but keeps his head on swivel, being situationally aware as ever.

I don't give a shit about what's around us. I don't care to see Philly at night. My eyes, they're glued to him.

Dion grabs my arm and tugs me back right as a runner races past us and across the crosswalk, trying to catch the light. "You're gawking at me like you haven't seen me in forever," he says, shaking his head.

"Uh, we haven't seen each other in over year."

He snickers, squinting his eyes. "We had a video call on WhatsApp last week to talk about this weekend. And the week before that after your first Beat Slave show in LA." Alright, he's got a point. Technically, I've *seen* him once or twice a month for the last six months or so. On top of pretty much texting on and off every week since we agreed to be friends a year ago, and calling each other a few times a month to catch each other up on life, I also make him video chat with me when he gets home from work once in a while. When he's home alone. That means I have until 2 P.M. Pacific time to get my Dion time in before *Jessica* gets back from work. Considering I'm never doing much after my kickboxing class gets out at 11 A.M., I use the opportunity to bug him. And he rarely misses a call. Because we've become best friends.

But he's more than just my BFF. Dion is my support system, my rock, my therapist, my advice guy. I do my best to be all of those things for him too.

"For someone who appreciates face-to-face interaction over video chats, you should understand my excitement over our reunion." I say, nudging his arm.

"I guess you're right," he says, eyes still front.

I look him over. He seems a bit guarded. Tense. Not the way he used to be around me. Not as relaxed as he comes off during our video chats. "I was a little, uh… surprised to see that you didn't use that second ticket I gave you to bring the girlfriend," I blurt out. "Things okay with you two?"

He finally turns to me. "Oh, yeah. We're good." His eyes search mine. "She's back in Lancaster doing girls' night with her old roommate and our friend Karla."

"Oh… I suppose the question is, does she or does she not know that you're here to see me?"

"She knows."

"Oh… Does she think you're here with your boys or something?"

"Yeah. Because I did come here to visit some college friends too."

"Mm-hm."

"I did! I told you I'm staying at my buddy Chris's apartment. Peep my Snapchat and you'll see that I was drinking with him and a few guys from our old party crew before the show."

"Smart move leaving a data trail for the girlfriend, Mr. CIA countersurveillance man." I smirk.

He scowls. "That's not why I did it."

"Mm-hm," I hum, staring at the light, waiting in silence for it to change. When the light goes green, I clear my throat. "Does she really know we talk as often as we do?"

"Well, maybe she doesn't know about the frequency of our chats or that we video chat… but I have told her about my friend out west who's a professional dancer. And I tell her that I keep in touch with you."

"Does she know that we…" I reflexively bite my lip at the memory of him taking me to ecstasy four days in a row.

"Banged each other's brains out for a week? Hell no."

"Ooh. So there *are* secrets."

"It's not a *secret* per se. We just don't talk about past sexual experiences. She's only had one boyfriend before me and no hookups before me or him. She's… conservative like that."

"As opposed to me and my body count, *right*?" I say with attitude.

"You know that's not what I meant, Izzy."

"Just teasing ya." I look at my phone, then grab his shirt before he's about to step off of the curb, tugging him to the right instead. "This way," I say, zooming in on the map. "Be honest, is Jessica boring? She sounds like she's pretty boring."

"Don't do that. Please."

"What? Share my opinion?"

"No, take shots at her. That's what my best friend Mikayla from high school did the week after I started dating my girlfriend. I found out two years later that she liked me and she was jealous the last half of senior year." He side-eye's me.

"Chill, I'm not jealous."

"Don't act like it then."

"I'm not! All I'm saying is that she doesn't sound like someone who excites you in the way that I know you want to be excited."

"If you say so."

"Psh, don't downplay how well I know you, Dion. Because I *know* you. Very well. Intimately." I bump up against him the way I used to when we'd take strolls together. He nudges me in return, scoffing. "And I know *exactly* the kind of things you like. I know what drives you wild. And I'm pretty sure I know what your dream girl looks like, acts like." The smirk that stretches across my face feels so devilish.

His eyes flick back and forth between mine, his expression neutral, his mind surely scrambling to analyze my words and intentions. "I'm not sure if I should say raunchy sauce right now or not."

"Hmph." I look down at my phone, then look up at the sign ahead. "Oh, would you look at that. We're here!"

Dinner has a weird vibe at first, probably because of what I said outside earlier. Dion seems unable to keep eye contact with me and he doesn't seem as engaging as he was during that week together a year ago or even when we talk during our friendly catch-up sessions. I want to chalk it up to the fact that he worked from six until two today and is probably tired. But my gut tells me that isn't the case.

Is he just nervous or straight-up guarded?

He's here with *me*, the girl he was crazy about just over a year ago. Maybe he still is. If he is, he's been hiding it very well, but there are cracks in in his guard, and that way he used to look at me slips through every now and then. Given our past, being here with me while his girlfriend who he's been living with for six months is back at home probably has him beating himself up. He is noble like that, after all, so I can't blame him for being weird.

After guzzling his first beer and half of the second, Dion becomes less tense and then he's back to joking and talking to me the way he used to. He's looking at me the way he used to. And that adoring gaze with a hint of longing makes my whole body tingle.

This feeling… This is what's been missing in my life.

When he left LA, I felt as broken as he probably did. Breaking him made me realize how broken I was. I didn't date or hook up for months after that day, because I just didn't have it in me. No Chase. No DJ TyDie. Nobody. Then, in the weeks after Dion and I rekindled our friendship, seeing all of his pics with Jessica started stirring something up in me. Seeing them happy prodded me to hop on Bumble. I went on date after date, trying to find someone to temporarily fill this void that I'd suddenly became aware of. I had a bit of a promiscuous month but, even after being more selective than I've ever been and hooking up with the best I could find in LA, I still felt empty. Disappointed. Dissatisfied.

Random hookups just didn't do it for me anymore like they used to. Sex was like a drug for me—a temporary high I could use to feel good for a while, something that'd make me forget about my troubles. After Dion, it became a reminder of what I missed. It was a reminder of letting that photographer try and bang the feelings out of me. Sex reminded me of all the times I'd hooked up for all of the wrong reasons. What should have been pleasurable became punishment, and not in the kinky way.

Following that month, I kind of went abstinent and just stuck to strictly dating. Connection was what I thought I was missing. There were a few gentlemen. A couple of nerds. Some fairly wealthy entrepreneurs. A male model. A famous guy. Now that I was being super selective, barely half of them made it to date two. Because none of them made me feel the way that I did that week Dion came into my life. None of them ever looked at me the way *he* did. And a longing gaze that reminds me that I'm worth more than I realized, that look of adoration mixed with desire that lets me know a man's playing for *keeps* are absolutes I require before I can give myself over to someone now.

The constant disappointment got annoying, so somewhere in the middle of October, I took a break from dating altogether. For a long while. Months. That was my longest stretch without guys since the span between birth and freshman year of high school. And it was nice. I learned to please myself. I learned to be okay with being alone. Losing myself in dance helped. So did the few spiritual workshops. I even saw the intimacy coach that Riley recommended to me. Through giving up on guys and working on me, I discovered a newfound sense of self-respect. Giving up being a camgirl really helped with that.

It wasn't until, like, two months ago that I finally jumped back into the dating pool. Not on an app though. I met a fairly decent guy during a video shoot—a dancer named Jude. We went on quite a few dates, when my schedule allowed, and I enjoyed his spending time with him. But we didn't connect the way I wanted us to. Not at first. Not in the weeks that followed either. And those intimacy classes didn't do squat to make me enjoy the two times we screwed. Big dick, stamina, and good technique from sexy-ass Adonis still panned out to be a *meh* rating for me.

The connection right here and right now, though? It's electric.

Today wasn't just supposed to be a much-needed reunion between friends, it was also supposed to be about me discovering that Dion wasn't the solution to the void I needed filled. Too bad it's feeling like the opposite might be true.

I'm buzzing, and it's not from the half-glass of wine, either. Being together again has me all giddy and smiley and antsy, which makes no sense because we're not even remotely flirting. For the first time in seventeen months, I feel... whole.

This is exactly what I both wanted and didn't want to happen.

Dion and I talk all too often, for hours at a time, yet we still somehow manage to chat from the time we're seated until the time our dessert arrives. What's next for me dance-wise, things that happened with us this week, him bitching about work, me rambling on about finding a new place are topics we've covered so far. Things with Jess are what we're on now.

"So," I say, raking flavorgasm-worthy chocolate cake off of my fork with my teeth. "When are you going to propose to Jessica?" I smirk as I chew.

He closes the bill book that he just signed and holds my gaze as he returns his double cash-back card to his wallet. "Not quite sure we're there yet."

"Having doubts now that you've been living with her for half a year?"

"Not really. I'm just not in a rush. She hasn't brought it up yet so..."

"I'm sure she's thought about it, though."

"Probably. There was a while there where I thought I was going to have to marry her before we finally—"

I raise my palm to him. "You can stop there. I can fill in the blanks, m'kay?"

He smirks. "Quite the reaction there, Izzy."

"Hey, you don't get to tell me about your sex life if I can't tell you about mine." We talk about anything and everything, including people I'm dating and milestones he's hitting with Jessica. The minute after she brought up moving in together, he texted me. Anything super intimate beyond kissing is off the table. The only thing that ever made me cringe is when he told me when they exchanged those *three* relationship-changing words to each other back in September…

"Fair enough… But I wasn't going to give any detail," he says.

"Either way, I'd rather not even skirt the line."

He smiles knowingly, eyes scanning me intensely. "What's up with you and that dancer guy?"

"Jude?"

"Is there another one?"

I grimace. "There's, like, three."

He pulls his chin back to his neck and blinks rapidly while shaking his head like I'm spritzing him with water.

I giggle. "Kidding! I pretty much broke things off with him before I left for this tour." And after I did, I seriously debated if I might be a lesbian… Tonight's reminding me that I'm not though, because I'm having all kinds of thoughts about the guy in front of me.

The corners of his mouth twitch. "What? That was three weeks ago. How are you just now telling me?"

My brows raise as a grin stretches across my face. "Don't look so relieved, buddy."

"I'm not relieved. I just had a feeling it wouldn't last more than a month. I'm just happy my calculations were correct."

No, you're fucking relieved, and I get that you can't admit that.

After I told him about dating Jude, he bailed on several of our scheduled calls for two weeks and sparsely replied to the memes I sent him over text and Instagram. That was him being salty that someone made it past date two. "Oh? And why did you think it wouldn't last past a month?"

"You never seemed excited when you talked about him. Your date recaps always... lacked enthusiasm."

"Yeah... Well, Jude didn't exactly light up my life. And feeling alone when I was with the person I was dating didn't sit right with me." *There's really only one person who never made me feel alone.* "I guess my standards ain't what they used to be, so it's hard to get excited about something that's disappointing."

"That's for damn sure."

Are you hinting that Jessica is disappointing you? "Speaking of disappointing things. I've got to say, it's funny how you always seem a bit bummed whenever I tell you I'm dating someone and so excited when I tell you it doesn't work out."

"That's not true."

"Your micro-expressions when I told you me and Jude were done? It looked like someone was tickling your nuts under the table and you didn't want anyone to know."

He clenches his jaw and tries not to laugh. "Raunchy sauce."

I snicker. "And, news flash, anytime I tell you over the phone that I'm going out with someone new, your voice drops an octave and your tone gets all flat for the rest of the call. Did you forget I notice those little things too? You taught me a thing or two, you know."

He looks away for moment. "Alright, maybe hearing about you wanting to date months after telling me you weren't ready triggers a sore spot for me."

I laugh for some reason. "Why do you even care? You're happily committed." My voice comes out more bitter than intended.

"Yeah, but some memories… take a while to heal."

A pang of guilt strikes. "Okay, well, that's understandable." I gulp down the last of my second glass of wine, then set it aside. *Change the subject before this night takes a bad turn.* "While we're on the topic of things we forgot to tell each other, you said you were supposed to be hearing back this week from your friend in Boston about getting you an interview at her lab, right? Did you?"

"Oh! That's what I wanted to tell you! I got an email from Adaptic Pharmaceuticals at lunch today!"

"And?" I almost shout, perking up.

"And I have a Skype interview next week!"

"So, you don't have to fly out to Boston for an interview?"

He shrugs. "If I crush this first round, they'll probably ask me to fly up to do the official one."

"Ah! So exciting! I hope you get it, hon! I'm tired of you sounding so drained and miserable after work all the time." *God, I sound like his wife…* That thought sends a chill down my spine. A pleasant one, at that.

He smiles. "Psh, I'm tired of *being* drained and miserable."

"I know you are." My stare lingers. "You need to be somewhere where they can utilize that big brain of yours and where they'll pay you what you're worth."

"Would you mind calling up some companies and telling them that for me, please?"

I giggle. "For you? Of course." I check my phone. "Shit, it's almost eleven."

"Holy hell… Already?"

"Yeah. No wonder I'm so tired."

He slides the plate of cake that was sitting between us toward me. "Shove that in your mouth and let's roll."

I snort-snicker. "Raunchy! Sauce!"

He cracks up. "Shit, I didn't even—"

"What, mean to tell me to shove something the color of your skin in my mouth?" My pointer finger finds my bottom row of teeth and I nibble my nail, smiling naughtily.

Dion just shakes his head as he rises along with me.

"I intend on squeezing in all the time I can with you this weekend, so walk me to my hotel room and I'll summon you an Uber as tribute."

He lowers his eyelids at me, pressing his lips into a thin line. "I'm insulted that you didn't think I was going to walk you back no matter what."

"Silly me, I forgot I was in the presence of a protective gentleman. My hero. My black knight."

"That's racist."

A cackle escapes me.

Dion walks me the four blocks to the hotel, then escorts me all of the way to my hotel room.

Once I get the door open, I prop it open with my butt, getting lost in his eyes against my wishes. "You're going to meet me here at nine thirty, right?"

"If I get up in time." He flashes a troll grin.

I scowl. "Well, get up in time. I want to explore as much as we can before warm-up time tomorrow at five."

"As you wish, Dancing Queen."

That makes me blush. "Alright, Abba." I open my arms. The second he wraps his arms around me it feels like I'm home. "Well, thanks for walking me to the door. And for dinner."

His embrace tightens. "No problem."

"And thanks for coming all the way here after work."

"Well, Saturday alone didn't seem like enough time for a proper reunion."

"Not at all." My fingers claw gently at his back. "Sorry we couldn't bar hop tonight. Jet lag. Show. Yada, yada."

"You don't have to apologize, Izzy. Getting sloppy tomorrow night will be enough."

The thought of him leaving me for the night makes me squeeze him tighter. "Good night, Dion," I whisper.

His head nestles against mine as he rocks me side to side. His chest heaves against my breasts. Suddenly, he pulls away like he just realized it's me and that our hug lasted longer than it should have. "Good night, Izzy." He gives me one last lingering look before turning and starting toward the elevator.

My jaw hangs and my lips twitch before I stop myself. It takes everything in me not call out his name, to ask him to stay the night with me. Not even to make love, just to talk until we can't anymore… and maybe hold each other. Innocently, of course.

I'm not sure that the words still won't slip out until he waves goodbye before disappearing into the elevator.

23
Isabella

Saturday

A BANGING BREAKFAST OVER coffee, a morning stroll through a new city, lunch with mimosas at a fancy establishment, the museum of art, and more exploring that ends with me getting ready to dance on stage—it's like that day in San Francisco all over again. Minus all of the kissing and hand holding. And the lovemaking that bracketed the day. As I'm stretching and warming up for tonight's final show of the tour, all of that missing affection and copulation is what I'm thinking about…

Having Dion in the front row for the second consecutive night show makes me feel like I'm supported in a way that I've been craving since my career with RTA began. It makes me realize how alone I've been feeling. His presence lights me up and calms me at the same time, just like back then. And it's not just while I'm up on stage, it was last night and all day today. Every second of our time together was like a dessert I couldn't get enough of—that I savored as much as I could because I didn't want it to end.

I never understood why spending time with me during his spring break meant more to him than hooking up, but after being together again, I get it now.

For the first time in a while, my heart's not in my performance. It's because my head is elsewhere. It's in the future, in the minutes after the performance. That's what I'm dancing toward. And it makes this performance feel like the runtime of *Titanic*.

When it finally ends, we walk on back to my hotel room. I shower fast to make time for prettying myself up. I slip into the sexiest, shortest-without-being-skanky, form-fitting dress in my wardrobe—the dress I bought specifically for a night on the town with him. My makeup, I keep modest since that's what he likes. A little foundation, winged eyeliner, and lipstick the color of wine to match my dress.

I haven't gotten glammed up like this in a while. Not for a guy anyway. If I do, it's usually for a photoshoot or an event. But this is for *him*. He's been a good boy since we reunited, though a bit more friendly today. He's playing it cool, but I want him to want me. I want to test the waters tonight to see if he still does. That's it.

As I'm stepping out of the bathroom, Dion is setting out the sandwiches we picked up on the way back from the museum.

"How do I look?" I say in the sexy voice I used to use during my camgirl days.

His eyes widen and his jaw hangs as I do a twirl, striking model poses every so often. "Hot damn… Are you ovulating and in search of a mate tonight?"

"That depends…" I look from his eyes to his crotch, then I look back up and give him a wink.

"Raunchy sauce."

"Do you likey or not?" I turn my ass to him again, looking back at him to gauge his reaction.

"Yes. It's a hot-ass dress and you look spec-fucking-tacular in it. Your makeup…" He gets lost in my eyes. "On point, per usual."

"Aw, thank you!"

"Mm-hm. Good color choice for the dress too. Burgundy. Your favorite."

"Aw, you remembered my favorite color."

"Nope. I just googled it."

I clear my throat, then I sniffle. "Ugh, my sarcasm allergies are acting up."

He just smiles.

I grab the whisky from the kitchenette and two glasses. "Are you ready to have some fun tonight? Because I am."

"Indeed," he says, grabbing two Stella Artois from the minifridge—the Stellas I bought to remind him of the night we met. "Let's try not to get too obliterated, though. I don't want my drive back or your early-ass flight to be too miserable."

"Psh, don't worry about tomorrow, hon." I pour a double in his glass. "Tonight, we're living in the *now*." My glass gets the same treatment. "That means we're getting wild A-F, baby!"

He snickers. "Not too wild, now," he says, picking up his glass, his brow cocked.

I clink my glass against his. "Yeah, let's just play it by ear, mm'kay? You don't get to be lame tonight."

"Cheers to a dope night then."

"Yass! Cheers to that!" I say with a grin.

We throw our shots back, slam our glasses on the tiny table then chase with Stella.

"Ahh," he says after swallowing the cold pilsner like it hit the spot. "So, what do you want to get into tonight?"

"Uh, I say we hit up the bars we picked out at lunch. Then, we go dancing!" I cheer.

He looks apprehensive. "Aren't you tired of dancing?"

"Nope." I pour us another round of shots. "The booze will numb me against any fatigue that may arise."

"I don't know… Going dancing might not be the best idea."

"Oh, don't be like that!" I say, sliding his glass closer to him. "It's just dancing, dude! Promise me one dance. Just one. We'll keep it tame."

His eyes search mine, then he sighs. "Fine. *One* dance."

"Yay!" I say, stamping my heels on the floor, clopping away like I'm trying to get a drumroll going.

We cheers again, then throw another double shot back.

24
Isabella

Saturday

THREE BARS. THAT'S HOW many high-end watering holes we hit up for drinks and rounds of fancy, overpriced appetizers before heading to the club. Thankfully, we don't have to wait in line because the owner of this place is a friend of Trevor Wahl and our producer got the whole cast on the list for the weekend. I'm glad I don't see any of them here. Even in the three crowded bars we hit earlier and in streets crawling with people, it feels like we're the last two people on Earth, and I want to keep that going without distractions.

The more Dion drinks, the more his eyes seem hypnotized by mine, the more they wander to my lips. I catch him sneaking peeks at my body and I think he's starting to miss all of this.

Seduction complete, I think, sucking my Long Island iced tea through the straw while I look up at the smiley guy across the high-top table from me.

The more I drink, the more I flirt, but I'm doing my best to keep it low on the raunch-scale. I take every chance I get to touch him and he doesn't seem the least bit bothered by it.

The higher our BACs go, the hornier I get, and the more I sense tension building between us. I feel like a cat in heat and all I want right now is him against me, him inside me. That's all I'm thinking about as I stare at him while I sip my drink.

Dion smiles knowingly. "What's on your mind, Izzy?" he says just loud enough for me to hear over the music.

"I have a confession."

"Uh oh… What is it?"

"I'm really fucking happy you didn't bring Jessica."

He grins. "I thought you would be."

"Admit it, you're glad she didn't want to come!"

His lips curl into his mouth and he averts his gaze.

"Dion… Thinking it is just as bad as saying it so just fess up. It ain't like I'm going to rat you out."

"I don't know… You might have a motive." He smirks.

I raise my brows. "Oh? And what motive could I possibly have?"

"You tell me."

I stare at him while I sip. "Answer my question, please."

"I'm glad she didn't come either."

I cheese hard. "Ha! I knew it!"

"It wouldn't have been the same with her here. Or anyone else for that matter."

I plant my elbows on the table, pushing my tits together as I rest my chin in my palms. "You wanted me all to yourself, huh?" I say through puckered lips in a sweet, child-like voice.

He crosses his arms on the table as he leans forward, smirking. "Yes. Because I missed you and I wanted a proper reunion. Just me and you, like it used to be." Something like guilt flashes on his face.

"I missed you too, hon. *Badly*." My foot finds the inside of his calf, and I make a slow pass up his leg.

He doesn't budge. He does, however, suppress a smile. "Had you convinced me to move to LA seventeen months ago, you would only have to miss me when you left for tours, Vegas shows, and music video shoots…"

The wave of regret that follows makes my stomach flippy. "Here's a thought… How about you move to LA instead of Boston." My voice comes out sultry. My foot caresses his leg again, prompting him to inhale deeply. "Then we wouldn't have to miss each other anymore." Now I get all pouty and bat my lashes.

Dion instantly goes from looking drunk to appearing sober. "What are you asking me right now, Isabella?"

I giggle, looking down, brushing my hair back, my hand rubbing my neck afterward. "I don't know… Maybe I'm getting tired of the time zone difference between us."

"I'm not sure Jessica would want to be that far from her family. Convincing her to move to Boston is already a challenge."

"Well, if you still want to move west and she doesn't, long-distance is an option."

He scowls. "As I recall, you once said, '*Screw long distance. That shit never works.*'"

"Her problem, not mine."

"*Oh,*" he laughs out, "so it's just her problem and not *mine?*"

I shrug. "You tell me… You're two hours away from home looking at me like it's spring break all over again."

A short huff of a laugh escapes him.

"If you were as madly in love and as happy in your relationship with her as you claim to be, you wouldn't be here getting shitfaced with *me* of all people. I know that because I *know* you. I know the kind of guy you are." I point back and forth between him and me. "This wouldn't be happening without there being a good reason for it." *And that reason is you still want me and you're here to find out if I still want you. Say it!*

"And what exactly is happening here?"

"Oh, you know, two besties hanging out, realizing they are both feeling happier and more alive this weekend than they have in a while."

"Is that right?"

"Mm-hm. I know it just like you do… And perhaps these friends are both imagining what'd it be like if there wasn't a country between them."

He leans a little bit closer. "Isabella, is there something you're trying to tell me?"

"Yes." I run my foot slowly up his leg, watching his face react to the temptation he's enjoying too much to ward off. "I want me and you to finish these shots, then I want you to dance with me like you promised." My foot stops halfway up his thigh and then I retract it, reaching for my shot glass.

Holding my gaze, he taps his shot against mine, then we throw them back, neither of us breaking eye contact as we do. Judging by the look in his eyes, he's in bad-decision territory right along with me.

I rise from my seat first and grab his hand. He resists at first, but he caves and rises, following me obediently to the dance floor.

Mine. You're mine tonight.

We start a few feet apart like it's a middle school dance. I belly dance and work my hips, making sure to spin and showcase that ass I'm confident he's thinking about palming the way he used to. Slowly, I close the gap and take his hands, placing them on my hips. My arms go around his neck. With every change in hook and chorus, I inch my way closer to him. By the end of the song, I do a 180 and back my ass into his crotch. As I do, his hands return to my hips like obedient dogs called back home.

That's right… show me that you want me, too.

I throw it back into him. Then I grind hard against him. His hands start to wander down my legs before shooting back to my hips like a chaperone just caught him. Feeling Dion Johnson's *johnson* plumping up against me is an immediate turn on. And what a surprise it is that he doesn't back off.

You want me to know that you still want me, huh?

Arms in the air, I work my way into a squat and his hands caress me up my sides to my arms until his hands find and hold mine. Then I rise, turning to him and wrapping my arms around him, and pull him in close, until my breasts are mashed against him and his dick is against my crotch, until our bodies are writhing against each other like we're doing a carnal mating dance. His fingers play against my back as I bring my face closer and closer to his. I'm smiling while giving my lip a bite, giving him fuck-me eyes while he's entranced by me.

I bring my lips as close to his as I can without brushing them and we dance like that for a good bit, breathing into each other's mouths, teasing each other with temptation to the point of maddening desire.

Dion's rock hard. I'm drenched.

Just like the first time we danced together, the only thing left to do now is leave.

I pull my mouth away from the danger zone and lean toward his ear. "My feet hurt!" I shout over the music.

His hand finds the small of my back. "I'll get us an Uber!" He guides me toward the exit.

The Uber is close, so by the time we get out of the bathrooms, our ride is outside waiting for us. I sit right up against him, laying on shoulder, talking the whole six-minute ride back. Once at the hotel, Dion gives me a piggyback ride from the car to the elevator. When it opens, I loop my arm under his and make him escort me to the door like an usher at a wedding.

"You thirsty?" I say, slapping the keycard against the scanner. He nods. "Dehydrated."

I nod toward the door I just opened. "Come on in then."

He follows me inside.

We sit up in bed, my leg and arm pressed against his, talking about random shit while we guzzle water. I keep up the flirting and touching. Sexual tension keeps building. When my hand finds his thigh after he makes me laugh, he inhales deeply.

"It's getting late," he sighs out.

"You can stay with me. There's enough pillows to build a barrier if that's what you want."

"It's probably best I go."

I nibble at my lip, giving him the best longing look that I can muster as we stare at each other in silence. "Who knows when we'll see each other next, though… Stay. Let's talk until sunrise."

He shakes his head. "I have to go, Izzy." He swings his legs over the bed and grabs his phone from the nightstand.

"Fine, you buzzkill," I say, getting out of bed.

We walk to the door in silence and, when we get there, I sigh.

He turns to me and blows air through his lips. "This was… fun. Much needed."

I grab fistfuls of his shirt. "Let's do it again soon?"

He nods. "We'll work something out."

I tug him toward me, wrap my arms around him, and hold him like we both might die if I ease up. He embraces me just as firmly, rubbing my back. Our embrace lasts even longer than last night's. The whole time, his heart is thumping away just like mine is. It almost feels like our palpitations are in sync.

I pull away just a bit, hands clutching the back of his shirt, eyes meeting his gaze. I smile. So does he. That's when I lean in and plant my lips against his. At first, he doesn't kiss me back. After the second peck, he does and a tingling sensation rushes across my scalp, continues down my spine, and arcs across my limbs. My heart skips a beat.

Yes. Yes. Yes, I think with each peck.

Our tongues greet each other eagerly at the same time. The escalation makes me slam his back against the door. His hands caress my back, slowly inching to my ass. My hand finds his balls, then I work my way up from the base of his erection to the tip.

Dion pries me away, leaning his head back against the door to tilt his lips up to the ceiling. "Izzy… I can't do this."

"You want to."

"I'm drunk."

"You've wanted to since you saw me last night. I know it."

"God damnit, Izzy… I'm in a relationship."

"You look at me the way you used to. You held me like you did back then. You kissed me back. If you were happy with her, you wouldn't have caved. If you wanted to go the distance with her, you wouldn't be here."

"I didn't come here for this. I came here for *you*. Dirty dancing and making out were drunk moments of weakness—"

"Oh, don't pull that bullshit! You are the most in-control drunk I've ever met. Weirdly so. I know you wouldn't do anything that you didn't absolutely want to."

"Isabella, what is it you want from me?"

That gives me pause. "One night where we get lost in each other so we can satisfy this fucking yearning I know we've both had since we started talking again. Me and you reliving all of our greatest hits in one night. I need that because no one has ever made me feel drunk with bliss the way you do… No one."

"Well, sorry, but that's not something I want. I'm in a relationship. A serious one."

"Really? Pretty sure you said way back when that you'd break up with someone for me if I wanted to try. How is one night of passion somehow a dealbreaker then?"

He looks appalled. "Is that a serious question?"

"Yes! Because if you're willing to give up an engagement for me, I thought that you meant you'd cross any line for me."

"Yeah, well, that's not what I meant… Getting *lost* in you for *one* night is not what I want, Isabella. It's not enough for me. It wasn't then and it's not now… What I meant was that I was willing to sacrifice something good and stable for a chance of trying to build something amazing *with* you. Not one night of amazing. Amazing that could go on for months. Maybe years. Forever if I was lucky."

My knees go weak and it feels like the wind was knocked out of me like that time I took a bike handle to the belly. "Oh… wow… So, I guess you *did* lie to me about being over me."

"Confessing that there hasn't been one day since we met that I didn't think about you didn't seem like a good idea after what happened the last time I told you how I felt."

"I mean, I don't blame you… I did do a number on you, after all."

"You really did."

I sigh. "If it makes you feel any better… I haven't exactly stopped thinking about you either, hon. You fucking haunt my thoughts. All the time. Hell, sex hasn't even been the same since you." I laugh, shaking my head at myself for letting that slip. "I've literally cursed your name after every failure to come the way you used to make me."

His expression is a mix between a cringe and a smile. Then he goes neutral while searching my eyes, scanning meticulously, longingly. "Isabella?" he finally says, breaking the trance he put me under.

"Yes?"

"I'm in love with you."

I sigh hard, looking away with an eyeroll. Or maybe that wasn't a sigh. Maybe he just took the breath out of my lungs again. That must be it, because I'm lightheaded and breathless.

Dion takes my hands and I immediately squeeze them like I just found him after wandering alone in the dark for days. "I have been in love with you since that dinner on the beach. Hell, maybe since I first saw you walking into that bar the night we met. But it didn't occur to me until after I caught myself looking forward to our talks a few months after reconnecting. If you feel the same way, tell me right now. If you can't, no worries. At least just tell me that you're willing to *at least* try now. We'll take it slow. Tell me that's what you want and I will call Jessica right now and break up with her on speaker phone and then I will kiss you and lick you and dick you until you are completely satisfied, until you're unable to keep going."

His words make my body shudder. If something went down right now, foreplay could definitely be skipped because I am primed and ready to receive his package.

"And then I will spend every moment after trying to make you happy until my last fucking breath," he continues.

Anxiety wreaks havoc across my body. *RUN* is the only thought in my head, but my legs feel like overcooked pasta, which makes that feat impossible. I probably wouldn't get far because it feels like I'm on the verge of hyperventilating. My head's involuntarily shaking from side to side, the way it did when I heard the word *terminal* to describe my dad's cancer diagnosis. "I can't. I can't tell you what you want to hear."

"Then say you're not crazy about me too. Tell me that you don't want to be with me."

"I can't…"

"Then give me a reason! Please. That's all I'm asking for."

"I can't, because I'm still fucking terrified that I'll somehow ruin things and lose you forever."

"You won't. And even if you did *ruin things*, I'd stick it out and we can work through whatever happens. Because you're worth it. You're worth fighting for."

"You can't promise that. You can't promise that, somewhere down the line, we won't end up breaking up and never speaking to each other again."

"If we want to be together bad enough, we'll make it work."

"That's the same kind of *hopeium* thinking you lectured me on, hon."

"Nah, this isn't hope. I'm sure about this. And I've never been more sure about anything in my life."

"Well, I'm not," I laugh out. "I need you in my life and I'm not willing to do anything to risk losing you."

"What if you were going to lose me anyway? What if I told you that being *friends* and talking almost every week and always texting and hearing about you going on dates is torture and I can't take it anymore?"

"Then we'll talk less. I won't talk about my relationships and hookups. You don't talk about yours."

"I love having you as a friend, I love having you in my life, but I can't *just* be your friend when I feel the way I feel about you. I can't keep *just* being friends and pretending that's enough while I'm in a relationship with someone else. It's… maddening."

"So, what are you saying?" The panic in my voice is overt as hell.

"I don't think I can do this anymore. It's either we end up together or we cut ties completely until I'm over you." He shakes his head. A sob of a laugh escapes him. "No… who am I kidding? I'll never be over you. Maybe it's best we just cut ties for good."

"You can't be serious."

"Oh, I'm very serious. As long as I have you in my life, Izzy, I'm going to be miserable over the fact that I'm not with you. I'm always going to be holding out for you. I dread the day you end up with someone else. Even if I marry Jess and start a family with her, I'm going to be miserable every single time your name pops up on my phone with a text or Snapchat or Instagram message, because there will always be some ember of hope in me that you'll come around. That's not fair to me. Or Jess. Or you, if you feel the way I do."

"I can't lose you."

"Then don't lose me! Tell me you want to be with me and I'm all yours!"

"I don't know that I'm ready to take that risk yet."

"If you're not willing to risk our friendship, then you clearly don't feel the same way I do. Because I would take any risk if it meant that there was even the smallest chance we could be together."

"Well, guess what? I'm not you."

"Guess you're not." He sighs, rubbing his hand down his face. Then he takes a deep breath. "I can't debate this anymore. I can't."

"Then let's stop. Let's forget about that kiss and my proposition and this conversation and let's just talk until we fall asleep like I wanted. Okay? Let's not end the night like this."

"I think it's better if I go. And, so you know, I'm sticking to my guns. The goodbye that follows this will be our last goodbye."

My lips curl into my mouth and my eyes burn like that time I got teargassed at a protest. "Call it false hope or hopeium or whatever if you want, but there's no way this is it for us."

"It has to be."

"It can't be."

"There's only one way it won't be," he says.

"Because you're being stubborn! Maybe I just need a bit more time before I'm ready for what you want!"

He just shakes his head. "Maybe I can't wait anymore."

My eyes are welling up with tears now. "That's not fair."

"This situation isn't fair."

I huff. "After tonight, how about we take a break from each other? A few months. Then we can reconnect and go back to being besties! Okay?"

He grabs me gently by the elbow and pulls me in. His arms wrap around me and he holds me tightly. "Goodbye, Izzy."

I squeeze him as hard as I can, digging my fingers into his back so hard it hurts. "I'm not saying goodbye to you! I won't." I shake my head against his chest. "I will spam you with texts like a crazy ex until you come to your senses and thing go back to normal."

His lips press onto the top of my head and then he pulls away. But I don't let him go.

"If I text you, you better respond. I can't take you ghosting me. I can't!"

He blows out hard. "I'll do my best to be cordial. *When* I'm ready."

I pull away and look up at him, batting my lashes to clear away the tears.

His thumb finds my cheek and then he wipes away my tear. With a pitiful smile, he opens the door and heads for the elevator. And from the time he presses the button until it arrives, he doesn't look back at me once.

Nine Months Later

25
Isabella

Saturday

ALL OF THE BIGGEST influencers and celebrities in Maisie Marie's circle have been invited to this Hollywood Hills mansion for her book launch party, including Chase, who gives me a friendly nod when he sees Riley and me walking toward the backyard bar. Maisie and I being friends who sometimes hang out probably would have been enough to get me an invite, but I'm pretty sure it's my 600k Instagram followers, 300k Facebook fan-page following, 150k YouTube channel, and 800k TikTok audience that landed me on this shindig's VIP list.

Three months after the award-winning Beat Slave tour and our appearance on *The Ellen DeGeneres Show*, there was a bit of a lull until my next gig. No gigs meant no money and more free time than I knew what to do with. Such is the unpredictable nature of being a dancer for hire, I suppose.

The time off was not wasted. I still attended dance classes and I even started teaching an entry-level contemporary teen dance class at RTA a few times a week. Being on an award-winning dance cast might have been the boost in credentials I needed for that, given I've only been at this just over two years.

Still, I had more free time than I could tolerate. And I needed to keep busy to fill up that emptiness I was left with after the best thing that ever happened to me removed himself from my life. So I decided to focus on my modeling career. I booked a bunch of photo shoots. I posted those, along with a bunch of ass-shaking thirst traps, bikini pics at the beach, exercise videos, and makeup tutorials on Instagram—a wide net to catch a wide audience. I kept the content flowing regularly and my following grew bit by bit. Dion still followed me on Insta, but his name was never amongst the hundreds to thousands of likes. I know because I checked…

It wasn't until I saw a random ad posted of a girl on my feed that it occurred to me to do the same. So, I read some blogs and a few books, watched a couple of YouTube videos, and then invested some of the money from my camgirl nest egg and pushed ads to my Insta. Boys between the ages of eighteen and thirty got the thirst traps, girls around the same age group got the makeup and exercise videos. It was fall-winter-ish when my page started booming. Then, one by one, brand deals for clothes, beauty products, and food slash drink products started trickling in. Around that time, I signed with a modeling agency and a few offers came through soon after.

Professional dancer? Check.

Model? Check.

Influencer who gets free shit and gets paid to post content about it? Check.

Gone are the days of me showing up to these kinds of events as a desperate groupie looking to get noticed. I've made it. On my own. And I didn't have to whore my way to get all of the things I want.

Well, maybe I didn't get *everything* I wanted…

And having achieved all of the things I've wanted my whole life by the ripe ol' age of twenty-two doesn't feel as great as I thought it would. The *fame,* the dream career—though I love the life I've built for myself, none of it fills the emptiness left in me since losing what Dion and I had.

"Who's the caramel Adonis who keeps looking over at you?" Riley, my forever plus one, asks.

He's staring at me because I've been ogling him from the time that I spotted him from the bar, and every chance I got when making mingling rounds. I glance at the other side of the pool and lock eyes with the curly-haired, mixed-race stud, smiling back the second he offers a confident smile. "Pretty sure that's Maisie Marie's publisher or whatever... Marcus something. He was in her Insta story earlier."

"Wait, *he's* the one who organized and paid to host and cater this party at a mansion?"

"Mm-hm," I hum, sipping my whisky sour. "Renting a mansion for a night isn't that impressive. It's only like, two grand on Airbnb."

"I mean, that's still a lot of money for the average American to shell out. Also, why do you know that?"

"I asked about renting mansions back when I did that music video shoot for an indie artist last summer."

"Oh... still... why aren't we on our way over to that young entrepreneur?"

"Because I ain't that thirsty, Ri. If he likes what he sees and wants to talk, he'll come over." *Because I know my worth. I don't chase anymore. I don't throw myself at every hot, wealthy, or well-connected guy I cross. I deserve to be chased. By someone worth letting into my life.*

"Izzy, I know I've said you need to start putting yourself back out there, like, a million times these last few months, but tonight I mean it. I think you *really* need to jump back in and get your feet wet with this guy who can't take his eyes off of you. And if you're not, pass him off to me."

"Well, Maisie is right by him. How about we go say hi and congratulate her first, then we'll see if he takes the opportunity to come on over." I lead us through the crowd.

Maisie is standing near a round table with stacks of her memoir *Of Laughs and Love* and a poster board of the cover behind her. From what she told me the last time we did yoga together, it contains essays chronicling her journey from making it big on YouTube to becoming a comedian and an actress and all of the relationships that happened in between.

"Maisie!" I cheer, opening my arms to the biggest hugger that I know.

"Izzy! You made it!" Maisie hollers back.

"Of course, girl! You know I couldn't miss this momentous day!" We clash with a hug. "Congratulations!"

"Thank you so, so much!"

"Congrats, Maisie!" Riley says next.

Maisie hugs her. "Thank you, Riley! And thanks for coming."

"Of course!"

Maisie looks at something behind us. "None of this would be possible without this guy right here!"

We turn around and find her publisher approaching with a warm, swoon-worthy smile, a beer in his hand. The closer he gets, the more evident it is how fit and handsome he is. His dapper fashion sense is a plus. I'm also really digging that curly, Hispanic-looking hair of his.

"This is Marcus Jones, best-selling thriller author turned indie publisher. Marcus, I'd like you to meet Isabella and Riley," Maisie says, pointing from me to my bestie.

Marcus extends a hand to Riley. "Nice to meet you, Riley."

"Hiya!" Riley almost squeals.

Marcus and I shake hands next. "And a pleasure to meet you too, Isabella," he says coolly, a knowing smile on his face. Despite his curious smirk, there's something... sad in his light brown eyes.

Maisie nudges him. "Marcus is a talented visionary, a brilliant marketer, and a goof like me. And… he's single, ladies!" she says in a silly, Oprah-like voice.

Riley and I giggle.

Marcus laughs, shaking his head. "Thank you for trying to sell me, Maisie."

"Hey, you're selling my books to maybe tens of thousands of people. The least I could do is sell *you* to my single gal pals."

Marcus's eyes shoot right over to me and the look he gives me is far from lust-filled or sleezy. It's more like awestruck attraction.

"Sooo," Riley drags, "how did you end up taking on my yoga student as your author?"

Marcus looks to her.

"Well," Maisie pipes up. "When I was talking about trying to get published on my live stream one Sunday, fate sent him to the comments at the right moment."

"She replied to me pretty much right after, too!" Marcus says. "Maisie gave me her email live and I contacted her ten minutes later."

"The power of social media," I say with a smile.

"Indeed," he says, gawking at me. "Speaking of social media… if I'm not mistaken, I think you might be someone I follow online too."

"Oh?" I say, playing aloof and confused. In reality, being recognized flatters me.

"Yeah, you're Isabella Monroe, right? Izzy-Does-It on Instagram?"

I shrug. "What if I am?"

"If you are, I've been a fan of yours since *way* before you blew up."

My heart bangs in my chest when I feel like he might be referring to my camgirl days. "From?" I blurt out.

"You were on *So You Think You Can Dance* a few years back, weren't you?"

I grin, letting out a sigh of relief. "Why, yes I was! Not that I did great enough to warrant any fans."

"I disagree… I thought you were *very* talented."

"And very hot too, I bet," Riley mutters.

Marcus looks slightly embarrassed. "Yes, that, too… But I was all about your routine. And your technique was better than probably a third of the people they let through that day. You got robbed."

I blush. "Well, thank you! Can't say I disagree." A shameless laugh escapes me.

He grins. "I suppose it doesn't matter that they didn't take you to the next round since you made it pro anyway! *The Ellen Show.* Vegas shows. A tour."

My front two teeth gently scrape against my bottom lip that just curled inside my mouth. "Sounds like you're quite the fan, Mr. Jones."

His kind eyes search my face. "Maybe. Or maybe you post so much that it's impossible not to keep up with all your life events."

I roll my eyes. "Or that."

"Oh, hey, you!" Maisie says, walking off.

"Would you look at that," Riley says, holding up her empty martini glass. "I need a refill. Excuse me for a moment, would you?" She gives me a wink as she struts off.

Marcus and I end up chatting for a while. It's his vibe and our immediate connection that keeps me around. That and the fact that he's witty, sweet, suave, intelligent, and has something caring and kind about his eyes. If I'm being honest with myself, the only reason I let him dominate my attention, the only reason I start flirting with him after a few more drinks is because he reminds me a lot of a taller, more light-skinned Dion…

Marcus is from upstate New York and he now lives in Boston, just like Dion does. Like Dion, he also graduated with a degree in biology and he worked in a lab right up until he decided to quit and chase his dreams of being an author. And now that he's achieved the success he's always wanted, he's working to help others tell their stories. Very admirable.

Once all of my mingling for the night is complete, Marcus and I reconvene by the pool, continuing to get to know each other. Around midnight, the guests start to trickle out and the crowd thins around us. Riley shoots me a text that says she ready to leave.

The one I send back reads: **Yeah, I'm gonna stick around... Text me when you're home safe!**

Riley: ***Ooooooooooh... Get it, girl!*** An eggplant emoji follows that.

The next thing I know, it's just me and Marcus alone in the backyard of a mansion. He looks over at me, not like a douchey horn-ball lusting after me, but like he's in awe. His gaze is respectful, taking in the features he likes while possibly searching for a sign from me that I want him to kiss me. As much as I want him to look at me like I'm the only girl in the world, he doesn't. That doesn't take him out of the running for a potential hookup though. Because I'm long overdue for some loving.

"Are you hungry by chance, Isabella?" Marcus finally asks. "Because I've got the drunk munchies and there's a stash of food in the fridge that I really want to warm up."

"You don't know how happy it makes me that you just said that, Marky Marc," I tease in my best Bostonian impression even though he doesn't even have one of those *Family Guy* accents.

He offers me a hand and helps me up from the pool chair. As I stroll beside him, he rattles off the list of meals he squirreled away before the guests arrived.

"Perogies for sure. Maybe some of that chicken, too. And that Mexican rice. Please!" I say as he's opening the fridge.

"Mind passing me the foil? It's in that pantry over there, I think."

"I don't know how things work where you're from, hon, but putting foil in the microwave is a no-no." I flash a menacing grin.

"I don't like microwaved food, so I'm going to pop it in the convection oven for a little bit. I hope you don't mind waiting an extra eighteen minutes."

"Ugh," I say with an eye-roll. "Not you, too... Is it a scientist thing or an East Coast thing to not like your food microwaved?"

He cocks a brow and smiles in confusion. "Microwaved food always tastes weird to me. Maybe because I'm over-analytical when it comes to flavor. So it probably is the scientist in me. Who else do you know like that?"

The memory of Dion complaining about his microwaved leftovers plays in my mind. "Oh... uh, some guy I used to talk to."

Marcus searches my face like the ache in my heart is evident. "Judging by that look on your face and your change in demeanor, I'd say that he was more than just *some guy* you used to talk to."

"He was pretty special to me, but we didn't date or anything. Not that we really could. He lived in Pennsylvania at the time. And I wasn't really looking for anything serious after we... spent time together."

He nods and then takes a drink of beer. "I see... So, what happened?"

"He couldn't take just being friends, so we kind of just stopped talking..."

"Oh... I get that."

"Do you now?"

He nods slowly. "All too well... Was losing him the worst thing that's ever happened to you?"

"Nope. But it's right up there. Losing my father in ninth grade to cancer—nothing can top that."

His lips curl into his mouth, his eyes widen like my words triggered a bout of PTSD. It looks like he wants to cry. "I'm sorry, but I get that too. I uh… just lost my mom a few months back. Colon cancer, stage four."

"Aw, you poor thing." I wrap my arms around his muscular form and give a nurturing hug while rubbing his back. "I'm so sorry."

He holds me tightly like he's known me forever. "Thanks. Losing her still has me broken, if you couldn't tell."

"Hey, there's nothing wrong with that. Doesn't make you any less manly. And, honestly, sensitivity is kind of hot to me."

"Good to know," he says, laughing quietly against me.

"It took years for me to cope with losing my dad… Even until this day, I cry every time I achieve a goal because I think about how I can't share it with him." Great, now thinking about all of my recent successes makes me emotional.

He sniffles. "That's where I'm at now. My mom always said I'd be a best-selling author someday, but I was a few months too late on that *prophecy*. And that's my biggest regret… That's why I go for what I want any chance I get now. Because life's too short to wait for the things you want." His embrace loosens around me.

His words make me think of Dion.

I pull back and look up into his red and teary, sorrow-filled eyes. For some reason, his vulnerability and our common wound has me wanting to get lost in him.

Judging by the look in his eyes, he's feeling something too.

I crane my neck forward, my mouth hanging open just a bit. *Kiss me* is what I'm trying to convey. *Kiss me so I can forget, damn it.*

And he does, gently, thoughtfully. Sparks don't fly, but things get hot and heavy pretty quick in that way they do when two drunk people hook up. His hands explore my body, respectfully at first, until I move his hand to my ass. Now he's squeezing my cheeks like it's his first time grabbing ass. I go back to clawing at his back and those muscular arms.

The next thing I know, he steers my ass toward the kitchen island and he lifts me up onto it, moving his waist between my legs. We make out passionately like that for a while. As we do, I don't think about who's kissing me, I think about who I wish was slipping his tongue into my mouth right now. Thinking of our last time together, remembering our last time in bed has me slick and horny as all hell. I remove Marcus's hand from my back and guide it up my skirt. I plant both palms against the counter and throw my head back, imagining it's Dion who's kissing my neck and giving my folds and clitoris an over-the-panties rubbing. It makes my chest heave. It makes me pant like a marathon runner in the middle of a race. It makes me upset like it's August last year all over again.

At that moment, the convection oven beeps.

I palm his chest and give him a pat. "Don't hate me, but I really, really want to break for food quick," I say, panting.

His hand withdraws as he pries his mouth from my neck, his eyes searching me. "Yeah, that's totally fine," he says with a bright smile.

Marcus slips on some oven mitts and sets the food out on the table. "Help yourself. I gotta pee quick."

"Alrighty," I say, watching him hurry off.

What the hell is wrong with me?

26
Isabella

Sunday

I LOAD UP MY plate with enough to tide me over, then I have a seat. As I blow on my chicken, I open Instagram and pull up Dion's profile. He hasn't posted anything in a while, aside from a few photos of him hiking around some lake in Massachusetts with Carmela, his friend from PSU that got him the job in Boston, and his new friends. Below that are some pics of him and his friends from his going-away party. Nothing of him and Jessica has been posted in months. It's the same on Jessica's Insta, which is odd considering all she did was post pics of them. Weekly. I know because I checked. Daily. I'm guessing they're not together anymore. And if they did break up months ago, it really effing hurts that he still hasn't reached out to tell me. The idea of reaching out to him terrifies me because I don't want to find out that he may have moved on to someone else. That's the only reason why I haven't asked Riley to message Mike for me yet.

I scroll my way down to his posts from two years ago until I find the ones of him and me during our road trip. I pinch out on the picture to zoom in on us.

"Is that him?" Marcus says quietly from behind me.

I jump like a startled cat and drop my phone on the table. "Geez! Make some fucking noise, you stealthy sonofabitch!" I say with a deranged smile, checking my screen for cracks.

He chuckles. "Sorry, I don't like to make noise."

I shake my head. "Neither did he," I say, closing Instagram and staring at the food I'm poking around until the embarrassment subsides.

Marcus portions food onto his plate, then sits across from me, sighing as he does. "You know how earlier, when you were talking about how your guy couldn't take being just friends and I said I get it?"

"Yeah," I mumble with a mouth full of rice and chicken.

"Well, there was this girl I was friends with for years. We were close as hell and there was always something undeniable between us. I took too long to act and then she ended up dating some guy she met in some calculus class her second year of college. There were times when I knew she wasn't happy with him, times she would be all up under me when she wanted to piss him off. I missed so many opportunities to tell her how I felt. But now it's too late because they're engaged and happy-ish. Being friends with her is hard. Unbearable. For years I tried getting over her. Not being friends who see each other almost once a week was hard on me. It would've been easier if we weren't, because then I wouldn't be wondering *what if* when we're together."

"Are you over her now?"

Marcus bobbles his head side to side. "Yes and no? Sometimes I find myself feeling some kind of way when we hang out, but I've met someone else since their engagement. Someone who makes me feel like I've never felt before. This girl might just be one."

"Wow... And what's going on with that lucky lady?"

He smirks, keeping his lips pressed together. "She wasn't exactly single when we met. And... uh, let's just say that, by the time we realized we had feelings for each other, it was too late to act on them. Because she was taken off the market too."

"Oh... You're one unlucky dude."

"You have no idea... So, what about you? Tell me about this guy you clearly can't move on from."

How Dion and I met, the week we spent together, talking for a year, our weekend in Philly together—I drunkenly spew it all to this man I was making out with like he's my therapist. "And since that day we stopped talking like we used to, there's just this fucking hole in me that no amount of success, fame, or money can seem to fill up. To make shit worse, I can't connect with anyone like I could with him. It's to the point that I don't even want to try. No offense."

"None taken. If it makes you feel any better, I've been a bit emotionally detached after my mom passed away and after missing out on the only two girls that I could ever see myself with. Getting myself to even want to hook up is hard sometimes. If I wasn't buzzed enough to numb my sorrows before I saw you, I wouldn't have put myself out there either, no matter how beautiful I thought you were or how much of a social media crush I had on you before my life went to shit."

I smile. "Aw... That's understandable, hon."

He smiles back, then takes a sip of beer. "You know, from what you told me, one thing has become clear about your situation, Isabella."

"And what's that?"

"That you're in love this Dion guy."

I poke the last few grains of rice around my plate in silence.

"Could you go through the rest of your life without him?"

"No."

"Is he all you think about?"

"Yes."

"If you found out you were terminally ill, is he the person you wished you were with in all your good days and in the final minutes?"

"Without a doubt."

Marcus nods. "Listen, I'm going to give you a glimpse into your future. You ready?"

I nod reluctantly.

"Until you explore this thing with him, every guy you meet from now on, you will be comparing to him and despairing over the fact that none of them are him. If you get past that and you do ever end up with someone, you'll never completely be happy with them, because it'll never be good enough and you'll always wonder what could've been. Now, should you just choose to hook up when the need arises from now until the foreseeable future, you'll feel good for a little while, but as soon as it's over, you'll be left with nothing but disappointment. Trust me. Unlike my situation, you absolutely know if your person of interest loves you."

"What if he doesn't anymore?"

"You said it's only been nine months, right?"

I nod.

"It takes a lifetime to get over someone you truly love. If he was seriously willing to give up being engaged for you back then, chances are he probably still is. Reach out to him. Tell him how you feel and that you're ready to try. If you don't now, one day it'll be too late and you'll live with regret for the rest of your life. And life is too short to regret, Isabella. So don't fuck up like I did. Text him. Text him right now!"

I giggle. "You must really not want to get laid tonight."

"We both know that you didn't stop us from going any further just because you wanted to eat." He searches my eyes then nods when he observes the reaction he was waiting for. "That's exactly why no one is getting lucky in this house tonight."

I nod subtly.

"Text him, Isabella."

"It's, like, four in the morning in Boston, Marcus… I don't want him thinking this is a drunk booty call."

"Good point… Then text him in the morning. First thing. If you want to stay here in one of the six bedrooms, I'll be happy to remind you when you get up to contact him."

I shake my head. "You're unbelievable."

"Am I? Or am I just a sucker for love after watching rom-coms and *How I Met Your Mother* with my mom for years?" He gathers up the dishes. "I'm a good judge of character and I can tell you're someone who deserves happiness. Since I missed my shot, I'm thinking at least one of us deserves to be happy in this life, don't you think?" He heads to the dishwasher.

"I think we both deserve it. You never know, maybe things with your girl will work out down the road."

He inhales deeply and blows out hard. "I hope so."

"If the opportunity presents itself, make it so that she realizes she's with the wrong guy."

"Maybe I will… If things *do* work out, I'll text you. If they don't, and if I find out that you don't get your guy, what do you say we reconnect when I'm less broken and when you're all out of hope?" He grins.

I giggle, shaking my head. "Deal. But if he does for some reason still want to try and we happen to stick it out long enough to maybe get married someday, you're invited to the wedding for being the reason I took the leap."

"It'll work out. I'll keep an eye out for your engagement ring pics on Insta, then I'll DM you my address for the save the date."

Marcus and I sit around talking until the Uber arrives. The second I climb in the back seat and shut the door, I open up my conversation with Dion and start drafting a text that I'll send first thing in the morning.

27
Dion

Sunday

A SMILE AND A shake of my head is how I react to seeing a text from Isabella pop up right as I'm glancing at the windshield-mounted phone that I'm currently using as GPS.

Our *relationship* has been relegated to sparse texting throughout the last nine-ish months. There was no contact between us until two months after Philly, when she checked in to see how I was. I replied and asked how she was, of course, because I couldn't torture her like that. I cared way too goddamn much and that wasn't going to change in sixty days.

She texted me again on Thanksgiving.

I texted her November 30th for her birthday.

Izzy texted me December 14th for my birthday.

Christmas, she texted me first.

New Year's at midnight, I texted her first because I was hammered and got in my head about her, wishing she was who I was going to kiss when the ball dropped.

In January, I texted her that I got the technical writing position up in Boston, just because moving and finding a new job was something we talked about often.

A few texts with her followed in the first quarter of the year with updates about dancing gigs and brand deals, things I already knew from Instagram.

"How are you? What's new?" followed each exchange, but our exchanges fizzled out after three or four back-and-forth messages. Then there was nothing for weeks.

Today is the first time she's texted me in over three months, and I'm both eager to read it and dreading opening it.

Anxiousness persists the entire rest of the drive to this Costco in Everett, Massachusetts that I can never remember how to get to. As soon as I pull into a spot, I snatch the phone from the mount and open the text.

Isabella: **Hey! Long time no talk, Dion. Hope you're well. Listen, I've been thinking about you and I miss you dearly. Not having you in my life is depressing as hell and I can't deal with it anymore. If I'm someone who still matters to you, would you please shoot me a text and let me know when it's a good time to call you?**

Eight A.M. Pacific time is a little early to be thinking about me, I think, thumbing my reply. *And there's no way she's drunk at this hour...*

Me: **Hey there. You'll never not matter to me. You should know that. I'm free now until 9 tonight my time.**

I don't move to exit the Jeep. I just wait.

Isabella: **Can I call you now?**

Me: **Sure. If you wanna, I can hold off going into Costco.**

The phone rings barely ten seconds after I hit sent.

"Good morning," I answer, confusion in my voice.

"Morning, Dion," she says sleepily, taking a deep breath and groaning after. "Let's talk about how happy I am that you were willing to chat."

"Sounded like you really needed to talk. Didn't want to neglect a friend in need."

"So, we *are* still friends?"

"Of course. I just—"

"I know. You don't have to say it."

I sigh. "Is everything alright with you? It's a little early for a phone call from someone who despises mornings just as much as me."

"Yeah... I just... couldn't sleep. A lot on my mind."

"Did you need me to play therapist for you like I used to?" I smile.

"Hm... No. I just wanted to talk in general... Hear your voice. Catch up. If that's okay. Is that okay?"

"Yeah. That's fine."

"Yay! So, tell me about your life. How's the new job?"

"It's a job. Not slaving away in the lab with death compounds that could fuck up my genes. Now I'm slaving away in a cubicle combating heart disease from sitting down all day."

"Do you hate it? Are you miserable there too?"

"Eh, it's boring, but I'm liking it better than the last one. For now. I can see myself hating it in another year or two."

"Then what? Did you figure out a passion project that you could turn into a business yet?"

"After writing pharmaceutical reports in my last job and writing documents and reports for this lab, I'm rediscovering my passion for writing. Maybe I'll get into freelance science writing. Something I could do from home to avoid commuting, you know?"

"There you go! I knew you'd figure out something eventually."

"Yeah. Guess I just had to try a few things to see what I hated. As it turns out, what I hate is working for people."

"People like us don't do well chained to a desk and being micromanaged. We're rebels, hon."

"Damn right... What about you? How's life?"

"Life's okay. Same old. Looking for a change. Thinking about becoming a choreography instructor for a while instead of going weeks without knowing if I'll get work."

"Figured that uncertainty would be stressful after a while."

"Yeah, but it's not so bad with the brand deals keeping the money coming. And the revenue from those beauty product affiliate links that you told me to use way back when."

"At least all of those podcasts and videos paid off for one of us."

She laughs. "Yeah. Maybe they will for you once you stop planning and start doing."

"Yeah, you're right."

"Of course I am. Let's see, what else…" She hums in the silence that follows. "Oh! I'm thinking about moving."

"Oh yeah? Where to?"

"Not sure yet… Going to see if my RTA contacts have any openings someplace good before I set my heart on anywhere in particular."

"Smart call. Nothing worse than getting your hopes up and then not having it work out." *That was a jab at you.*

"Mm-hm… So… anything new with you? Engaged yet?"

I laugh silently at the question, as I was waiting for her to inquire about my relationship status. "I'd have to be in a long-term relationship in order to be engaged."

"Wait, what happened with you and Jessica?"

"I uh… broke up with her before I made the move to Boston."

There's rustling on her end, like she just sprung up out of bed or almost dropped her phone and caught it. "Shit. I'm sorry."

"It is what it is."

"So, what happened? And how are you just now telling me this? I mean, I know we're not talking like we used to but this is a pretty big fuckin' deal and we still usually tell each other about the big life events!"

Her attempt at playing at being concerned has me grinning to myself like an idiot. "I'd rather not get into it if it's okay."

"That's fine."

"And I didn't tell you because I wasn't ready to."

"I guess I can't blame you." Silence follows.

I don't say anything. Not sure what there is to say.

"Have you met someone new up in Boston?"

"Eh, kind of? I've been sort of talking to a girl from work. Nothing serious. Trying to avoid getting involved with a coworker, if I'm being honest."

"Always a good idea." Her words trail off.

"Mm-hm."

"So, you said you were getting ready to go into Costco?"

"Yup. Sunday shopping. It's my usual routine these days."

"Gotcha… Alright, I guess I'll let you go then… But before I do… There's this thing I've wanted to send you for a while. Can I have your address?" A pen clicks in the background.

"Yeah, of course. Uh, 14 Audubon Road, Wakefield, Massachusetts. Apartment 335."

"Got it! Thanks! You might have to sign for it, though… If I sent it in the next week or so, will you be home to receive it?"

"Um… Yeah, I'll be home. If not, the front desk will hold onto it for me."

"Excellent. I'll text or call when it arrives, mmm-kay?"

"Sounds good, Izzy."

"Alrighty! Well, it was really nice talking to you!"

"It was good talking to you, too."

"Let's do it again soon?"

I take a deep breath and exhale slowly, quietly. "Yeah, for sure."

"Kay, bye!"

"Later, Izzy."

28
Dion

Saturday

"*BE HOME SATURDAY AT, like, 3ish,*" is what Isabella texted me right as I got home after Costco last week. All week, I've been distracted as hell trying to figure out what she could possibly be sending me. Because I hate surprises and I like to predict things before they happen. And if I can't, it stresses me out.

Tickets to a show.

Some random expensive gift.

A large sum of cash.

A hard drive containing intel on a legitimate conspiracy of some kind.

A wedding invitation…

Neither an invitation nor a plane ticket would require a signature, so those options seem highly unlikely. Thankfully. If it was a wedding invitation, I would drink myself into oblivion the second I got back from checking the mail. I highly doubt that she'd mail me cash unless she found a bag of drug money laying around and couldn't send it over PayPal or something. And a hard drive with world-changing secrets wouldn't surprise me given that she's the queen of conspiracy theories, but something tells me that's not the case.

That just leaves an expensive gift.

Waiting for this mystery thing made what would normally be a slow week drag on like a bad weed edible high, making every hour of mundane work feel like two. Last night I couldn't sleep. This morning I woke up early. After breakfast and two cups of coffee, I did laundry and watched Marvel movies all day to keep occupied, checking my phone every five minutes just in case she texted saying it was coming early.

But the wait is almost over. It's 2:55 P.M. now. Part of me wants to wait in my luxury apartment's common area so I can watch the maildrop from the couch instead of racing down the hall and down the stairs like five-year-old me on Christmas morning.

I anxiously scroll through Facebook and Instagram, only because when the notification comes through, I'll know right away.

"What the shit," I say to myself when I see it's 3:26 P.M. and I still haven't heard anything.

My phone screen switches from the YouTube video I'm watching to the picture of Isabella as the phone begins to buzz in my hand. I stand up and head to the door before even answering.

"Howdy," I say, stepping out of my apartment.

"Hey, hey!" she says cheerily, wind blowing in the background. "You picked up fast."

"I was watching something on my phone when your call came through."

"Porn?" she says in a sultry voice.

I enter the stairwell. "No, Raunchy Sauce."

She laughs. "Ah, I missed hearing that… You home? I got the confirmation your package has arrived."

"Yup. On my way down now."

"Yay! You alone?"

I scowl. "What the hell did you send me?"

"Something I don't want you to share with anyone else. Now are you home alone or not?"

I emerge into the first-floor hallway and start powerwalking. "Yeah, I'm alone."

"Good. Stay on the line. I want to hear your reaction when you get it."

"If you insist, weirdo."

She giggles. "Oh, come on. When's the last time you got this excited about anything?"

"Honestly, I couldn't even tell you."

"You're welcome. I just hope the gift lives up to the hype. I know you probably spent all week trying to figure it out."

"You're enjoying torturing me, aren't you?"

"Yes."

I pass the bathrooms, then the community recreation room and turn left to the lobby, where the security desk lies beyond the wall of glass. Packages are usually either behind the security desk or on it. "I don't see any packages."

"Maybe check outside," she says as I'm tugging open the heavy glass door.

I look from the lobby to the entrance ahead. There's a honey-brown-haired hottie with blond highlights who's dressed in high-waisted shorts and a burgundy and white striped tank top. She's standing right outside with her back to the glass double doors, a medium-sized suitcase beside her.

"There's nothing out there, either, Izzy."

Isabella scoffs. "*Nothing?* Really?"

The girl outside twirls around.

Reality seems to shatter before me, and my heart damn near explodes at the sight of her.

29
Isabella

Saturday

CONFUSION. HAPPINESS. EXCITEMENT. IT all shows up on Dion's face at once. And his reaction makes me blush.

"So, I'm nothing now?" I say with a smile as he approaches the doors, dressed in his black T-shirt, black basketball shorts, and black Adidas.

He's grinning and shaking his head the way I imaged he would when he saw me today. Slowly, he lowers the phone and yanks open the door. "What... What are you doing?" he laughs in bewilderment, approaching me ever so cautiously, like I'm a mirage.

"Good to see you, too, hon." I wink.

"This is *not* what I was expecting."

I grimace. "Bad surprise?" I say through gritted teeth.

He shakes his head. "Unexpected surprise." He opens his arms and I almost knock him over when we collide. "What are you doing here?" he whispers again. Though his hug is apprehensive, he still feels like home.

I tighten my embrace, groaning as I squeeze him. "I told you I was looking to move, didn't I?" I whisper back.

"The last time we talked, you didn't even have anywhere on your radar."

"Well, I made a couple calls since I told you that."

He releases me and searches my eyes. "You're telling me that, in the hour that I went shopping and drove home last Sunday, you found a potential job here?"

I nod with the smuggest look I can muster. "What can I say? That's the power of being well-connected."

He's half-smiling, half-scowling. "And what made you choose Boston?"

"Uh, I liked it when I performed here with Beat Slave... Uh... *you're* here."

He takes a deep breath, the excitement in his eyes melting away into what looks to be heartache.

"Before you say anything, let me disclose that I already had the plane ticket in my cart before you told me about... your relationship status."

His face is neutral but the corners of his mouth quirk. "So, what's the initial reason you were planning on coming here then?"

"I really wanted to see you," I whisper back. "So... here I am."

"Here you are..."

I grit my teeth. "Is it okay that I surprised you like this?"

"Yeah, Izzy. Believe it or not, I'm happy to see you. Happy, albeit super caught off guard."

"Goodie! Does that mean I can crash with you for the week?" I grimace. "I didn't exactly book a hotel."

Dion cocks a thumb to the right. "There's a Four Points hotel right down the road," he says flatly with a straight face.

That hits like a punch in the gut and I flinch. "Yeah, I saw that when I was mapping out this trip."

"I'm kidding, Izzy. Of course you can stay with me."

I sigh in relief. "You asshole."

A menacing grin spreads across his face as he takes my luggage. His head then bobs toward the door. "Let's get you in the air-conditioning."

The building is fancy as hell—more so than where Riley and I live. There's a gym. An upscale lounge with a pool table, a kitchen, a fridge, a coffee station, and what looks to be an 80-something-inch flat screen. Beyond that is a pool. A grilling area with tables and chairs lies beyond the pool's fence. The halls are clean. Everything smells fresh.

Dion's apartment is neat. Minimalist. All of his furniture is black and sleek. There's an Alexa Echo Show on his countertop. His bookshelf is full of books. His Xbox games and Blu-rays are neatly stacked in the TV stand.

"Here's the bedroom," he says, gesturing to the open room as he hoists my luggage beside the dresser topped with a 52-inch flatscreen. "The bathroom is right here right across from it." He flips on the light. "Bed's all yours."

I eye up the bed with a black headboard and comfy-looking navy-blue comforter and sheet set. "Yeah, no… You're not sleeping on the couch in your own home, hon."

"And I'm not letting you sleep on the couch or the airbed."

"I mean… there is another option."

With a sigh, he shakes his head. "You thirsty? Hungry?"

"Both."

The fridge opens with a rattle. "Water, beer, or juice?"

"Water, please!"

"I don't have much to eat. Grocery—"

"Shopping is tomorrow," I finish for him. "I remember you telling me your routine last week." I smile.

He offers a faint smile in return. "I typically go out to eat on Saturdays."

"Did you have plans tonight?"

"Nope."

"When I was creeping on your address on Google Maps, I saw there were a bunch of restaurants across the street from ya. Take me to your favorite place. I'm buying. No if ands or buts."

"As you wish. Let me get changed quick."

It's only a twelve-minute stroll down Audubon Road to the restaurant he frequents called Yard House. Since it's nice out, we both vote on walking. Plenty of time for us to break the ice that has formed between us since Philly. Dion seems a bit distant, so I drive the conversation to get him to open up, probing him about new friends and what he's been doing around here for fun.

Yard House isn't super busy, so we're seated right away. This place is basically a mix between chill and classy, which is right up my alley.

"Hello! My name is Nancy! What can I get for ya?" the waitress says in a strong Boston accent that makes me both cringe and smile.

"Loaded nachos and two Stella Artois for now, please," I say to her while staring at him. "And please put everything on my tab now so this gentleman doesn't sneakily pay for me." I whip out my credit card.

He just smiles, sliding his ID over to her.

I hold mine out, still holding his gaze.

"Coming right up!" she says, setting down our IDs before hurrying off.

Dance and all of the things I've done in recent history, the details about my upcoming interview for choreographer instructor at RTA's Boston division this Wednesday, what's been new with him, how he's adjusting to being in a new city—we cover the last nine months over appetizers and two beers. By the time dinner and our third round of beers arrive, he's noticeably looser and getting back into the goofy groove I've missed.

"Here," I say, cutting my entrée up, "try this salmon." I extend the chunk of pink meat that I've just stabbed with my fork. "It kind of reminds me of what we had in San Francisco at that Japanese-Mexican fusion spot."

Though he's hesitant at first, he lets me feed him. "Mmmm... That's pretty good. It does remind me of that fish! It's something with the glaze."

That exchange leads to us reminiscing over our road trip together. That leads to us reflecting on how much fun we used to have together, how close we were.

It's maybe twenty minutes to dusk by the time we leave the restaurant. Halfway to the apartment, I work up the courage to segue our conversation in a way that will allow me to bring up what I wanted to say all day. All week. All year. Years ago.

This conversation needs to happen so he doesn't insist on sleeping on the couch tonight...

Dion glances at me, his mind clearly working—probably trying to bring up what he's been dying to ask me, what's been on his mind all day. *What are you really doing here?* "Izzy, I gotta say... it's absolutely blowing my mind that you're here right now." Everything about him is relaxed now.

"It's blowing my mind that you're single," I say.

He snickers. "Really? As I recall, you said more than a few times that Jessica wasn't right for me... You knew this was inevitable."

I smile. "Because I know you like you know me, hon."

He faces front. "I suppose we do know each other pretty well."

"Yes. We. Do," I say, poking him in the arm with each word. "And that's why I knew she wasn't the kind of girl you should be going the distance with. Just like how you knew I'd eventually come to my senses about all of those things that weren't clear to me when we met."

His head snaps in my direction, eyes squinting curiously as they scan me, his mouth twitching like he's fending off a smile. "And what are these things I enlightened you to exactly? That was so vague and it's been so long, I'm having a hard time remembering."

I slap his firm chest. "You know, like, changing my behavior once my dreams started coming to fruition. Wanting certain things to happen after it might be too late for them."

Dion sighs, then tilts his nose up as he surveys the sky above. "A meteor is hurdling toward Earth and it's going to hit the Atlantic Ocean and wipe out the entire East Coast. You have ten minutes to tell someone something you've always wanted to say. Who do you call and what do you say?"

"Seriously? What is up with you and tsunami scenarios?"

He chuckles. "Maybe it's because they're a reoccurring motif in my dreams. But I think it's because it's the most plausible threat that you can calculate arrival time for."

"I forgot how much of a nerd you can be."

He smirks. "Clock's ticking. The wave is coming…"

"You. I'd call you. Or I guess I'd turn to you right here and tell you that… by the end of that week we were together two years ago, my butt really hurt."

He shakes his head. "Um… what?"

The look on his face make me cackle. "My butt hurt because for, like, five days straight, you kept sweeping me off my feet and I fell harder and harder each time. Right on my ass. I fell so hard and so fast that I didn't know what was happening. To end up feeling so strongly about someone new in such a short amount of time? To have them feel just as strongly about me? To make such an intense connection the way we did? For someone I barely knew to make me happier than I've ever been in my entire life? I didn't know how to handle any of that. It made no sense! It scared the ever-living shit out of me."

"If it makes you feel any better, it scared me too."

"At least you vocalized your feelings like a sane person. I just denied them and blew up what we had... Which, just so you know, left me feeling sick to my stomach for weeks. Not just because I hurt you but also because I thought that I lost the best thing that ever happened to me forever. I didn't realize how alone and empty I was until I lost you then got you back. Because reconnecting and talking week after week made me realize I wasn't whole without you. But you were with Jessica, so I tried to enjoy the single life like I'd wanted to."

"I don't want to hear that."

"Just let me finish."

"Fine. Go on ahead."

"Thank you. As I was saying, I couldn't enjoy any of it. Hookups left me feeling empty. I mean, they always have, but it was worse after you. No matter who I dated, it never felt right. Every day, every minute I spent with another guy, every fiber in my being was screaming against it because none of them were you. Like, I pined for you. Daily."

"So, what you're saying is...?"

I scoff, scrunching up my face. "I fell in love with you when we met and I never fell out of love with you. Not for a second."

He smiles and the heartache in his eyes goes back to that longing adoration he's been hiding from me all day. That gaze sets me on fire. "That's what I thought you were trying to say."

"Oh, hush."

"So, that last night in Philly?"

I sigh. "It wasn't until last weekend that I realized why I didn't say I loved you too."

"And that reason was?"

"I wasn't ready to be loved, because I didn't love myself enough to give all of me over to you. Because I didn't think someone as amazing as you could ever love someone like me. I didn't think I was worthy of all that you had to offer. You saw everything I was and all of my worth from the beginning, but I didn't see it until recently. I think I had to grow into myself, you know?"

He nods, giving me a pitiful look.

"And, some time since I last saw you, through a cycle of having you and losing you, I ended up becoming some version of me that loves who I am and who feels like I deserve happiness and to be loved, someone who's worthy of something amazing with the only man I could ever see myself with. I didn't realize that until the night before I texted you last week. And it wasn't until I was lying in bed that night that it dawned on me that you only get a few true loves in your life. Your parents, if you're lucky. Your kids. And your soulmate. When I lost my dad, I lost the only person that ever loved me unconditionally. Until you came along, that is. I didn't cherish the time with my father like I should've, because I thought I'd always have more time. I'm never making that mistake again."

I search his face as we walk. "So, I guess what I'm trying to tell you is that the only thing I want more than anything in this life is *you*. Me and you. Together. I just hope that I'm not too late."

Dion keeps walking in silence.

The seconds tick by and his lack of a response ramps up my anxiety. I halt abruptly. "Can you say something, please? I'm teetering on a fucking panic attack here."

He taps his key fob against the lock and pulls the door open, stepping aside for me. "You made me wait nine months—no, two years—for this, so I'm going to go on ahead and make you wait a few agonizing seconds." He smirks fiendishly.

I shove him as I pass. "Alright, maybe I deserve that... But show some mercy, hon."

His silence continues as we walk down the hall past a few people dressed like they're heading to the gym.

"Seriously, Dion?" I say as we're approaching the elevator.

The elevator arrives. "I broke up with Jessica because of you," he says as I follow him inside.

"Wait, really? Why? What happened?"

"The short answer? She wasn't you."

I smile. "And the long answer?"

"No matter how close we got or how much time we spent together, I never felt the way about her that I did about you. Anytime I said *I love you* to her, I never meant it, not the way she did. Not the way I was supposed to. Not the way I meant it when I said it to you. I realized I was only still with her because I didn't want to be alone. Because I couldn't force myself to look for something better when I knew there was only one woman out there for me that was worth my energy. My time. My attention. All my love." He searches my eyes. The vision of him blurs behind walls of tears.

The elevator opens and he leads us out.

"I settled for her because she was *good enough*," he continues. "But that wasn't fair to her. Because I fell in love with you two years ago and I never stopped loving you, even when I was pissed at you. Even after Philly when we stopped talking. I gave you so much shit about holding out on unrealistic hopes but, even when I was mad, I was high on *hopeium*," he says with finger quotes, "from that spring break until now. High on the hope that one day you'd come around." Holding eye contact with me, he unlocks his apartment door.

"News flash, Dion," I say, walking past him. "It wasn't false or unrealistic hope. You were waiting because your analytical ass can predict shit that simple folk like me can't. You knew I'd realize you were right and I would come around." I turn my palms up to the ceiling, eyes welling with tears even though I'm smiling. "Me flying here to gift you my heart? This is what coming around looks like, hon. So, do you still want to try with me or not?" I manage to choke out.

There's silence as he steps closer, searching my eyes. "More than anything. But remember, this is for keeps… You know that, right?"

"Letting you go again is the last thing I would ever want to do. Hell, I'd give up my career and my following before letting any of that get in the way of us."

Smiling, he takes my hands. "You don't ever have to give up your dreams for me. If you have to travel, I'll go with you. And if I can't go, I'll be here when you get back. I'm in, no matter what."

"Good," I say, getting lost in his eyes like he's getting lost in mine. "Now kiss me like you missed me and take me like I'm yours."

His hand cups the side of my face. His thumb caresses my cheek, wiping away a tear like he did during our last goodbye. Then he plants his lips gently and thoughtfully on mine, electrifying me in a way that feels different than all the times before.

Each kiss is deeper than the last, more passionate. His hands explore my body with a gentle caress. My fingers play against his sides until they get minds of their own and grab fistfuls of his shirt. I walk him back to where I think the couch is. When the backs of my legs hit the couch, I use all my weight to toss him onto the middle cushion. Grinning, he scoots back to the armrest and I mount him. And we kiss. We touch. I hump. I strip him of his shirt. He removes my tank top and bra. The second my shorts and panties are off, he maneuvers me gently onto my back and kisses me, probing my mouth with his tongue. Then he pecks me from my lips to *lips*. Then his tongue probes again and I can't help but cry out in sweet bliss.

Like he promised me in Philly, he tends to me until I finally cry out, moaning, "Oh god… That's enough, babe. Up here. Now. I need you inside of me."

He comes up from chowing down and we kiss as I guide him in. Bliss surges through me with that first slow thrust of his. With each stroke, I get closer to euphoric, brain-scrambling ecstasy. An orgasm comes in minutes and my hips buck into him of their own accord. Once I'm done contracting around him, he stops tunneling in an out of me then lifts me up, carrying me to the bed that I already imagined us making love in the second he showed it to me.

Deeper, faster, he gives it to me the way he knows I like it. Another orgasm comes, plus two more aftershocks before he finishes with me on my fourth and final quake, which makes my entire core spasm in a way that I thought porn stars only did in exaggeration.

"My body loves you as much as I do," I pant out.

Laughing, he collapses on top of me and we make out like we can't get enough of each other, panting into each other more than actually kissing.

When he rolls over, our hands find each other as we both lie there, staring at the ceiling like we got too high off each other to make sense of reality. Breathless, tingling all over, lost in a daze. Somehow I feel spent and energized at the same time.

I turn my head to him right as he's turning to me and we both smile, laughing quietly.

"That was worth the two years, two months, and three-week-long wait," I say, still working to catch my breath.

"It might take me that long to be ready to go again." He grins.

I scoot over, lay my head on his chest, then cuddle up to him. "It better not, sunshine. We've got a lot of catching up to do this week. And after I make that move."

We lie there, staring at each other, cuddling and mapping each other's bodies with light traces of our fingers the way we did our last time together in LA. Dion asks me what I want him to cook for me for tomorrow. While we're on the topic, he requests that I also make a list of what I want for the week. All I can see is our future together. And not even, like, making love or romantic vacations. It's cooking together and grocery shopping and laundry and binge-watching TV shows and having lazy days where we do nothing together. I look forward to doing all that normal shit I do alone with him tomorrow and every day after that.

That's how I know this is love. That's what love looks like to me. It's finding joy with someone who completes you during all those little moments everyone takes for granted between the dates and the lovemaking and the supporting of each other. And no matter what it takes, that's what I'm going to give my all to keep alive for as long as he and I are alive and breathing.

Dion and I, happy and together. For good. That's what I hope for.

No… screw hope. That's what I WILL for us! I will it into existence, just like I've willed the success I've always dreamed of.

Epilogue
Dion

One Year Later
Saturday

"OUR BABY IS GROWING up so fast!" Isabella squeals, wrapping her arms around me from behind as she joins me in gazing at what we've created together.

I chuckle. "Tell me about it. I never thought *this* is where I'd be at twenty-four years old."

"Right? But with me and you going at it as passionately as we were, there's no way that this wasn't going to happen," she says in a sultry voice.

I look back at her with a smirk.

Our first big leap was moving in together two weeks after finally becoming a couple. Even during her transition east, there wasn't one day that we were apart. The day she got the call about landing the choreography instructor job, I called out of work sick last minute and flew out west with her to help her pack. At least, that's what I told her. The surprise going-away party that Riley and I coordinated was the main reason for my impromptu vacation.

Living together so soon didn't seem like a bad idea to either of us. It's not like we'd just met. After that fateful week together in LA, and the year we spent talking, we forged a connection that was stronger than anything either of us had ever shared with anyone else. Likes, dislikes, hopes, dreams, fears, where we both stood on the topic of kids and marriage, quirks, habits, and pet peeves—there wasn't much we didn't know about each other by then.

Neither of us could imagine a scenario where cohabitating so soon after becoming a couple could backfire. And a little over a year later, it's clear we weren't wrong. Open lines of communication and a no-secrets policy have led to a relationship with no quarrels.

Isabella and I have achieved an unwavering oneness. She caters to my every want and need, and I to hers. Love dominates our home all day, every day. Somehow, our honeymoon phase seems to be renewed with each morning, probably because her sexual appetite still hasn't waned.

The next big leap was taking her to Pennsylvania to meet my parents on that first July 4th weekend together. My parents loved her. She loved them. While I was doing the post-breakfast dishes, Mom leaned over to me and whispered, "*I can tell she's the one for you.*" She said that after day one. She'd never said that once during any of the dozens of times I had Jessica over.

That was all the confirmation I needed to be sure that Isabella was the right woman to spend my life with.

My phone chimes in my pocket. "Ugh," I groan, opening the message. "Guess who pushed back the lease signing by an hour," I say, thumbing a response back to billionaire real-estate broker that we met at his Mass-a-Millions Spring Social—the rich-folk networking party we attended back in April.

"Mr. Brayden Never-on-Time McManus?"

"Wow! You guessed on the first try, babe!"

She flicks my nipple. "After he was late to the office space signing and after he rescheduled two house showings and showed up smelling like liquor to one of them, we shouldn't really be surprised."

"Seriously. That's the consequence of enlisting the Bruce Wayne of Boston, I guess. Though, in his defense, he was having relationship issues with you know who at the time."

"Either way, it's unprofessional as hell. I'll definitely shop around before enlisting someone to look for our LA home."

Most babies make couples hemorrhage money. Our aforementioned *baby* named Florus makes us money—enough money to afford a small office with three employees, a house twenty-five minutes outside of Boston, and hopefully a house out west in the near future. Not that we're making upper-class income off of an adorable lovechild with a progressive hipster name. Neither of us is ready for children. Yet. She wants kids, just not until meeting her dance career goals. As for me, I'm in no rush to tackle fatherhood anytime soon.

Florus is the limited liability company that Isabella and I founded together. While she was content being a contemporary choreography instructor, she wanted to get back to dancing in big shows at some point. But she didn't want to travel without me.

It was one evening during our first month together after I got home from work when she said, *"I'm tired of seeing my baby coming home looking so miserable. It's about time we both get our financial independence on."*

Brainstorming went down during dinner that night.

With her massive social media following, there was no doubt in my mind that we could leverage her traffic to sell a product. That was evident from her engagement levels and her affiliate link clicks, which I spent hours analyzing. All we needed to find was something that we were passionate about. A few weeks later, during our 8 P.M. tea time, it clicked.

"You know what?" I said, scrolling through her Instagram as I sipped the English breakfast tea that gets shipped to us for free because of her brand ambassador deal. "We're both health fanatics who drink herbal teas two to

three times a day. Why don't we just launch our own brand? Start-up costs are pretty low compared to other supplements." That was something I'd learned when I was researching the supplement business on and off in the years after college.

"Um, that's a fantastic fucking idea! Everyone knows I'm, like, the tea-queen!" she cheered. *"Ooh! I feel like my CBD posts have a lot of comments about how people say they can't go without it. Maybe we can do an infusion since that's big now!"*

"Yeah! And maybe we can do a nootropic blend to help with focus. You know, like how I drink tea after my coffee to counteract jitters and help me stay in the zone!"

"Fuck yes!"

"And we market from a scientific standpoint. You know, use my degree as a selling point that our claims have been properly researched, yada-yada."

"Oh my god! Yes!" She hugged me and planted a big wet kiss on my cheek. *"Yes! This is it! This will be our thing, babe!"*

Flor is Latin for flower. That called out to Isabella while she looked up translations of the name ideas she had. *"Flowers for us,"* was the motto she threw out there. As someone who's been making portmanteaus of words for years, *"Flowers for us"* became Flor for us. That got mashed into Florus, then boom, the brand was born.

A supplier with private labeling was sourced. We connected with a girl named Antha who runs a high-quality CBD lab in Colorado. The domain name and social media handles were acquired. The LLC paperwork was filed with the state. The logo work was outsourced while I worked on the FDA-compliant labels and blog posts. In four months, our business was live and we had two flagship dried tea products ready to go—the Flow State focus blend with added caffeine, and the CBD-infused CannaZen relaxation blend.

Isabella began marketing in late September, supplying her influencer contacts with free samples to promote. On October first, we launched.

"I want you to quit that job," Isabella told me in bed the Friday after crunching week eight's promising numbers. *"It's time for you to be happy."*

I kissed her. *"I've got you. Nothing can make me happier."*

"You're happy with me, but you're miserable at work. And I want my man to be happy in all areas of his life. You don't need to play it safe anymore, hon. Trust your spreadsheet." She pecked my lips. *"Trust me."* Another kiss. *"This is going to work out just the way we imagined it."*

I quit the following Monday.

Now, here we are, raking in well over seven figures, about to launch the next wave of pre-bottled drinks and premium dried tea blends that should take us into tens of millions in sales by quarter three next year.

The fact that we built this amazing thing together without one disagreement speaks volumes for our relationship. Because businesses and relationships can be messy all on their own. Mixing the two can be catastrophic. But not for us. Whether it's being partners in love or in entrepreneurial ventures, there's no doubt in my mind that we'll be together for the long haul. Not that being business partners is a metric for how well a relationship will work out, but given that we're great at handling a legally binding commitment that can have serious consequences should we split before the wedding bells have a chance to ring, I think it's a good sign. Though, looking at the rock on her finger, and considering how happy we make each other day after day, all other metrics indicate that we'll make it to the altar and beyond.

A Week Later

Our new five-bedroom, four-bathroom home at 385 Highland Street here in Weston, Massachusetts is bustling with people. Thanks to Isabella's preemptive furniture shopping and a team of movers, we somehow turned this house into a home in four days—just in time for our housewarming/late engagement party.

Everyone who matters to us is either here or on the way. My parents have been in town since Thursday. Riley got in last night. My spring break crew came in this morning, with the exception of Jeremy, who became a Boston resident back in late March after landing the job at Altus Marketing. It's a company owned by Isabella's contact, Marcus Jones, the last guy that she made out with before we finally ended up together—the guy who made her finally admit to herself that the reason she couldn't find happiness with anyone else was because she was in love with me. For that, I bought the guy a beer when we met up with him and his girlfriend.

Anyway, Jeremy has actually been handling the marketing for Florus over at Altus since joining their team. The deal was that they could have our business if they hired him on, so long as he alone handled the account the way we trained him to.

Isabella prances by and grabs my hand, tugging me away as she skips along. "My mom and Kirsten are here!" Isabella announces, leading me from the backyard patio, where it's been a struggle to stay cool in the early-August heat, and into the much-needed air-conditioned house. It's good to see her so excited about having family in town.

It was a little before her mom's June birthday last year when I talked her into reaching out to her mom. Time had dampened her mother's disappointment in her. Isabella's lifestyle change and dossier of achievements coaxed her mom into accepting her again.

After months of rebuilding their relationship with weekly chats, her mom invited us down for Thanksgiving.

"Hell no! I'm not ready for a big family holiday," is what she told me after hanging up the phone.

It took a lot of convincing to help her find the courage to want to reunite with her family after being shamed the way she was. *"If I didn't have you as my rock, I don't think I could go through with this. Not yet."* That's what she said when we were buying the plane tickets.

A warm, supportive welcome was what she received from her mom and the rest of her relatives. Praise for all of her successes showered her the entire four-day weekend. Witnessing her rekindle bonds with her loved ones and find acceptance is what made me the happiest. Finding out that her mom and all of her fairly conservative family loved me was just a bonus.

Following the grilling and cornhole tournament, everyone files into the living room to watch the engagement video that Riley put together for us.

"Wait, wait," Mike says, shaking his finger at Riley, "how were you involved in the proposal and we weren't?"

"Um, maybe because I live in LA and you don't?" Riley says, pulling the video up on the wall-mounted 4K flatscreen. Now she steps in front of the TV and raises her champagne glass. "As future maid of honor, I'd like to say a little something about this amazing couple that I envy so very much sometimes."

Mike opens his arms and makes a come here motion with his hand. "Get with your boy Mikey Mike and let's give them a reason to be jealous!"

With an eyeroll, Riley shakes her head. That's all she can do after already reminding him twice today that she has a boyfriend. "Anyway… What can I say about Isabella? She's the best girl I know. She's super talented, sweet, smart, and, for as long as I've known her, I never thought she'd settle down. Then she met Dion.

And she was happier than I'd ever seen her before in the three years I'd known her. I'm talking day one when they met at the bar. And after that first date, and following their road trip, and in the moments after that last kiss before he went back east. Isabella was the girl who I thought would never commit, but after seeing them together, I think I knew it before she did that Mr. Dion Johnson here was the one who would change that." She glares at Mike, smirking. "That's why *I* had to help him with this proposal. Because I knew before anyone that they'd end up here eventually." She raises her glass. "So, let's raise our glasses and drink in celebration of the love these two have for each other so we can watch this video I spent weeks editing!"

"Cheers!" the group says almost in perfect harmony.

While I actually bought an engagement ring the month before Florus launched, I didn't plan on proposing to Isabella for maybe two or three years. Given how averse she was to relationships, there was no need to rush things. But then the hints kept coming.

"The idea of marriage used to make me sick, but I kind of get it now," she said to me one night after watching *Hitch*.

"Are you still going to love me when I'm all wrinkly like that?" she asked after passing an elderly couple in the park.

"This is the kind of reception I'd want to have," she whispered to me while we danced at my friend's October wedding. More wedding talk followed that night after she got drunk.

On March 16th this year, three years to the night that we met, three months shy of our one-year anniversary, we flew out to LA and I proposed to her after dinner on the beach somewhere in the vicinity of where we had our first date. Riley was lurking behind a beach umbrella to inconspicuously record Isabella's mild freak out, and the sobbing-laugh that almost made her response of, *"Of course I'll marry you, Dion!"* inaudible.

When the video ends, our parents retire upstairs for the night while us "youngins" all head to the backyard to drink around the fire pit.

Surrounded by the best friends anyone could ask for, owning $1.5-million home with my dream girl, being the co-owner of a successful business—I don't know how the hell I got here when, three years ago, I didn't even know what I wanted to do with my life or even what my ideal girl looked like. But then I met Isabella, and everything just became crystal clear.

Me and Izzy together. Once that happened, the rest would fall into place. That was what I told myself after Philadelphia—after I broke up with Jessica.

To be honest, our business could tank tomorrow and I wouldn't even care. Word could come in that the world will end in a week and, as long as we have each other, I'd still go out the happiest guy on Earth.

Isabella's hand slides into mine when she catches me staring at her. "What are you all smiley about, babe?"

"I'm just imaging our future together." I lean in and kiss her.

She blushes. "So was I. It was the near future for me, though."

I smirk. "Oh yeah? And what does that look like?"

She brings her mouth to my ear. "Baby-making horizontal dance routine practice as soon as you're ready to call it a night," she whispers.

I pull out my phone. "Oh, shit. Would you look at that... We forgot to schedule that Florus promo to send tomorrow morning. I better go do that."

Isabella springs up from her seat. "Oh yeah... I should probably go with you. To proofread. You suck at spell-checking when you're drunk."

Riley and Mike give each other a lingering look, grinning devilishly like they're considering following suit like they did the night they met. Despite both being in long-term relationships, there's undoubtedly still some sexual tension there. Hell, Mike asked me three times if Riley was coming without her boyfriend this weekend, which is definitely why he didn't invite his girl.

"Try and keep it down tonight," Riley lectures. "Remember, your parents are upstairs."

Isabella giggles. "Whatever could you be talking about?"

"Gosh darn it, I just can't wait to be an uncle," Mike says with a grin.

Like me, Isabella shakes her head. "See y'all bright and early in the morning!" She drags me toward the house before I can even say goodnight.

Next up in The Messy Business of Love Series...

Marcus Jones helped steer Isabella into taking the leap, catalyzing her happily ever after with Dion. Now get ready to experience his journey of love in the even steamier, heart-tugging, swoon-worthy story, *Detachment*.

Debuting This Winter!

Signup below to get a few chapters of *Detachment* early & to get other goodies for FREE:
https://www.masterlesspress.com/romance

Craving more of Isabella and Dion? Yeah? Great! Because there's more of them to come in the Messy Business of Love series, so keep an eye out for them in the next few books, especially in Riley and Mike's book, ***Sunrise Nights*** where they'll be frontline and center as secondary characters. Also, you'll definitely want to see what happens as the friend group blends with Marcus and Kylie leading up to Izzy and Dion's **wedding**…

Oh, and Brayden McManus, the real-estate mogul from the epilogue? Yeah, you'll see Dion and Isabella interact with him during their house hunt while he finds love in ***Suite Haven***…

Author's Note to the Reader

Dear reader,

In the *Angels of War* series, an alternate universe where society collapsed after a global war, freedom fighter Dion Johnson met an enemy soldier named Isabella Monroe, and they became allies, friends, and so much more. During the end of the last book (*Terminus*), Dion wondered what would've happened if the world never went to crap and if he happened to meet Isabella during that spring break trip to LA he never got to have. *Hopeium* was born from that idea, and I was compelled to write it because of how much I loved writing their complicated relationship during the *Angels of War: Talion* and *Terminus*. Also, meeting the love of my life during a chance encounter while on vacation has also been a bit of a fantasy of mine. That's probably because my parents met while my dad was on vacation, and I've always thought that'd be better than meeting my future wife at a bar or work.

Though I suppose meeting the love of my life during an apocalyptic war would surely top that...

From the bottom of my heart, thank you for buying and reading *Hopeium*. If you loved Isabella and Dion's story as much as I loved writing it, please feel free to let us know by leaving a **review**! Reviews help authors more than you think, and they also help your fellow reader. It would also mean the world to us if you could tell all your romance-loving friends about this story!

Thanks again for being a part of this journey!

Peace and love,
D.J. Thompson

Acknowledgments

A huge thanks to the remarkable editor, Julie Mianecki, and the beyond superb proofreader, Brooks Becker! You ladies did an outstanding job making sure this story was as strong as it could possibly be. Can't wait to team up with you all again in the future!

To the wildly talented cover designer, Vanessa Mendozzi, you have done a stellar job with the cover for *Hopeium* and for *Detachment* too! A big thanks goes to you for your hard work, and we can't wait to see what you come up with for the rest of the books!

To Katie Reeb, a special thanks (from D.J. Thompson) for always supporting me and for being my go-to person to talk about relationships, all things love, and about the human condition from psychological and scientific standpoints. I'm incredibly thankful to have a friend like you in my life.

Most importantly, a special thank you to all of you amazing readers out there who have bought and read *Hopeium*! Your support means the world to us, and we couldn't be more grateful that you've gone on this journey with us. If you loved this story, please drop a review on Amazon or Goodreads and let us know! You can also like/follow us on our social media accounts if you below if you want to give any feedback or just talk love stories with the authors (Check the following **About the Author** pages)! There will also be an exclusive reader group coming soon to https://www.facebook.com/AdrianEverlyWrites.

Also, check out the Masterless Press social media for other exclusives and freebie announcements:
https://www.instagram.com/MasterlessPress/
https://www.facebook.com/MasterlessPress/

<u>About the Author:</u>
Adrian Everly

A New York-born, full-time author who loves all things love just as much as writing, good food, & memorable times. Whenever there's a rare break in obsessively writing stories, Adrian can be found watching rom-coms, reading, and spending time with friends.

Keep an eye out for Adrian's upcoming books:

<u>The Messy Business of Love Series</u>
Detachment (Kylie & Marcus) (Winter 2020)
Suite Haven (Elyse & Brayden) (Spring 2021)
Sunrise Nights (Riley & Mike) (Summer 2021)
Reverie (Senna & Trey) (Fall 2021)

Signup here for release date updates & to get the first few chapters of each book early: https://www.masterlesspress.com/adrian-everly

Follow @AdrianEverlyWrites here:

https://www.facebook.com/AdrianEverlyWrites

Keep an eye out for the Adrian Everly Private Facebook group where you can talk romance with the author!

About the Author:
D.J. Thompson

D.J. Thompson is a scientist-turned-author and owner of Masterless Press. He lives in Pennsylvania where he writes full-time while also working to help others share their stories through his indie publishing company. While he loves writing techno-thrillers like the *Angels of War* series that read more like prophecy than fiction, he took a recent departure into New Adult Contemporary Romance with *Hopeium* to expand the Masterless Multiverse of stories.

Other Books by D.J.:

<u>The Angels of War series</u>
<u>(Dystopian Technothrillers)</u>
Angels of War: Veritas (Book 1)
Jezebel (An Angels of War Novella) (Book 1.5)
Angels of War: Talion (Book 2)
Angels of War: Terminus (Book 3)

Check them out here, and find out how Dion and Isabella's relationship played out during a hellish, multiyear war:
https://www.masterlesspress.com/dj-thompson

Follow @TheDJThompson on:

https://twitter.com/TheDJThompson
https://www.instagram.com/TheDJThompson
https://www.facebook.com/TheDJThompson